A Victim of Magic
Magic and Mischief Book 3
N. R. Hairston

I0667584

Cover Design: Lou Harper https://coveraffairs.com/

Published By

OTHER TITLES BY N. R. Hairston
Magic and Mischief Series
A Magical Reckoning,[1] Book One
A Symptom of Magic,[2] Book Two
A Victim of Magic,[3] Book Three
Sun Cursed
Cursed Magic,[4] Book One
Savage Magic[5], Book Two
Lethal Magic[6], Book Three
World Breaker

---

1.   https://www.amazon.com/Magical-Reckoning-Supernatural-Betrayal-Mischief-ebook/dp/B071P7HQVH/ref=as_li_ss_tl?s=digital-text&ie=UTF8&qid=1495929540&sr=1-1&keywords=a+magical+reckoning&linkCode=sl1&tag=fbp02-20&linkId=53cd93b9dc96241660ae8b41ec2bdefe

2.   https://www.amazon.com/gp/product/B07489BQVL/ref=series_rw_dp_sw

3.   https://www.amazon.com/Victim-Magic-Stories-Supernatural-Mischief-ebook/dp/B07H5FHBFB/ref=sr_1_6?ie=UTF8&qid=1536873999&sr=8-6&keywords=n+r+hairston

4.   https://www.amazon.com/dp/B075YDZZ45/ref=sr_1_3?s=digital-text&ie=UTF8&qid=1506478708&sr=1-3

5.   https://www.amazon.com/Savage-Magic-N-R-Hairston-ebook/dp/B094DXP7J1/ref=sr_1_6?crid=2BGRD37EYPF31&dchild=1&keywords=n+r+hairston&qid=1620470219&s=digital-text&sprefix=n+r+%2Cdigital-text%2C148&sr=1-6

6.   https://www.amazon.com/dp/B094DQ663R/ref=sr_1_10?crid=2BGRD37EYPF31&dchild=1&keywords=n+r+hairston&qid=1620470219&s=digital-text&sprefix=n+r+%2Cdigital-text%2C148&sr=1-10

Rogue Magic,[7] Book One
Bloody Magic,[8] Book Two
Battle Magic,[9] Book Three
World Breaker Beginnings (Novellas set before the events in Rogue Magic, though you don't have to read one to read the other.) Read this series for free when you join my mailing list, here.[10]
Rebel Magic,[11] Book One
Stolen Magic,[12] Book Two
Crooked Magic,[13] Book Three
Dirty Magic,[14] Book Four

---

7. https://www.amazon.com/dp/B075YGLN4P/ref=sr_1_1?s=digital-text&ie=UTF8&qid=1506478708&sr=1-1

8. https://www.amazon.com/gp/product/B094DR-RQH7?ref_=dbs_m_mng_rwt_calw_tkin_1&storeType=ebooks

9. https://www.amazon.com/dp/B094DS7WLQ/ref=sr_1_8?crid=2BGRD37EYPF31&dchild=1&keywords=n+r+hairston&qid=1620470219&s=digital-text&sprefix=n+r+%2Cdigital-text%2C148&sr=1-8

10. https://landing.mailerlite.com/webforms/landing/h2l3b2

11. https://www.amazon.com/gp/product/B075YD3B6V?notRedirectToS-DP=1&ref_=dbs_mng_calw_0&storeType=ebooks

12. https://www.amazon.com/gp/product/B075YTLVZK?notRedirectToS-DP=1&ref_=dbs_mng_calw_1&storeType=ebooks

13. https://www.amazon.com/gp/product/B075YF35XX?notRedirectToS-DP=1&ref_=dbs_mng_calw_2&storeType=ebooks

14. https://www.amazon.com/dp/B094DSC8ZX/ref=sr_1_5?crid=2BGRD37EYPF31&dchild=1&keywords=n+r+hairston&qid=1620470219&s=digital-text&sprefix=n+r+%2Cdigital-text%2C148&sr=1-5

Feral Magic[15], Book Five
Lawless Magic[16], Book Six

Rise of the Dragons

Fire and Ash,[17] Book One
Smoke and Flame,[18] Book Two
Dust and Cinder,[19] Book Three

Atina and Ridge

We Got Powers Too,[20] Book One
We Wreak Havoc Too[21], Book Two

---

15.   https://www.amazon.com/dp/B094DQHDHY/ ref=sr_1_3?crid=2BGRD37EYPF31&dchild=1&keywords=n+r+hairston&qid=1620470219&s=digital-text&sprefix=n+r+%2Cdigital-text%2C148&sr=1-3

16.   https://www.amazon.com/Lawless-Magic-World-Breaker-Beginnings-ebook/dp/B094DPBVHN/ ref=sr_1_11?crid=2BGRD37EYPF31&dchild=1&keywords=n+r+hairston&qid=1620470219&s=digital-text&sprefix=n+r+%2Cdigital-text%2C148&sr=1-11

17.   https://www.amazon.com/Fire-Rise-Dragons-Trilogy-Book-ebook/dp/B076VFSGTZ/ref=sr_1_4?s=digital-text&ie=UTF8&qid=1531259254&sr=1-4&keywords=n+r+hairston

18.   https://www.amazon.com/gp/product/B076V3N5H8/ref=series_rw_dp_sw

19.   https://www.amazon.com/gp/product/B076V14N8H/ref=series_rw_dp_sw

20.   https://www.amazon.com/gp/product/B07F8D55LL/ ref=dbs_a_def_rwt_hsch_vapi_taft_p1_i10

21.   https://www.amazon.com/dp/B094DQSMS5/ ref=sr_1_9?crid=2BGRD37EYPF31&dchild=1&keywords=n+r+hair-

We Got Witches Too[22], Book Three

Rebel Writers Anthologies

Street Spells[23]

ston&qid=1620470219&s=digital-text&sprefix=n+r+%2Cdigital-text%2C148&sr=1-9

22. https://www.amazon.com/dp/B094DP9PNQ/ ref=sr_1_13?crid=2BGRD37EYPF31&dchild=1&keywords=n+r+hair-ston&qid=1620470219&s=digital-text&sprefix=n+r+%2Cdigital-text%2C148&sr=1-13

23. https://www.amazon.com/gp/product/B07F6GXSWV/ ref=dbs_a_def_rwt_hsch_vapi_taft_p1_i11

Five Stories of Supernatural Carnage

Five stories of supernatural carnage.
Including five kick-ass women.
With five unique powers.
On five different worlds.

Rye Unchained:

Agent Rye has always been able to depend on her skunk DNA in a fight, but when a vicious man with fly DNA kidnaps someone close to her, it sends her into a tailspin with consequence so severe she may never be able to claw her way free.

Delia Uncaged:

Elemental Delia is in the fight of her life when something ancient and feral stalks her with one goal in mind, killing her for horrific, hideous crimes it claims she will one day commit.

Leah Untamed:

Telekinetic Leah exists in the rough world of gambling, so she's used to a challenge. But when a ruthless man with superspeed comes after her for a debt, it leads to a showdown so bloody and brutal few will be left standing when it's over.

Kerry Unrestrained:

To stop the reign of terror of a man named Zeke, Coalition Agent Kerry will have to push her powers to their peak.

Her team is brawling, casualties are falling, to liberate this rhyming world, they'll have to put their all in.

Then a distraction, the unthinkable happens, Kerry can't control her reaction, there's no coming back from this infraction.

Kia Unleashed:

Succubus Kia's wrath is uncontrollable, as she hunts down those responsible for hurting her lover and makes them pay.

Take the title literally, there will be carnage here, and lots of it. Just a warning!

This book contains side characters who identify as LGBTQ, please don't read if that's not your thing.

This book contains a few strong words.

Rye Unchained

Chapter 1

I hated when they ran. Jumping out of the way of a wagon being controlled by telekinesis, I rounded the corner and saw Brad skirting around the block. *Here we go.*

"He's coming this way, Rye!" my co-worker Garrett said into my com.

"Nope!" he yelled, sounding more than a little pissed. "Changed directions. Drena watch your left."

Drena was also my co-worker. The three of us worked for Scope, an arm of law enforcement that only dealt with major and specialized crimes.

I cracked my neck, having had enough of this guy. We'd been chasing him for over thirty minutes, but he was faster than most, and always slipped away at the last second.

The phone in my pocket buzzed for like the third time in the last five minutes. My eyes flicked in annoyance. I didn't know who was on the other end, but this Brad guy I was chasing, he'd been caught trying to sell people like me, those who had skunk DNA.

You get caught selling skunk oil, and it's life in prison, no way around it. Skunk oil, drawn from the lateral glands in our backs, can heal anything from a persistent cough and broken bones, to open and gaping wounds. Some use it for skin protection, others use it as a contraceptive.

Also, some rub it on their privates and orgasm for hours. I usually carry some with me, especially when I'm working, as it allows me to heal quickly.

But I carry my own. Getting the oil from our backs can be painful, but my boyfriend Jax can literally pull the grease out of a pizza, so he makes the process a lot easier for me.

I rounded the corner and saw a flash of blue. "I think I got him," I said to Garrett and Drena, giving them my location. There was nothing that skunk oil couldn't heal you from and that in itself made it valuable, but the number one reason people use it is to get high.

Skunk oil, when heated to a certain temperature, could get you so high that you didn't come down for days. That coupled with everything else made it one of the most expensive and sought-after drugs around.

The problem was, drug runners needed skunks like myself to get it, which put a target on every skunk's back. That's why the penalty for dealing it was life, no exception.

Brad jumped onto the roof of a building, and I stumbled and almost skinned my knee following behind him. Getting my balance back, I blew out a breath, having had enough. Sweat dripped down my face and my bones ached for me to stop.

Knowing one way to get him now that I was closer, I held up my hand, shooting out my thiols. Thiols was that awful smell that we skunks used to protect ourselves from would-be attackers.

We could also turn it sweet and have you eating out of our hands, though that one we didn't use much as it was a terrible drain on our powers and caused a breakdown in our bodies that left us without thiols for days until it built back up.

I wrapped it around his neck and made the smell so inhuman that no one could stand it. The thiols was silver mixed with purple, a clear sign that I was pissed off.

If I wanted to clear a room, I'd shoot it out like a mist, where it'd take the form of a large mass floating wherever I directed it.

This time though, it came out in a hard, straight line. I made it tangible, and strong, as I wound it three times around Brad's neck, choking him until I saw his eyes pop.

His hands went to his throat, clawing desperately to no avail. I lifted him in the air and slammed him hard to the ground. See, us skunks were not without protection. We learned early on how to defend ourselves against all those who'd seek to hurt us for our oil.

At my feet, Brad groaned, his tan skin going ashy. "Got him," I said, just as my phone rang again. It wouldn't fucking stop.

"You going to get that?"

I looked up to see Garrett headed my way, Drena not far behind. Garrett had dragon DNA, and from the way he walked, you'd think he owned the whole damn world. His hair was black spiked with red tips that matched the deep red of his eyes, which was in contrast to his pale skin. He'd been on the force a lot longer than me, and I figured I still had a few things I could learn from him.

The phone continued to ring. "Could be Jax," Drena said once she reached us. I gave her a sour look, then brought

Brad to his feet, turning him around so that Drena could place the power-stripping cuffs on him.

Drena was my top mentor at Scope. She had short, curly brown hair and stood about five feet six. She appeared slim but had just enough muscles to let you know she wasn't to be fucked with.

She was of turtle DNA, and at times like this, her skin had a slight green tint, a sign that her shell was close to the surface. Though some could hide it, one look at Drena and most knew she was an agent.

Drena was older than both Garrett and myself. I was twenty-eight, and Garrett thirty. Drena was eight years my senior. She'd taken me under her wing when I'd first entered the force and I'd only be half the agent I was now without her.

All I'd ever wanted was to be a cop, that's it, nothing else. Bringing down the bad guys and standing on the side of good was important to me. You didn't get to wreck people's lives and cause harm to others without suffering the consequences. Not on my watch.

Brad was placed in the car by other agents who'd arrived on the scene to help secure him, and the look on his face said he knew he wouldn't be seeing the outside world any time soon.

The area was now crawling with Scope because the use and sale of skunk oil was that big of a deal. I mean, my life depended on us having a zero-tolerance policy, so...

As the other agents drove Brad away, my phone shrilled once more.

Drena rolled her eyes. "Just answer the damn thing!" By now she was probably irritated that I'd let it go on this long, but I'd say catching Brad was a little more important than a freaking phone call.

"Hello," I said, pressing the thing to my ear, a little annoyed that the person on the other end couldn't take the hint that now wasn't the best time to talk.

"My brother is missing," I heard an angry voice say. "Now what the fuck do you know about it?"

Chapter 2

His brother was missing, and he thought what... that I'd taken him? No, that's not what he'd said. I got Drena and Garrett to go with me to his house, because this was Vin, and Vin didn't like me.

His brother Drew was what I called one of my late-night friends, or he used to be before Jax stepped into the picture. Ironically, the first day I'd met Jax had been the last time I'd seen Drew.

I shook my head, thinking back to that day. My best friend had been kidnapped, and Jax himself, who is also in law enforcement, working higher above my pay grade at the government agency Albright, was helping me find him.

I'd promised Drew a new pair of shoes, but he'd come over for a little fun too that night. I remembered being irritated and scared for my friend Cam, so I'd stuffed eight twenties into his hand and pushed him out the door.

I'd promised we'd meet up again later, but I'd gotten caught up with Jax, and all of my late-night friends had kind of faded into the background.

Nervous orange thiols swirled around me as I stood on Vin's front porch beside my fellow agents, waiting for him to open the door. Drew had called a few times after that night, and I'd finally gone ahead and ended it with him and a few others.

I liked them all okay, but I'd never committed to any of them. We had fun, and if I wanted to buy them something nice, or pay their rent, I did that too.

Some may have had something to say about that, but I never really gave a fuck. I liked my men to look a certain way, to live a certain way, and I didn't mind paying for them to do it.

Some had accused me of having a harem, but that wasn't really the case. I'd had friends, and a lot more than one. That didn't matter now anyway, from the moment I'd met him, Jax had been the only man in my life.

The door flung open and I braced myself for what was about to come. Vin had convinced himself long ago that I had his brother caught up in some weird ass skunk spell. It's what he thought, and there was nothing I could do about it. Right now, I just wanted to know what was going on.

Vin stood at the door, arms at his sides, chest rising and falling. His brown skin, which was a few shades lighter than my darker tone, gleamed with sweat as he watched us.

His tall, muscular frame filled up the doorway, though he still looked every bit the stuck-up, stick-in-the-mud lawyer that he was.

I pushed thick black hair out of my face. If anybody wanted to know who'd invented the term, stiff upper lip, well, it had been Vin, for sure.

My hair fell into my face again, and I cursed under my breath. Skunks all had one thing in common, which made us easy to identify. It didn't matter your skin tone or eye color, we all had black bushy hair, with a large white stripe. No matter how many times we tried, we couldn't dye it; couldn't change it. Our hair color always remained the same. The only thing we could do was cut it off, though I'd never entertained that idea.

"Come in," Vin said, his voice gruff yet still managing to sound like he could buy the whole universe, if only he wanted to.

I gave Drena and Garrett hard stares as the three of us walked into the fox's den. Those with fox DNA, like Drew and his brother Vin, could not only absorb poison, they could also use it to fight with, which made them dangerous. They also liked to pounce, could move swiftly, and their retractable claws meant they could climb anything.

I was always on my guard when coming up against a perp with Fox DNA, though Vin and Drew were not a threat, so I felt only slightly nervous being here now.

Foxes were excellent at blending in. Truth be told, if they didn't want to be found, they wouldn't be. Their hair also changed colors with the seasons. Right now, I practically had sweat forming small pools at my feet.

It was summertime here in my small town, so Vin's short hair was dark black. In the fall it would be brown, in the winter white, and in the spring a reddish orange color. Vin looked nice with black hair, as did his brother.

I cleared my throat as we all stepped inside. This was a first for me. I mean, I knew where Vin lived, but I'd never actually had a reason to come here.

Vin waved a hand toward a couple of chairs, offering us a seat. I looked around, impressed. It was a nice house, not all that warm, but nothing was out of place, dust apparently didn't live here, and of the deep-seated black furniture in his living room, every bit of it looked sturdy and well-taken care of.

I sat on the edge of the couch, while Drena plopped down on the love seat, and Garrett sat down in one of the recliners. This way we all had a good view of Vin, who took a seat in front of us.

Garrett, who was in 'I don't give a fuck' mode, threw one leg over the edge of his armrest. My eyes went wide, and Vin gave him a wry look.

He inclined his head to the side as he looked at Garrett, an unreadable expression on his face, then he turned my way. His voice was laced with authority when he spoke. It was the voice I'd witnessed him use many times in the courtroom, and I noted with interest that he felt the need to employ it now.

"Rye." He said my name like something had curled into his mouth and died. "You last saw or talked to my brother when exactly?"

My brows might have risen to my hairline. He was really questioning me like I had something to do with Drew's supposed disappearance. "I don't know." I ran a hand through my hair. "It's been a while."

He narrowed his eyes, then shot a look at Garrett, whose leg was still thrown over the chair, only now it was swinging back and forth. Garrett stared back, his eyes never leaving Vin's face, not even for a second. Talk about laser focus.

"Why?" Vin asked, turning back my way. "Why has it been a while?"

What does this have to do with anything? I was losing my patience. "Vin, I didn't kidnap your brother, but I can't help you if I don't know what's going on."

His hands folded in front of him, his shrewd eyes fixed on mine. "I usually talk to him once or twice a week. We had some things that needed discussing so I started calling him the day before yesterday. He never answered, nor did I receive a callback. I took it upon myself to go to his house today."

He reached into his pocket and twirled around a key on his fingers like I didn't already know he had one to Drew's place. "It was ransacked, and my brother was nowhere in sight." He stared at me again, eyes unblinking, not saying a word.

"Find any clues?" I asked, after about three seconds of his unnerving gaze.

"No," he said, managing to look very disappointed with me. "I already told you what I found was a mess."

From his place on the recliner, Garrett let out a small chuckle. I gave him a sharp look. What about this was funny to him?

"Let's do this," I said, still not convinced that Vin wasn't overreacting. "We'll go to his house and see what we find."

I stood, thinking he would hand the key over, then fought from rolling my eyes when he stuffed it into his pocket. I started to object, but one look from Drena had me closing my mouth. "Show us what you found," she said to Vin, a calm smile on her face.

Chapter 3

Drew lived in an upscale neighborhood called Fringe. He hadn't lived here when I'd first met him but had moved here after we'd been talking for about five months. I hadn't made him move, hadn't even suggested it, but I had given him the money for half the down payment.

Drew had money, he worked as an investment banker, but still, I liked to treat my men whenever I got the chance. All except Jax that was, but he was different from all the others anyway.

Decorative red rocks crunched under my feet on the path leading up to the driveway. The house was a large red blue brick, four-bedrooms, three baths. It'd always been exceptionally clean whenever I'd been over, not a scrap of paper in sight, not a thing out of place.

Vin opened the door without ceremony and we all stepped inside. My heart stopped for a few seconds, and for a minute I forgot how to breathe.

Stuff was everywhere. Clothes were thrown about, furniture knocked over, and the glass table, which had been the centerpiece of the room, was busted with glass littered all across the floor.

The wall by one of the windows in the living room was caved in with the impression of someone slamming hard into it. I stood in the middle of the mess, hands clenched at my sides, trying to follow the progression of the fight.

He'd been caught unawares, he had to have been. Foxes were lethal in battle, which meant that someone had to have caught him completely off guard and attacked. The question was why? Angry purple thiols swirled around me as the scene of Drew's capture played out in front of me.

I could feel my pulse jumping. They fucking dared! Someone dared touch one of the guys under my protection. No, I didn't own Drew, but just like my other late-night guy friends, there was a hands-off policy, and everybody knew it. So, who would dare cross that line?

I walked through the mess, kicking clothes, overturned plants, and knickknacks out of my way. My eyes went into microfocus, scanning every inch of the place, looking for something, anything to give me a clue as to where he'd been taken.

I finally found an item under the couch, way back in the left corner. Already on my hands and knees, I reached for the small metal ball-shaped pod that was not yet covered in dust.

Slight apprehension ran down my spine as I looked at the thing because I knew what it was. A message pod, some-one had left us a message pod. At least I hoped this was from the people who'd attacked Drew and not some random friend of his.

I stood, and brushed myself off, then pushed a small button on the side of it. "Hey," I said to the other three in the room, getting their attention.

I let the message pod go and it hovered, then opened to reveal a hologram message. The dude looked like he was standing right in the room with us, especially since this had been taped right here where we now were. Beside him stood Drew, looking like he could barely stay upright.

I took a step back, Garrett and Drena coming to stand on either side of me. Vin stood off to the left, his eyes wide as he looked at his brother.

The hologram man was tall with olive skin and a tattoo of a fly on his face, below his right eye. His hair was a dark black, his brown eyes hard and mean. He was of fly DNA, I could tell from the three pin sized dots on his jawline.

They were called deloux, and only flies had them. They were danger receptors that warned a fly when something harmful was coming their way. In a fight, flies could anticipate your next move, long before you made it, and keep themselves from harm.

In flight, their deloux warned them if they're flying into a danger zone, allowing them to change course midair. It also helped them in business dealings and other aspects of their lives.

Garrett was of dragon DNA, his wings only came out when he wanted them to, and the same was true of flies. This dude, and the more I looked at him the more familiar he looked, anyway, this dude had his wings out now.

Unlike a dragon's wings, which were several feet long when unleashed, a fly's wings were only a few feet wide and closer to their inner backs. This guy's wings were silver, as were the retractable claws that he made sure to have out.

I took in the whole picture and realized that he wanted there to be no mistake as to who he was, but my only question was what did him being of fly DNA have to do with anything?

"Hi, Rye." He waved. like one did when meeting a friend on the jogging trail.

I inhaled sharply, and something in me went cold. So, this had been a message to me. He'd deliberately gone after Drew to get my attention. I shook my head because I wasn't sure doing all this would be worth it once I found his ass.

"Almost a year ago now," dude said, his eyes looking straight ahead, straight at me actually, because I was the one standing directly in front of the message pod. "You chased my brother Jerald to the top of Estes then used your dragon boy to bring him down." Estes was the highest building in our town, a couple hundred stories up.

I squinted at the man before me, then snapped my fingers, only now realizing why he looked so familiar. My brain must have short-circuited for a minute because this was Ham, Jerald's brother.

I'd brought Jerald in after a six-month-long investigation. Like those with fox DNA can absorb and carry poisons, the same was true when it came to those with fly DNA and diseases. Someone with fly DNA could inject you with any of the numerous diseases they hoarded, if they chose to hoard diseases that is.

The only way they could inject it into your bloodstream was by using their toenails, fingernails, or teeth. Flies were telekinetic, so it wasn't hard for them to drag you close and then do whatever they pleased with you.

Though we suspected Jerald of dealing in everything from skunk oil, to deadly frog spit, we hadn't been able to catch him on those things. A fire rolled in my gut, and purple thiols swirled around me like an angry storm just waiting to descend.

We'd caught Jerald dead to rights, injecting women between the ages of twenty-five and thirty with deadly diseases. In some cases, he'd mixed it up, then documented, and taped every single second of their demises.

He had a history in science, and we'd figured out he'd been working on a new super drug, something to sell on the black market, and these women had been his unwilling test subjects.

Jerald was a psychopath, and I truly believed he'd wanted to see just how these women would handle each disease, and how a combination of diseases would affect them. None of the ten women had been of the same DNA path, which he'd also carefully documented.

This had me even more convinced that he'd gotten some kind of joy out of seeing how someone with say fox DNA handled a disease versus someone with wolf DNA.

He'd gotten off on it, I knew he had, and to me, life in jail was exactly where he deserved to be.

Ham used his telekinesis to raise Drew in the air, holding him in an invisible choke hold. Drew's eyes were swollen and bloodshot, and he had an open wound on his neck and his right cheek. He was losing blood fast, and his face was starting to pale.

From the left of me, I heard a sharp intake of breath and turned to see Vin with his claws out, eyes fixed on his brother, who honestly didn't look so good.

"I'm not an unreasonable man," Ham said, squeezing his hand, making Drew choke even more. "I know these things take time to maneuver. You have five hours. Get my brother out of jail in a way that it's not questioned, leave him on the same building you caught him on, and pick up your boy at the bottom. If not..."

He squeezed a little harder, and Drew shook, white foam coming out of his mouth, as his eyes rolled to the back of his head.

A pain hit me deep in my chest, and the thiols around me turned darker, angrier. How. Fucking. Dare. He. My body trembled with rage, and I felt myself losing control as thiols filled my eyes and shot out of my fingers.

I was going to kill that motherfucker. I was going to hunt him down and peel the fucking skin from his body while he begged for me to stop. I was going to take his eyeballs out of his head and crush them under my feet. I was going to grind his bones down until they were nothing.

He'd violated on the deepest level, and this was a hit that I could not let go unanswered. Drew was one of my guys, under my protection, and the moment Ham had touched him, he'd signed his own fucking death warrant.

Warm arms wrapped around me from behind, and I heard Drena whisper in my ear. "We follow the law, we uphold it, but one thing we never do is break it because that would make us no better than them. You will not hurt this man unless you have no choice. Yes, I see the abuse that he's inflicting, but he'll have his time in court. You will bring him in, and he will answer for what he's done. But just like everything else, we will do this the right way. Do you understand me?"

My eyes watered, and I took deep breaths, trying to calm down. She was trying to save me from myself, and I'd thank her for it later, but right now, I had a fly to catch.

Chapter 4

I called Scope mid-transit to let them know what was going on, and was given a task force under my command. Ham was suspected of a myriad of crimes, but until this very obvious kidnapping, we'd never had enough evidence to put him away.

Which meant he was desperate, or he'd misjudged me and really thought I'd keep this quiet. Maybe he didn't care either way. We'd never been able to get him before so...

I sent some members of my team to Jerald's house, others to the known addresses we had for Ham. As for myself, Drena, and Garrett, well, we three along with five other agents, went to Elonx Boulevard.

Elonx Boulevard was about ten miles long and had every type of outdoor shop, store, and club you could think of. There were no bricks and mortar here, everything was out in the open, under large tents, canopies, and gazebos.

There was nothing you couldn't find here, from the finest restaurants to the hippest clubs. It even had grocery stores, clothing shops, gambling spots, and so much more.

Local law enforcement usually patrolled it, but they let a lot of things go here that they wouldn't anywhere else. Which was a good thing. I think we all needed a place that we could just come hang out and not worry about cops looking over your shoulder every five minutes.

We walked through, looking at familiar faces, most of whom knew we weren't there to harass them. Unless one was in the process of committing murder, abuse, harming another, or had skunk oil or some other type of drug, then they wouldn't be on our radar.

Ham, we knew, had at least three businesses here: a club that catered to those who liked live music, no DJ's allowed, a gambling joint, and a car washing and detailing spot.

Drena stood to my left, Garrett to my right, and Vin on the other side of him. Vin. We hadn't been able to get rid of him yet. He insisted on sticking around, and as long as he stayed out of our way and let us do our job, I figured I'd let him.

Besides, I didn't know if it was in Garrett's face, or maybe his eyes, but I felt a small bit of attraction going on and something told me he didn't want Vin going away anytime soon. Garett could deal with him then. I had other matters to focus on.

"We need to split up," I said to all three of them. "If he's here, he could be anywhere. We'll check the shops we know he owns, but he could be in any one of these spaces."

Drena nodded. "I'll take his gambling tent, Garrett..." Her eyes narrowed as she looked from him to Vin. "You two take the detailing shop." She turned to me. "You can handle the club."

I didn't care. My hands flexed at my sides, and I was just happy to be able to do something. Every inch of this place was covered, yet there was still enough room to walk comfortably from one canopy to the next.

Around me, I could hear sounds of both laughter and arguing as people relaxed in a place where the rules didn't really exist. On my way to Ham's club, I passed by three more dancing spots, plus a clothing shop, and a fight ring.

The smell of cooked pork, barbequed chicken, and deep-fried fish followed me as I went by one food place after the other, the smoke from some of them hitting me in the face. My stomach growled in response and I realized it'd been a while since I'd eaten. It didn't matter though, the last thing on my mind right now was food.

Shop after shop was filled with the life and energy of the people inside of them. The boulevard hummed and vibrated, a separate entity all on its own. Someone looking from above, especially at night, would see so many different colors and lights that it may even look like a firework show.

Ham's club was toward the end of the boulevard, sandwiched in between a coffee shop that sold food all night long, so stumbling clubgoers could come in and feed their stomach after a good night of partying, and a hair shop. If you sweated out your hair at the club, you need only walk over a few steps to get it touched up, and then go right back to whatever you were doing before.

The club was under a ten-thousand-foot gazebo that Ham had probably had specially built. Most shop owners here customized their own space, and Ham was no different. The gazebo was black, with silver etchings of people laughing, drinking, and dancing from the top and down the sides.

The carvings glowed brightly, and since the figures were holographic they even danced and turned.

The floor was also black and silver, made of wood and sanded over to look like tile. It ran the length of the gazebo and also stayed lit up. There were strobe lights everywhere, in every size and color. The music from the band on stage blasted out a cool, heart-throbbing tune as about two hundred people swayed and danced.

There was a bar at the front of the club and another one toward the back. I went to the first one I saw, and the bartender held up a few beers, asking me what I was drinking.

I shook my head to let him know that wasn't in the cards for tonight then squinted as I looked around. "Trying to catch up with Ham," I said to the guy, and since Ham was his boss, I was pretty sure he knew who I meant. "Have you seen him?"

The dude, who was kind of on the tall side, put a hand through his red, slicked-back hair. He looked like he took his job pretty seriously and didn't seem to notice the activities around him as he poured one drink after the other.

"Not tonight, not yet anyway," he said, then turned to focus on the couple beside me who were yelling for refills.

I gave him a thank you, then looked back over the crowd. Would Ham be here, hiding in plain sight, or was he even trying to conceal himself at all?

Figuring I wouldn't get any answers unless I moved about, I made my way to the back of the club, where the other bar was set up. Since this was an outside setting, there were also shops around the back side of the club.

One such place caught my attention just as I was stepping up to the bar. A group of people, looking to be in their late twenties, early thirties, sat on top of picnic tables, drinking and eating.

On the floor, three games of dice were in progress, and I noticed that a few of the tables had people around them, doing everything from watching small portable entertainment devices, to reading, or just munching on food. A hangout area, that's what this was.

With small beer tables, food tables, and popup shops lining the edges, I'd say the owner was very clever in how he made his money.

That hadn't been what'd caught my eye though. In the middle of it all, on one of the tables, surrounded by people and talking a mile a minute was Jax. I think it was very telling that Ham hadn't gone after Jax, a top trained Albright agent.

Yes, when I'd captured Ham's brother, Drew and I had been hot and heavy, but that wasn't the case now. Ham either didn't know that, or he was too much of a coward to go after someone who could slaughter him in a second.

Plus, Jax was an agent; try to kidnap him and there was no saving yourself from the many law enforcement agencies coming for your head.

Jax was dressed in blue jeans and a black T-shirt, definitely not his usual style. Beside him was Tonya, one of his co-workers, and she was dressed the same way.

"Ah," I said, realizing what was going on. They were probably undercover, getting a lead on some case they were working, and since I didn't want either of them to become distracted and lose focus, I quickly made my way over to the bar, hoping that even if they did see me they wouldn't give away anything visually that could blow their cover. They were both excellent agents though, at the top of their game, so there was probably little chance of that happening.

I walked up to the bar to see a woman with hair puffs and a nose ring mixing up a few orders. Unlike her co-worker, she appeared to be having a wonderful time, interacting with her customers, and swaying her body to the music as she talked and poured.

"Seen your boss?" I asked, hoping to get straight to the point.

She shook her head, then went right back to what she'd been doing.

I scanned the crowd again, wondering if he'd really be among the gyrating bodies. Deciding to move around a bit, I weaved through the dance floor, my shirt getting stained with everything from liquor to sweat as I reached the other end of the club.

He probably wasn't in here, at least I hadn't seen him anywhere. My throat tightened a little as the realities set in, and I realized that I might not be in time. Drew could freaking die today, and knowing Vin, he'd make it as painful as he could.

Nervous orange thiols surround me, as I let that thought eat me from the inside out. This was no good. I couldn't help Drew if I couldn't keep myself together.

Checking in every shop I passed, I soon made my way to the grass part of the boulevard.

Here people sat on towels and blankets, eating, drinking, reading, listening to music, watching TV on their entertainment devices, or enjoying the cool breeze coming from the clear blue lake in front of us.

I looked out at some of the boats on the water, and at the people on the bank, fishing. What were the odds that Vin was actually in the lake skinny-dipping and would jump out at any moment?

"Yeah, yeah, we can do that," I heard Jax say from behind me, and I stilled not knowing what he was up to. "Yup, tell 'em I said so."

He walked up beside me, a few feet away and I realized he was on his phone. "I'm talking to you, babe. Only way I can at the moment." His eyes were subtle when they cut my way, and I realized he wasn't on the phone at all. He was trying to talk to me, without anyone noticing.

"Remember the last time we were in a lake?" he said into the phone, his eyes shining as he looked out at the water, the lowering sun giving it a slight glow.

Biting my lip, and trying to hold in my smile, no matter the situation, Jax could always make me smile, I picked up my phone and pretended to punch in numbers.

"You mean the first time you got between my legs?" I asked. He laughed, before quickly covering it up with a cough.

"You okay?" His tone suddenly turned serious.

"Fucking Ham kidnapped Drew and has given me five hours to release his serial killer brother or he's going to kill Drew."

Jax brows furrowed. "Jerald the fly?"

"Yes."

He cursed under his breath, then walked forward, picking up a rock and tossing it in his hand. "The name Drew sounds familiar."

Someone jumped into the water, causing a small splash, and I smiled, thinking back to Jax's and I first time together. "When we first met remember, he came by the house while you were there."

"The shoe guy." He didn't sound amused, but he didn't seem upset either, which was a good thing, because we had more pressing matters to deal with at the moment.

"That's him. Are you and Tonya undercover?"

He turned my way, pretending to look over toward the trees. "Yeah, and I better get back. Saw Ham here about an hour ago, by the red dentist tent."

Right, because there were actually licensed dentists and doctors here. Hey, everyone made their living their own way. To each their own and all of that.

"Let me know if you need backup," Jax said, before putting his phone in his pocket and walking away.

I strolled past three dentist canopies before I saw the one with the red tent. Now, Jax hadn't said that Ham had actually been in the tent, only that he'd spotted him around this way.

I scanned the area, wondering just what he'd been up to. My eyes finally landed on a spot selling boats, scuba diving equipment, and a few other things to prepare you for the water.

It was a long shot, but I figured I had to start somewhere, especially since I'd yet to hear back from either Drena or Garrett.

The shop had three people working in it, all wearing blue shirts and white pants. I went over to a tall guy with short blond hair, who was sanding down a small boat. I pulled up the most recent pictures Scope had of Ham and showed them to him. "Seen this guy?"

He stopped what he was doing and gave me a hard look. "Ham? Not getting into that. I like living."

I stood there for a minute, then decided not to challenge it. If he hadn't seen Ham he would have said so. His no comment told me for sure that Ham had been here. Yet this guy obviously knew what happened to people who whispered Ham's name too loud, so he chose to keep his mouth closed.

I wandered around the store looking at the products trying to figure out what Ham was up to. Everything here was for someone about to go into the water, so...

I took a few steps out of the shop and looked over toward the lake. He wasn't in there. I didn't think he would be that obvious about it. I turned on my com. "Guys, I think he's ready to hit the water. Maybe he has a shipment coming in."

"I talked to a guy who said he saw one of Ham's people last week buying stationed lights," Drena said.

"Ah." Stationed lights were bulbs of all sizes that hung in the air, all on their own, and followed motion. If you moved, they moved with you, which meant you didn't have to waste your power or keep a low wattage flashlight in your hand.

They didn't come cheap, and I knew he wouldn't be using them in the water. "Longjack Beach! They have caves there, lots of them. If he's looking to dig or wander through one, he'll need a good light source. Those things are creepy dark," I said, shivering just thinking about them.

"I think you're right," Garrett said. "We talked to a lady who says she saw him loading up on crempes, maybe to keep the ragonds away."

Ragonds were small creatures, only slightly bigger than a softball. They were vicious little animals though. Their bodies were covered in white, black, or red fur and they were very territorial.

If they set eyes on you in their space, at least fifty would attack you at a time, clawing and biting until they ripped you apart. A shudder went through my body. I feared those things like nothing else. They were relentless in their attack and I avoided them at all cause.

They didn't come out the caves much, and as long as you stayed on the beach, and away from them, you were fine.

Crempes were a small, round, nutty, delicacy ragonds could actually eat their weight in and also sent them into a feeding frenzy. Throw enough of them around and you had a free pass, until they finished, or were too full to move.

As I thought about it, my mind drifted to Drew and I wondered if he was okay. Fear gripped my throat as I imagined what was being done to him. If Ham had hurt him in any way... my pulse jumped to triple time as the urge to tear something apart rose in me so fast that I had to stop and focus on my breathing to keep my thiols under control. "We better go get us some crempes then."

Chapter 5

Longjack Beach was five miles of brown sand and raging water. The caves were set toward the back of the beach and there were enough of them that we probably needed to split up, only none of us thought that was a good idea.

Ham knew we'd be looking for him, so this could very well be a trap. Also, the ragonds were deadly enough that none of us should wander around without backup.

We'd purchased some stationed lights on the way over and they now floated above us, moving every time we did.

"Okay," Drena said, standing before myself, Garrett, and Vin. "Remember that this could be a trap. If it's not, it may mean that Ham has reached the point of desperation, but for what? That's what we need to figure out."

I wondered that too. His brother had been in jail for the better part of a year, and it was only now that he wanted to get him out. I shook my head as I thought about it. Something didn't add up. We were missing a vital clue, I just needed to figure out what it was.

Garrett looked at the rows of caves stretched out before us. "You know I could just cover myself in crempes and fly through each one. Come back and tell you what I saw."

Vin gave him a wry look. "And I'm sure you would have a great deal of fun, but that's not why we're here."

Garrett opened his mouth to respond, and I held up a hand to stop him. "We have about three hours left to find Drew, so I'll say we need to get moving."

We went through cave after cave, throwing out crempes and moving as fast as we could, trying to catch some type of break. It wasn't until we stood back on the open beach that things started to turn around.

By now though, we were covered in dirt, grime, and I didn't even want to know what some of this stuff was.

Drena had somehow gotten a long scratch on her arm which had her cursing under her breath. "Ping is going to kill me when she sees this, and because I bailed on dinner, again." She looked disgusted with herself.

Ping was Drena's wife. They'd been married for ten years, and to be honest, that was a lot of broken dinner dates.

"You'll make it up to her," I said, a little out of breath. Trudging through the caves, fighting off ragonds, and other such creatures took its toll. "I think—"

I stopped mid-sentence when I saw what looked like metal gleaming from inside one of the caves. "Be careful coming in!" I shouted running toward that way, knowing that Ham and his cronies could be lying in wait.

I made it about two feet from the entrance before a line of fire blazed in front of me. I stumbled back, then looked up and saw a dude of dragon DNA floating above a cliff face.

He opened his mouth again, but before I could blink, Garrett had already taken flight. The two became entangled in battle and I went on guard looking around, knowing that he wouldn't be alone.

A large rock flew my way and I ducked and jumped back. Another came, and I saw Drena's skin hardening, becoming tough as a shell. When like this, nothing could penetrate it, which made it a very effective shield.

Knowing that it would put a big drain on my powers, I put up a shield of thiols. It wrapped around me, a large pink mass, blazing and protecting me from harm. It wouldn't last for long, this feeling of power coursing through me now. Soon it would start to wane, and my shield would drop, leaving me defenseless with weakened powers.

A few months ago, I'd protected myself from perps using a steel rope, and Garrett had given me a large metal chain in the shape of diamonds.

I pulled it from my side, and ran my hands over it, spreading red thiols onto it. By now, over twenty men and women had come into view, each powered up and looking like they meant business.

One of the men stood above the rest and had his hair cut close to his head. He held his hands out and two large rocks flew into them. A telekinetic then. I swung my chain and wrapped it around his feet. The thiols on the chain crackled and popped as it went through his clothes, biting into skin and bone.

He let out a howl, and I yanked the chain hard, slamming him to the ground by my feet. The red thiols was now working itself deep into his bones, and I pulled it back, not wanting him to lose the bottom half of his legs.

He was hurt though and wouldn't be able to move until he had medical assistance or at least a little skunk oil. I sprinkled some on his legs from the valve I kept around my neck.

Not enough so that he'd get up and be a threat again. But a sufficient amount so that in a day or two, he'd heal with no lasting problems.

Before I could fully wrap the small container back around my neck, five men with fly DNA flew from above and surrounded me.

I looked to where Garrett was still battling the other dragon in the sky, both of them using hand-to-hand combat and low kicks as they slammed each other into the cliff faces and cave tops.

Drena had two on her, a man and a woman. Unlike my shield, hers didn't drain her power, as it was a natural part of her skin. She knocked the woman in the face with a hard fist, then she dropped to the ground, and kicked the man's legs out from under him, before hopping back up, grabbing the woman by the throat and slamming her down.

I turned to where Vin was fighting three men. Foxes were swift and cunning, they absorbed poison and then used it for energy, which came in handy in a fight. They also had retractable claws, and right now Vin had his out.

He clawed a dude with wolf DNA across the face, then spit a line of yellow poison out of his mouth straight into the man's eyes. Then he called that same energy forward to his hands and soon they became covered with a blue and red energy that from what I remembered, was cyps and lones, two of the deadliest poisons foxes carried.

He shot a line at one guy, and it crept into the man's skin, turning it blue, exposing his veins as his breath became labored and he foamed at the mouth.

Vin's claws danced with the stuff, and when he raked it across the last man's face, the dude screamed, as his lips and eyes deteriorated in a matter of seconds. As those three fell away, five more appeared around Vin and I knew we were in for the fight of our lives.

I had to drop my shield. I couldn't keep fighting with it, because eventually, it would fail me, but not before it drained every bit of strength I had.

I went low into a crouch and spun around, swinging my metal chain. I wanted to hit all five of them in the face and let the red thiols slice through their skin. Instead, I only hit two, as the other three jumped or ducked out of the way.

The two I hit let out howls. One fell to the side, and the other stumbled back, blood gushing out of his face as he finally slumped to the ground.

Because of their deloux, those born with fly DNA could usually avoid most attacks. One of the three left was a tall woman with black hair. She flung her hands out to the side, and I noticed she had her claws out.

Apprehension went down my spine. If she could get those things in me, or even her teeth, she could inject me with any number of deadly diseases.

I cracked my neck. One thing about me was I loved a good fight and going toe to toe with a fly definitely fell into that category. Those with fly DNA could take most hits, as their bodies bent and reshaped itself with every blow. That only meant I'd have to leave my hands for someone else to catch. For these three I'd have to use my thiols.

I shot it out of my mouth, aiming for her face, but because of her deloux, she was able to lean back so it shot past her. Then the other two crowded in on me, and I noticed they had their claws out too.

My heart sped up... from... was that excitement? Yeah, I think it was. Pretty fucked up on my part, but not really something I could control.

I swung my chain again, and they fell back. I held out a hand as if to hit the man on my right with thiols, then fell flat on my back, whipping my chain around and slicing straight through the legs of the man on the left.

I then came back to my feet.

The woman held out her hand, and I felt my eyes strain and fill with water, as she tried to use her telekinesis to pull them from my head. I put my shield back up, just for a second, blowing her away.

Then I pointed a finger, wrapping red thiols around her neck, using it to pull her to me, as blood leaked from her throat and she choked and gagged.

Something hit the back of my legs. I stumbled and let go, but by then she was already too fucked up to move. I whipped my chain around again, but the guy who'd been on my right earlier was no longer there.

A hard fist hit the side of my head, and I dropped down, as everything around me began to spin. "Did you really think..." the guy started, then stopped when I shot a line of red thiols into his eyes, burning them out. He put a hand to his face and screamed, then dropped to his knees and fell over.

After that, I tried to come to my feet and noticed I was still dizzy. Drena had three bodies at her feet, and I stiffened when I saw that at least twenty more people had appeared. Then a body hit the ground beside me.

I let out a gasp, my pulse racing at the thought that it might be Garrett only to see him land in front of me. His clothes were in tatters, and he was covered in cuts, but other than that, he seemed okay, if not a bit exhausted.

Vin looked about the same, and he walked with a limp as he came to join the rest of us. "What about them?" He pointed to the guys balanced above us as they dove our way, ready to continue the fight.

I rolled my shoulders, not liking the odds, but willing to go down to my last breath if I had to. The only question I really had was, where the fuck was Ham? Had he even been here, or just sent in his minions?

As they got closer, we all went into a fighter stance, ready to carry on. Then one of the men's skin disappeared from his body. He dropped to the ground, painful screams echoing from his throat.

My head snapped up, and I saw Jax, Tonya and a few other Albright agents. One of them was Fred and another was Cynthia, both of whom I'd worked with on a previous case and liked okay.

Jax didn't say anything, just reached up his hands again, and then the arms and legs of our opponents begin to fall around us. After that, it was just chaos as we all jumped head first back into the fight.

I didn't know about the others, but I was feeling a bit refreshed that we now had some proper backup. In the end, the flies took off after ten more minutes of fighting, enough time for them or their friends to finish whatever they'd come here to do, no doubt.

"Don't worry," I said to the others around me. "I have a few Scope agents on the lookout. They should be able to track their movements."

Jax, whose black hair was now all over the place, looked at me, with a bit of... was that admiration? "Got Albright agents watching the exits too. They should be able to track them."

"Good," I said, my voice strained, my legs weak. "Because I don't think I can stay standing much longer."

Chapter 6

"**B**etter?" Jax asked, as he placed a kiss on my forehead and continued to rub skunk oil over my face, arms and legs.

"Hmm," I said, completely boneless under his touch. We were in the lounge of a conference hall that Scope agents used to meet up and regroup when out in the field. This place had three floors, and countless wings, so more than enough privacy.

Once he finished applying the oil, I immediately started to feel like my old self again, and the first thing on my mind was getting to Drew. I sat up a little more in my chair and looked around. "Are the others in the next room?"

Black curly hair fell into Jax's face and he pushed it away, his eyes never leaving mine. "Yeah, and we only have about two and a half hours left."

My mind went back to Drew's helpless face, unable to move while in Ham's grip and something in my stomach curled tightly as anger shook my whole body. "He doesn't deserve this. He did nothing wrong."

A feeling of helplessness washed over me, and I swiped angrily at my eyes. "I was supposed to protect him." My voice broke, and I wiped at my face again. "That's what I was supposed to do."

Jax let out a sigh and then pulled me closer to him, his rough calloused hands on my skin making it a lot easier for me to breathe. "You can't be everywhere at once, Rye. There was nothing you could have done to stop this."

"I know," I said, leaning my forehead against his. "But-"

He shook his head. "But nothing. So, you weren't there when he got taken, how is that stopping us from kicking in doors now to find him?"

I nodded, the urge to get proactive rising in my chest. Then I thought of something, and I pulled back and gave Jax a curious look. "You know, you're taking this very well, most guys would..."

"I *am* most guys," he interrupted me. "I've got all types of shit going on in here," he pointed to his chest, "seeing you so bent out of shape over another dude. But I know that's not what it's about, what we're about. We're agents of the law, and Ham is breaking the shit out of that motherfucker right now. Besides, I know what Drew and the others mean to you."

He paused for a moment, in a way that said he wasn't sure whether he should say his next words or not. "I know where it comes from." His voice went soft, and suddenly I had a very uncomfortable feeling that I wouldn't like where this was going. "You need to be in control, to be the protector, not the protected, I get it."

I looked at him with cold eyes and swallowed hard. I assumed he was talking about my grandmother, who I'd watched my whole life basically throwing herself at the feet of any guy that bothered to give her the time of day.

Yes, growing up, I'd said I would never grovel for affection from any man, and my mom was just the same as me. Why the fuck Jax thought now was a good time to bring all this up, though, well, that was something I wasn't ready to get into.

"I'm better now," I said, standing. I wasn't mad at Jax, I just had too much on my mind to think on all the shit he'd just said and what it meant for us going forward.

I shook off the feeling of discomfort going down my spine and walked into a conference room filled with both Scope and Albright agents. I stopped and turned around to look at Jax. "Will you guys get in trouble for helping us?"

He shrugged, and I noticed how his black T-shirt clung to his broad chest. "Have we ever?"

Shit, I didn't know. We were often called to share information and help each other out, but this was different, as no orders had come from higher up.

I wondered for a second if it was really going to be a problem, then my mind went back to the look in Drew's eyes right before he'd begun to gag, and my stomach twisted itself into knots.

"Just a little over two hours left, guys. Tell me what you've got." I took a seat on the edge of the table, swiping damp hair out of my face, and Jax went to stand on the other side of the room, looking as anxious as I did to find out what the group who'd gone over the caves had discovered.

Drena, Garrett, and a few Scope and Albright agents were already discussing something.

Drena turned to me when I walked in and lifted a brow, her way of asking me if I was okay. I nodded, and she placed a retag in front of me. Retags were about the size and shape of most tablets and held a wealth of information and had many functions.

The one in my hand showed the picture of a micro-sized piece of plastic tube. Under the tube was a caption that told me trace amounts of reanu had been found on it.

My head whipped to Drena and she just gave me a look. I let out a huff then sat back in my chair to ponder what this meant. Reanu was a combination of two drugs, each already potent enough on their own.

When mixed together though... I ran a hand through my hair, trying to fit the pieces together. Lyce was a plant that grew way out by the mountains. When smoked or inhaled, it often made you think yourself invincible.

Kylaz grew mostly in areas that were hot year-round. Which meant it had been imported here. Kylaz often made the user hallucinate, sometimes for days at a time.

Put the two together and you had people cutting out their own throats, using their powers to blow up buildings, blasting innocent bystanders' heads off, and all sorts of fucked up shit. Yet, still, people ate it up like candy, willing to do anything for that ultimate high.

My shoulders slumped, and I thought about the men and women hooked on the stuff, those who hadn't known what they were in for before they'd taken that first puff or sniff.

Drugs were something that drew you in, and once you were there, they held you tightly in their grip, making it a fight for your life to be able to let go. Many people, in many walks of life, succumbed to drugs, and no one could really know what'd led a person to their first taste.

It was my job to deal with the stuff from the moment it was made, until the moment someone took it and lost complete control. I wiped sweat from my brow because when it came to drugs like this one, there were no winners, only victims and those who would profit from them.

Not taking away personal accountability. The moment you decided to take a drug, you made a choice that not only affected you but everyone around you. That was one of the reasons I abhorred those who took skunk oil, because they knew they were getting high while skunks like myself paid the price for it in blood.

Dangerous purple thiols went up my arm, and I took a long breath and made an effort to calm myself down. This was serious, and if Ham was behind it, he had to be stopped, no questions asked.

"Anything from the flies who fled from the beach? Are we still tracking them?"

Garrett shook his head. "They disappeared after three minutes, and neither Albright nor Scope can find them."

Shit.

Drena looked down at the retag where the information about reanu was still lit up, and I saw a look of fear cross her face. "We've done good keeping that shit away from here. I think the closest case is over three hundred miles away."

Garrett sat on the opposite side of the table from me, while Vin leaned up against the wall, arms folded in front of him. Vin wasn't really supposed to be here, but no one had said anything because my fellow Scope agents probably thought he was Albright, and vice versa.

I could see the muscle in Garett's right jaw working and knew he was just as fucked up about this as the rest of us. "The question I have is, was the lyce and kylaz mixed together here or was it already reanu when it arrived?"

Jax walked farther into the room and I could tell from the look on his face his next words would piss me off. "We're going to find Drew. Everyone in this room is committed to doing that. But afterward, you guys are off this case. There will be no discussion. This falls solely into Albright territory."

He had that unyielding look on his face he got when that steel, the one that went down his spine, spread out to other parts of his body, and I knew he was unmovable.

The other Scope agents in the room, didn't know this though, and they begin to loudly voice their disapproval, Drena and Garrett included.

"Drew!" I said, making all eyes turn to me. "He has less than two hours so let's get on it."

I looked back down at the retag and something occurred to me. I typed for a minute, telling the device to search the plastic for what other elements might be lurking on it, even the smallest most insignificant thing.

I waited about five minutes before it listed other compounds that had touched or rubbed up against the plastic. One of them caught my eye, and I turned the retag around so others in the room could see it.

"Look at this." I pointed to where it said, Four-A Dye. Four-A Dye was used in making high-end clothes. It could transform that 'little black dress' into a garment that never faded, and stayed resilient, always looking like you'd just bought it the day before.

Jax went still, his face working through a range of emotions. "There are only three companies around here that work with that material, and all of them have factories."

Drena nodded, and from the glow in her cheeks, she must have thought he was on to something. "Ham is a big name around here. He owns multiple businesses. It's not surprising that one of these guys would throw in with him. Especially since reanu has the potential to earn you an extra hundred million a year."

"What else do those three companies deal in?" asked Garrett. "We can use that against the list of materials that've been shipped in lately, maybe narrow it down a bit more."

It was a good idea, and something else occurred to me as well. "Ham's people were probably down by the water because he had a shipment come in. The question is when, and who brought it?"

Jax held up a finger, excitement dancing in his eyes, and I knew he was officially on the hunt now and wouldn't stop until we completely nailed this thing down. He turned to three of the Albright agents in the room. "We need to know what's been in and out of that water for the last few weeks. Check with the Hailstate and see what they know."

Hailstate was law enforcement on the water. They monitored all ships and boats and kept detailed records. Enlisting their help could turn the tide on this investigation.

Adrenaline pumped through me, and then the look that'd been on Drew's face as he was being choked filtered through my brain. Anger made my fist curl. We had to get him back.

I knew, we needed to stop the reanu from hitting the streets, but we also needed to secure Drew's safe return as well. A lump formed in my throat and I tried to push it down as I looked at my watch. He really didn't have much time left now.

Chapter 7

We split up into three teams. Each taking one of the companies that made and worked with Four-A Dye. Jax, Drena, Garrett, Vin, and a few other agents were on the same team as me.

Drena and I went into the office building that hosted 'Premium Rags' while Jax and the others went into their large factory, about two hundred yards away.

The place was huge, and though a security guard had stopped us before we could enter the property, another one stopped us before we were allowed inside the office building.

Once we produced our badges, we were shown into a large room with white sterile walls, and a brown wooden table with twenty chairs around it. No one would suspect this of being anything but a place of business, I thought as I looked around.

The heat could be turned up to a hundred and I'd still probably freeze from the coldness of this place.

We only waited about two minutes before Todd Brenks, the owner and manager, walked into the room. He was a tall man with eyebrows that seemed to be daring you to cut them.

He had a bald head and wore a blue suit that probably cost more than most people's houses.

Drena and I both started to take out our badges, but he waved a hand, stopping us as he took a seat at the table. "I know who you are. Heard it from the guard at the gate and at the door. What do you want?"

I looked at the clock on his wall and felt my legs go weak. We had to move this along, as fast as we could. "I'm interested in your Four-A Dye. Can you tell me more about it?"

Todd's brows furrowed. "What do you want to know?"

Drena's eyes also went to the clock, but she was careful not to throw a look my way. Which was good, because I could feel the sweat going down my spine as I thought of all the things Ham could be doing to Drew at this very moment.

"Have you had a break-in lately? Maybe one you didn't report. Any employees suddenly quit? Anyone you don't recognize hanging around?" she asked him.

"No," he said, standing, but I could tell he hadn't thought about it at all. He didn't understand why we were here and he just wanted to get back to his work, without our interruptions.

"Have you had any shipments coming in? Anything go wrong on that end?" I asked, thinking maybe there was a connection that way. I was grasping at straws now, but we really didn't have much time.

He stiffened when I said that, and hope flared in my gut, making my pulse quicken as it did when I was on to a clue.

"We make Four-A Dye here," he said, and his eyes looked dark, like a man who thought his whole business was ready to crumble at his feet. "We still need the materials to make it though, had a recent shipment filled with supplies come in the other day. The usual foreman that oversees that part got sick. Been here twenty years and maybe only missed work five times. Came down with some forty-eight-hour bug. He's better now."

Drena started working keys on her retag. "He was out for the shipment, so someone else had to take his place. Who was that person?"

Todd licked his lips. "Frank Jiles. He's not here today."

We met up with the others as we were all leaving. "Frank Jiles," Jax said, holding up his retag with the man's address on it. Drena and I had gotten the address as well, before leaving the building.

"Also, Kerry Streens. She seems interesting," Garrett said. He also had her last known location.

Good. I could breathe again because at least now we had something to work with. Drena called the other teams. They'd come up short, but she gave them this Kerry person's address to check out.

We went to Frank's, getting a warrant while in progress. My hands shook with the urge to question the man, my gut telling me he knew something. I just hoped he was home.

Frank, being an employee of Premium Rags lived in a nice middle-class neighborhood. His house was red brick, and his yard neat and orderly.

Knowing that Frank may be our last chance to save Drew, I went to the windows and around the sides, while Drena and the others knocked on the front door. At first, I didn't see anything, then I heard a cough, followed by what sounded like someone puking their lungs out.

I took off for the front door, wondering if he was in there alone, but knowing I was going in any way. "Frank's inside!" I said as I skirted around to the front of the house.

They all turned to me, most looking confused like they hadn't understood what I'd said. I quickly repeated myself, so they'd know to be on their guard, then shot yellow thiols at the knob on the door, breaking it apart. Without a moment to spare, I ran into the house, the smell of death hitting me immediately and making me gag.

I ran down the hall, the others behind me, as we all looked for this Frank guy. He was in the last room on the right, and I gasped when I saw him, stopping short of going inside.

Frank's body was covered in boils, his skin had turned an ashen gray, his bones were pushing out through his skin, and his face was swollen twice the normal size.

Behind me, Garrett let out a curse. "Looks like Ham already got to him. Don't know what disease does all this though." He turned to me. "Can you help him?"

I was pretty sure he was too far gone, but Drena was already on her com, calling help in. I put up my shield, and then took a bottle of skunk oil from my pocket and passed it to Jax. "This could be highly contagious. You guys need to drink this. The skunk oil will kill whatever it is before it can hurt you."

I took a swig from the oil I kept around my neck, then taking a deep breath, and praying it wasn't my last, I walked into what had essentially become a death room.

Chapter 8

Jax came in behind me and closed the door. "Do you want me?" He pointed to my back.

I shook my head. I did need more skunk oil, and Jax was an expert at getting it, but I wouldn't expose myself here, not when we didn't know what we were dealing with.

I pulled the valve from around my neck. It was all I had left, as I'd given Jax and the others the extra supply I kept. I held it in front of me and let out a curse. There was only a small bit in there.

Frank was still breathing, so that meant there was still a chance. We'd been shown a picture of what he looked like, but under all the open sores and boils I didn't even recognize him.

I swallowed hard, and came to a decision, as I took off my shirt.

"Rye-"

"No, Jax. I don't want to talk about it. This man won't die, not if I can stop it."

Jax pulled me to him and kissed me hard on the lips. "Okay," he said softly. "Just keep your hands low."

Often times when skunk oil was removed from the lateral glands in our backs, thiols would shoot out, because well, it was unpleasant and felt like our insides were being torn apart.

"Get as much as you can without making me sick," I told him. Taking too much oil at once would render a skunk helpless, while draining us of oil completely would paralyze us for months, maybe even kill us. Unless we were given some oil to help us heal, but most who dealt in skunk oil didn't give a fuck about the skunks they were draining, unless they needed them again, of course.

"I'll take enough to give you a little too. We still have to find Drew, and you need your energy, okay."

I nodded then bent over, as he held out his hand. I sucked in a breath and then waited for what I knew would come. Jax had the valve that'd been around my neck, and I hoped it was large enough because he needed a lot.

"Hold on." Jax disappeared for a second and them came back with the extra bottle that I'd given to the agents in case this place was contaminated. It was empty, but that just meant we could fill it up.

Jax started the process and I tried not to scream as the oil was being sucked from my back, draining from my insides. Still, I had to do this. Yes, I knew that this Frank had probably been involved in all the fucked-up shit that Ham had done, but as agents of the law, we didn't get to pick and choose who we saved.

Frank would get his day in court, but I would have spent the rest of my days in a guilt-ridden abyss had I let this man die, knowing that I could have saved him. Nope, sorry, when I took a vow to uphold the law I meant it, with every fiber of my being.

Jax was almost finished and I closed my eyes against the pain, as thiols shot out of my hand onto the floor.

"Okay," Jax said, pushing hair out of my face and pulling me to him. "You first."

I shook my head and pointed to the bed.

Jax got that look of steel in his eyes as he held the bottle up to my lips. Knowing that we'd just waste time arguing about it, I opened wide and let him pour some in.

In a manner of seconds, renewed energy flowed through me and I was pretty sure I could climb a mountain and swim a hundred miles all within mere seconds.

Jax dropped to his knees, and while he took the valve and begin pouring it down Frank's throat, I took the bottle and started rubbing oil over his whole body. It would work quicker that way.

Drena had already called for help, so hopefully, they'd be here soon. Skunk oil was fast acting though, which is one reason it was in such high demand. The more I poured on him, the more I could see the boils and sores disappear.

His skin was returning back to normal, and the swelling in his face was going down.

"Is everything okay?" I looked up as Drena opened the door, only to whip my head back around when I heard Jax's voice.

"What the fuck!"

I looked at the bed where the skin was now clear, all the sores removed, the swelling gone down, and... Drew?

"It's a trap!" I yelled, panic rising in my throat as I threw up my shield to protect myself and everyone in the house.

A boom sounded, and then the roof caved in as fire licked at our heels. Even though I knew my shield would protect me, I still braced myself for impact.

Then, before I could check to make sure everyone was okay, another boom sounded, and then the whole house crumbled around us. Plaster and parts of the roof bounced off my shield, and I fell to one knee, as it was becoming too much of a strain to keep my shield up, especially with it holding so many people.

Then the walls were gone, and we were standing in the spot the house had once been. I gasped, as sweat rolled down my face and I knew I couldn't hold it for much longer.

Jax's arms came around me, as he held me close, his warmth making it easier for me to breathe. "It's all gone," I said as my shield fell away. Everything that hadn't been protected by my thiols was gone.

"He blew up the fucking house!" Garrett said, and I realized of us all, he probably was the only one who could have withstood the blaze.

But why would Ham do this, if he still needed me to get his brother out?

"He knew you would use your shield," Drena said, answering my unspoken question. "Either that or he has a backup plan."

I looked around. Drew and Jax had been the first ones to go under my shield. Jax was beside me, but Drew... I felt every emotion I had rage through me because Drew was nowhere to be found and in his place was a message pod dancing in the air.

Chapter 9

Of course, it was Ham's face we saw when the message pod began to play. "Give me my brother at the appointed time, or your dear Drew won't have a second chance."

With that, the message went blank. I tried to push down my anger at how thoroughly we'd been played.

"So, my brother was here, in that house just now. That was him lying on that bed?" Vin's lower jaw worked, and his black hair was plastered to his head. The way he stood all rigid and still made me think he'd lose it at any moment now.

Garrett walked up behind him and started talking to him while Drena conferenced with a few agents.

Jax stood beside me, the look in his eyes saying he was on to something. "What is it?" I asked, and he peered around, before crooking a finger and calling me closer.

"We're being watched," he said once I was close enough for him to whisper.

I looked at him strangely, trying to figure out how he'd come to that conclusion and he cocked a brow, waiting for me to figure it out for myself.

I thought about what'd just happened, my mind rapidly going through the steps because I knew we didn't have much time. "He didn't blow up the house until I had everyone under my thiols shield. He can't get his brother back if we're all dead. This was just a power play. Something to show me who's in charge."

Jax nodded, wiping sweat down his face, his black shaggy hair now a mess over his head. "He wanted to show us what he could do. He waved Drew under our noses and then snatched him back just because he could."

"Because he wanted to show us that he could," Drena said, walking up. She was covered from head to toe with her shield and I didn't blame her one bit. "He wanted to prove to us that he has us in the palm of his hands so that we feel we have no choice but to do as he asks."

Garrett and Vin walked up as well. "How many eyes do you think he has watching us?" Garrett asked, looking around. "No way he's able to do this alone. I bet he was probably somewhere across town when the house exploded."

I had to agree. Not only that, but if he did have people watching us then we needed to find them now and figure out what they knew. "Let's spread out," I said. "After that, we've got to get to Estes. I don't like how he's been one step ahead of us this whole time."

Garrett and an Albright agent who also was of dragon DNA took to the sky while Vin unleashed his claws and went to look in some nearby trees.

Drena, with her shield still up, went to the back of the other houses on Frank's street, while Jax held out his hand in a way that made me think he was trying to pull something to him.

What the heck was he doing? I mean, I knew he could pull the grease out of a pizza, but could he really summon someone before him? I imagined they'd have to be awfully close for him to do so.

My eyes roamed around, trying to figure out where would be a good place if you just wanted to sit back and watch someone. I was about to say something to Jax when the flap of wings had me looking up.

"Caught him in a car three streets over. It was his little spy equipment that gave him away." Garrett placed a tall guy with olive skin and a bald head down before us.

I held out my hand and stinky, funky, silver thiols appeared around me. If I hit him with this, he'd probably never recover. The smell would stay in his skin, his mouth, and every other part of his body for months. It would stop him from eating. It would corrode his insides, causing him to deteriorate and shrink away to nothing.

Or I could hit him with a weaker dose, but with Drew's life on the line, I was through being generous. "What the fuck do you know?" I asked as I got closer, the look on my face letting him know I meant business.

"Hey," he said, putting his hands up like that would really protect him. "All I know is that there's a big deal going down in about two hours. Biggest transaction of Ham's career." He licked his lips, his eyes full of panic as he looked at me, probably thinking of the horrible death that would befall him if I actually hit him with silver thiols.

I powered down for a minute, as I thought over what he'd just said because the answer was in there somewhere. I turned back to the bald dude, who looked like he was ready to shit his pants at any moment now. "Is Ham working with someone new?"

Dude shook his head. "No. He's been working with him all the time, just behind the scenes. Jerald is the one who usually meets the guy face to face."

That's what it was! I snapped my fingers and looked to Jax and Garrett. "If Ham has been pulling the strings from behind the curtain, then his supplier may not trust Ham. He may not even know Ham. Especially if he's only ever dealt with Jerald." Ham's way of keeping his hands clean, no doubt.

"Jerald may be the only person he was willing to deal with," Jax piped in.

"No Jerald, no deal," Garrett said. "Which explains why he wants him out so bad."

I nodded. "Dude just said it was the biggest deal Ham's ever done. He'd probably be willing to risk anything for that. Don't forget, reanu can earn you an extra hundred million a year. Lots of people would do some crazy shit for that type of money."

Drena and a few others came back to tell us they'd heard from the other agents and Kerry Streens had turned up nothing. Then we explained what we'd just discovered.

Drena snapped her fingers. "He doesn't have the reanu yet, then. I mean what we found was probably the discards of a very small sample shipment. That means the real deal is coming tonight. Which is why he needs Jerald to make the exchange"

She looked down at her watch, then back at me, a haunted look on her face. "Drew's time is up. We have to go."

Chapter 10

We arrived at the bottom of Estes as fast as we could. On the way there, Drena and Jax had both called in more agents. Whoever Ham's supplier was, he had to bring the stuff in some way. We figured it was a large shipment, so we alerted Hailstate, as well as air traffic control. We also had the roads being watched just in case he switched it up.

Anger made something hard and cold go down my spine as I looked up at the top of the building, the place Ham had wanted his brother delivered. Ham stood up there now, with about fifty men and women behind him. Maybe even more than that, but I couldn't see that far.

He had his left hand around Drew's throat, his disease-carrying fingernails poised to go right into his neck, as he drooped him over the building. "You better tell me that my brother is in a car on the way here. If not..."

He dangled Drew over a little more and my breath caught in my throat as rage boiled through me. Drew was under my protection. He'd done nothing to deserve this and if Ham thought he could just rub my tummy and have me do his bidding, then he had another thing coming.

As we stood there, more agents pulled up, and even an ambulance or two, which was good thinking on someone's part, because shit was ready to get bloody.

This dude, this Ham, had jerked us around all day and he didn't get to do that. He didn't get to violate the way he had and get away with it. Angry purple thiols swirled around me and I didn't even try to calm myself down.

Ham was busy saying something, while his followers looked upon him, probably with pride. Right now, he had both Albright and Scope at his feet, which in their eyes probably made him invincible.

I cracked my neck, my knuckles cracking on their own. Drew was too far away for me to see his face, but I imagined it held nothing but fear, and a pleading for us down below to do something.

Standing beside Ham was the dude Frank, and I knew then that we really had been played like a fiddle. My mind strayed back to thoughts of Drew, to his smile, to his carefree attitude, and no, dammit no.

He didn't get to do this, wouldn't get away with this. Ham shook Drew back and forth, and the rage that seeped into my bones, to every part of my core, just wouldn't be contained anymore. I turned to Garrett, a sneer on my face. "Catch him when he falls." My voice was low now, guttural sounding.

"Who? What?" he asked, but I had already turned away.

I wiped sweat from my face as I looked up to where Ham still had Drew. He was still trying to give out orders, but I was too far gone to care about what he had to say. If I'd been thinking straight, I probably never would have done this, but at the moment my mind was on a faraway boat somewhere. I had to be precise though.

Holding a hand out, I gave Garrett a look to let him know I meant *now*, then pointed my finger and used red thiols to slice each one of Ham's left fingers off at the knuckles, including the thumb.

Drew started a freefall in the sky, and some of the flies jumped, but Garrett had moved with lighting speed and folded Drew in his arms, bringing him to the ground and placing him in back of one of the waiting ambulances.

Ham let out a scream as blood spurted from his hand, and from the corner of my eye, I could see both Drena and Jax giving me wide-eyed stares.

I wouldn't explain myself, and I didn't have time to anyway, because Ham and all of his people jumped, hopped, flew, and bounced off the rooftop, all headed our way, some already throwing out fireballs or using their telekinesis to knock agents back.

Before they even reached the ground we'd already started a counter attack, and now the fight was on. A woman held out her hand toward me, and I shot red thiols into her eyes. She screamed and fell out of the way.

Someone grabbed me by the back of the head and slammed me face first into a nearby brick wall. Pain shot through me, and I let out a grunt as blood trickled down my face.

Then I sent an elbow back, and since it connected, the red thiols around my arm probably sliced into their face, which explained why I was suddenly let go.

I blinked, ready to turn left, but then a kick to my face sent me sprawling. I landed hard on my side. The guy who'd kicked me had his foot raised above my head, and I shot thiols at his legs, slicing them both out from under him.

A woman with wolf DNA picked Drena up over her head and slammed her down on the concrete. Drena hit hard, her shield wrapping around her, then she hopped back to her feet, sending a fist to the lady's face.

The woman's head snapped back, but even as it did, she kicked out her foot in an effort to trip Drena up. Drena jumped back, then brought her hard-shell hand around, cracking the lady's face open. The woman fell to the ground, but before she'd even landed, Drena had already jumped back into the fight.

Vin had another fox on him, pounding him in the face. The guy was relentless, and once Vin went down to one knee, I figured it was over. Instead, Vin used his claws to rip into the man's calf muscles.

The man let out a howl, as blood and tissue pooled around his leg, and Vin used the distraction to hit him with an uppercut, knocking him back. Vin grabbed the man's head and slammed it into the street, then he hopped back up and pounced on the guy to his left, who already had his hand up ready to attack.

Garrett was covered in fire, so only another dragon could get close. He had balls of fire in his hands, and he threw them at anyone who came near. Then a tall guy, built like a mountain, also with dragon DNA, picked him up and slammed him hard into the ground.

The guy then dropped down with him, holding up a fist, in a way that said he was ready to pound Garrett into the concrete. Garrett's foot kicked out and knocked him in the face. Then he went for the middle section, using his claws to rip into the guy's stomach, pulling the skin apart.

The guy let out a scream, and Garrett sunk claws into his eyes digging, into them. All the fight had gone out of the man now, and blood leaked from his face and stomach. Garrett, without missing a beat, then pointed his finger, a line of fire coming out. He wrapped it around a man with fly DNA above him, then slammed him hard to the ground.

A dude with fox DNA came at me, and since I knew any energy he used to fight with was probably full of poison, I shot out a hail of red thiols, ripping his face apart.

A girl with telekinesis got her hold on me and pulled me to her. I couldn't break free, try as I might, and I did try hard. I had no idea what she planned on doing with me once she had me, but as soon as I was close enough and she needed to refocus her energy for whatever she had planned next, I shot red thiols out of my mouth. She screamed as thiols ripped apart the inside of her mouth and throat.

Jax had one guy go low to his legs, trying to take them out, so he squinted, and soon the bones in the guy's hands were at Jax's feet. The guy's hands didn't have a cut or opening on them, and now he just screamed, as he looked at it, not sure what had happened to him probably.

Jax turned, just as a fist was coming to his face. His head bounced back, but his eyes were already squinted, and soon a red puddle was at the other guy's feet, as his skin lost all color. Jax had drained the guy of blood, because that's the type of shit Jax did.

Jax then turned and sent an elbow into the face of a different guy ready to attack him, before following it up with a kick to the face, then a chop to the throat. The guy fell on his ass, but then four more took his place and I knew Jax was outnumbered.

We didn't have any more skunk oil, we'd used it all, and I couldn't give any more, not for a few weeks, as that's how long it would take for mine to build back up.

One of the four was Ham, and I took off that way, and then watched in horror as Ham sunk the claws from his right hand into Jax's neck. My world stopped at that moment, as I watched Jax's skin go from its usual pale to an ashen pallor.

Boils and open sores covered his body, blood leaked from his eyes, his body shook, his knees hit the ground, foam poured from his mouth and through it all I stayed stock still, immobilized as what I loved most crumbled before me.

My heart beat out of my chest, rage curled in my stomach, and the image of Ham's smug face as he and his followers walked to stand in front of the building was enough to send me over the edge.

They'd just taken out a top Albright agent, not something many could brag about, and now they were feeling themselves as they stood before us, them on one side, us on the other.

Jax... My Jax... My every... Cold fury boiled in my gut as black thiols exploded around me and I knew I couldn't hold it any longer. My chest heaved with the effort to keep it in, and I knew that it... that I... wouldn't be contained.

"Run!" I said to my team, who were behind me, because what happened next was not going to be pretty. We were headed for a bloodbath, and anyone in my way would be a victim.

The image of Jax going down to his knees flashed before me and I let out a wrathful scream as red and black thiols exploded out of me. "Run!" I yelled again, not just to my team, but to everyone in the near vicinity.

Ham and his goons stood tall before me, and I didn't know if they didn't understand what was happening or truly thought themselves untouchable.

Instead of getting the heck out of there, they attacked. Telekinesis held up their hands, dragons threw their fire, foxes hurled their poison, wolves bared their teeth, the deloux on those with fly DNA must have been going crazy, yet none moved, all still seemed to think they were in control of this fight.

They hurled everything they had at me, and rage, hurt, and anger bit into my skin because they were trying to take my life. They were hitting me with everything they had, trying to kill me like they.... Jax... oh, Jax...

I screamed again as red and black thiols shot out of every part of my body, blowing everything they threw my way back. They wanted to kill me? To remove me from this earth? They weren't strong enough and I'd yet to meet the motherfucker who was.

You come for my throat, and I'll rip yours out, every, fucking, time. I rolled my shoulders; if they wanted a fight, then I'd damned well give them one.

By this point, my mind was gone, and I was reduced to my baser instincts. They were trying their best to kill me, and I wouldn't fucking let them. I walked toward them, my thiols so out of control that the red and black mixed together dropped them where they stood.

Head high, one foot in front of the other, I moved closer. My thiols went to the neck of a dragon, taking his head off. A telekinesis's eyes exploded. A wolf's whole body separated as he was split in half. A fox lost his hands, then his feet, then his guts exploded from his stomach. A fly's whole body was ripped apart as bloody pieces of him fell to the ground.

They all fell at my feet. I walked through them, black and red thiols shooting out, dropping them like beasts lined up to be slaughtered. By now they knew this was something they couldn't handle, and some tried to run, but I knew that Drena and the others were close by, and they'd better not let one of them escape.

They'd killed Jax... They'd... I let out a howl, as the wound from what I'd witnessed grew even worse. With most of his men scattered, only Ham stood before me now, and he was steadily backing up.

Gone was the smug look from his face, and in its place was wide-eyed terror.

"I told you to run!" I said, my voice barely recognizable. "You should have fucking listened!"

Something flashed in his eyes, and I didn't know if it was arrogance, that one such as me, could take out one such as himself, but whatever it was he ended up paying for it with his life.

Using his right hand, he unsheathed a long blade, bringing it toward my throat, and from the look in his eyes, he actually thought this was it, that he'd won. Black and red thiols crumbled the blade into confetti and then it shot out at him, and I heard him scream, as his body was turned inside out, ripped apart, and then he was reduced to random skin, blood, and tissue floating in the wind.

My legs went out from under me after that, as did my thiols and I heard both Drena and Garett calling my name. Jax... Drena's voice was tight as she held me to her and I wondered how she could dare touch a beast like me.

"It's okay," she whispered in my ear as Garrett wiped soaking wet hair out of my face. "It's okay," she said over and over again.

But it wasn't, the bloody body parts piled around us said so. "I told them to run," I said my voice breaking. "I told them..."

Garrett shook his head. "They attacked you, tried to kill you. What the fuck else were you supposed to do?"

I looked at Garrett then burst into tears, wrapping my arms around his waist. "Jax!" I screamed out, then Garett said words that made my heart stop.

"Jax is alive, Rye. One of the ambulance crew had skunk DNA. We took him right there, and dude covered him with the stuff, plus had him drinking it. Jax is okay, a little weak, but okay."

I let out a breath, and then everything went black as my world folded in on itself.

Chapter 11

Three weeks later

I sat on the floor of my living room, having been through the ringer these last few weeks. I'd be allowed back to work tomorrow as the investigation into my behavior was now complete and I'd been cleared.

Scope had known exactly what a skunk was capable of when they'd hired me. It was what those on the other side of the law were capable of that scared them most.

The thing was though, I'd waited for more of the deep-seated guilt to set in and it hadn't. I mean, I was upset and felt that it was fucked-up that things had ended the way that they had, but I didn't really feel guilty.

And that *scared* me just a little because I realized that maybe what I was, was a survivor. That wasn't always a good thing. It meant that I would do whatever it took, take out whoever was in my way, to stay breathing and though it was something important to know about one's self, it was also hard to accept.

At its most basic core, the will to survive would often override common sense, and the moral imprinting we'd been brought up with.

My stomach growled, and I realized I hadn't eaten since breakfast, and it was almost six in the afternoon. I would have called Drena to see if she wanted to grab something, but she'd taken the week off to spend time with her wife, giving her the love and attention she deserved. I didn't want to interfere with that.

I looked at the clock again. Jax should be off by now. Maybe he'd stop by like he usually did. I shook my head, clearing it of his body hitting the ground covered in sores and boils. He was better now, the skunk on the ambulance had taken good care of him and he'd been back at work for two weeks now.

Drew had also made a full recovery and I was glad to see that he was doing well. His brother Vin had gone hard for him, something I'm sure Garrett or someone else had already told him.

Speaking of Garrett, I could tell how interested he'd been in Vin, but Garrett was a player, a straight love 'em and leave 'em type. I chuckled when I thought about it because Vin was not one to be trifled with.

I heard a key jingle and Jax walked through the front door, his arms loaded down. I made a move to get up and help, but he shook his head.

"What do you have?" I asked.

He placed his stuff down on the floor beside me then went off to the kitchen, bringing back plates and utensils. My heart warmed as I watched him. His black hair was in shaggy curls all around his head and his silver eyes were lit up, making my heart lurch again, because damn, I was glad that he was okay.

"Smells like steak and cheese subs. Is it?" I licked my lips just thinking about it.

Jax let out a laugh then bent over and kissed me on the lips, his warmth radiating through me, and damn, just the thought that I could have lost him.

He took a seat on the floor with me, holding up a six-pack of what was both our favorite beer. "We can drink it warm."

I really didn't care. The only thing I wanted was sitting right here beside me, and that's all that really mattered.

Delia Uncaged

Chapter 1

My hands shook as I looked at the paper telling me I was to appear before the Council of Langen. The Council of Langen didn't really get involved in the everyday life of the people of the Isles, so when they did intervene, you knew it was a big deal.

No one even knew where the five Council members resided, only that they were all-powerful, and their word was law. I did a slow slide on to my couch, my throat suddenly dry. The council wanted to see me? Why?

The Isles were five hundred miles from where I lived, and truth be told, though most of my family resided there, I hadn't been in years.

The people of the Isles were very powerful beings, but pacifists to the core. So was I to a certain point, because it was how I'd been raised. Before I'd been born, my father had gotten a good job offer here, where I lived now, and moved the whole family away from the Isles.

But we'd always gone back there for long extended stays. So, I'd grown up splitting my time between here and the Isles, calling both places my home.

The sound of my phone going off startled me and I nearly jumped out of my chair, still wondering what I could have done to draw the attention of the Council.

Six years ago, I'd been put in a mental institution for a crime I hadn't commit. Having spent five years of my life there, I'd only been home a year, and sometimes the fear of being sent back took hold of me and would not let go.

Pushing those thoughts away, I answered the phone without looking to see who it was and was pleased to hear Leon's voice on the other end.

Leon was a cop who'd become a great friend. Though he had been the detective who'd arrested me and helped in the judge's decision to send me away, but he'd been fooled just like everyone else had. I'd been accused of murder, but you can't kill someone who's immortal so...

"Delia, what time are the twins coming?" Leon asked, and I almost kicked myself for forgetting they were coming to take us back to Kelm with them. Kelm was in an alternate universe we sometimes visited, as we had a couple of friends there.

I looked at my clock on the wall. "They should pop up in a couple of minutes." We hung up and I ran a hand through my shoulder-length black hair, knowing I should probably go over it a few times before the twins arrived.

Klenaya and Kyle were twenty-two years old and were from Kelm.

I stood and was just putting the finishing touches on my hair when I heard a voice that I didn't recognize. Anyone with blood from the Isles had a mental link with each other. No, we couldn't read or influence each other's thoughts, for that you'd have to be a telepath like my sister.

The voice was female, so I listened closely to see what she had to say. *The cage is open, the dog is loose, the cage is open, the dog is loose*. Over and over again that's all I heard. What the krankle? What was she trying to say?

"Ready to go?" a voice sounded behind me, and I turned quickly to see Klenaya and Kyle standing in front of me. My smile softened as I looked at them. These two never failed to put me in a good mood. I was six years their senior, but even with the age difference, we still got on great.

I gave them both the once over. They each had bone straight blue-green hair that stopped at their shoulders. Also, their bright purple eyes often lit up when they were excited or very pissed off. Sometimes they just lit up for no reason at all, which was something I thought was very cool.

Klenaya had on black pants that stopped about two inches from her calves. Kyle wore blue jeans and a white shirt. They both had dark bronze-colored skin, much like my own.

"I'm ready." I started to say something else, but then the same voice from before popped back into my head, tutting the same line. I let out a breath and closed my eyes, trying to suss out something to identify the person.

"What are you doing?"

My eyes snapped open and coming in the door was detective Leon Kravis. Leon had bright green eyes, pale skin, and shockingly red hair. He was a man about business, evident by the way he strolled into the room, shoulders wide, body alert. With him nothing came before that badge he wore, a lesson I'd learned some time ago.

The cage is open, the dog is loose. Okay, enough is enough. My face must have spoken to my feelings because when I looked back up I had three concerned faces staring back at me.

Something heavy uncurled in my chest. Growing up I'd never really had any friends besides my sister Lena, and that had followed me into adulthood. I wasn't used to people giving a crap about how I felt, so it always kind of threw me when these three showed that they cared.

Figuring I may as well let them know, I handed the paper over to Leon. His eyes scanned the words, a twin on each side of him, reading as well. He handed it back, his forehead in a crinkle now. "So, when do we leave?"

"What?"

Klenaya waved a hand. "You didn't really think we'd let you do this alone, did you?"

Kyle nodded. "Un-huh, she did. I can see it in her eyes. She never even gave a thought to bringing someone with her."

Well, he was right about that, but I wouldn't give him the pleasure of saying so. I'd never heard the end of it if I did. Kyle liked to stick his chest out from time to time and telling him that he was right about something was a surefire way of having him remind you of that forever.

A knot formed in my back and I rolled my shoulders trying to work it out. What I hadn't told any of them was that the council could impose any rule they wanted on me, which meant that once there, I may not be able to leave.

Chapter 2

The twins opened a portal and we went through it, landing in the family room of the big mansion they lived in. Since their father, Bale, was next in line to rule Kelm, he stayed there to take part in the day to day operations.

The current ruler, who would still have the seat for a few hundred more years, was Yama. That was another thing about the people of this universe. They were immortal. The only thing that could kill them was if they stopped taking the blue powder-like substance called tacium.

The mansion belonged to whoever ruled Kelm, and so right now that was still Yama. We'd probably only been there about ten minutes when he walked into the room, deep in conversation with Bale.

Bale was a short man with a bald head and like most people when they talked to Yama, he was absorbed in the conversation. I watched them, understanding all too well.

Yama was the light that made the stars shine at night, the flame that danced on the wood when it was cold, the ruffle of wind through your hair on a cool day... His ebony skin was a shade darker than my own, and his purple hair hung loosely at his shoulders.

His red eyes often looked right through you, and with every step he took, there was no doubt who was in charge.

"Delia, hey," he said, smiling at me, and making heat pool in my stomach. He gave Leon a nod.

Bale's eyes went wide as he looked up, and I could tell he hadn't known we were there. I sat on a long blue couch, Klenaya beside me. Kyle sat in the chair to our right, his feet dipping into the water from the floor.

Kelm was made up of ninety percent water. Its people were seventy-eight to eighty-three percent water. There was no dry ground here, no matter where you went, the water always came up to at least your ankles. That had taken some getting use to at first, but after coming here for almost a year now, it was just par for the course.

I looked down as it lapped around my legs. Controlling water is what I did. I'd always thought of it as a useless skill, but it came in handy from time to time.

Leon sat on the couch in front of me, looking at his phone, and I wondered if he'd caught a case and had to go. I sure hoped not. He swiped at his phone a few times, then nodded and put it away, and I knew that meant that everything was fine.

I let out a breath. If we were going to do this, then I definitely wanted him by my side. Leon was smart, quick, loyal, had the power of telekinesis and would never let you down, no matter the situation.

Bale went to sit around a big silver table, and I marveled at how it would never tarnish because the tacium was in that too. It was in everything here.

Yama gave me a look like he knew exactly what was going on and just wanted me to say it. He did that a lot and I let out a big breath, suddenly finding it hard to breathe.

His eyes crinkled as he looked at me, and I felt myself go boneless. I shook my head. What in the world was wrong with me? *The cage is open, the dog is loose.* "Ahh." I grabbed my head, then decided to push it down, because now was not the time.

"We need to go." I stood so fast I almost tripped over myself. The voice was driving me insane. What was it that she wanted?

Leon stood too, his hands in the back of his black jeans. "You're nervous, I get that. But you don't have to be ashamed in front of us."

I swallowed hard. He would think that, since when we'd met I'd been covered in my now ex-boyfriend's blood, screaming about how I hadn't really killed him, and that he was immortal and would rise again.

No one had believed me, and I'd spent five years of my life locked away in a sanitarium. Of course, Greg *had* been immortal, and without him and his devious plot to use me to take over Yama's rule of Kelm, I never would have met Klenaya and the others, so I owed him for that if nothing else.

My legs weak, I sat back down on the couch for a moment.

Yama came closer and then dropped to his knees in front of me, his red eyes intent on my golden ones. "Make it rain."

Huh? "I can't... Why?"

His eyes stared hotly into mine, making me gulp and lick my lips at the same time. He always told me to believe in my powers, to have more confidence in myself.

"Pull the moisture from the air and do it. Or..." He ran his hand through the water beneath us, then scooped some up and waved it under my nose. I took a big sniff, and... oh... all I smelt was him.

The signal I got from the water gave me glimpses of not just him, but everyone who'd ever passed through it, including myself and Leon.

His eyes watched me, never leaving my face for a second, and man did it feel like he was staring straight into my soul. "Do you see? Do you see what you can do? Now make it rain." Honestly, he believed in my abilities a whole lot more than I did, but...

Closing my eyes, I reached my hand out. It was nothing for me to make fog or steam, so I'd just approach this the same way. Once a good bit of moisture had accumulated around me and the air was dusty and dry, I flung my hands out and the water from the floor rose up in sprinkles, as more fell from above.

It pelted down on us, and as it touched my skin, my senses, and my psyche, I could tell every emotion that'd ever passed through it. My breath hitched, and a lump formed in my throat. "It's beautiful," I whispered, not knowing how else to describe it.

Yama smiled now, his shoulders losing some of the tension they'd had just a moment ago. "No. It's you, all you. You can do that, so don't tell me you can't handle what's coming later."

A calming warmth started in my gut and spread to the rest of my chest, because thinking of all the derogations, humiliations, and outright terror I'd been through in the last couple of years, handling the council should be easy.

I looked at Yama, wondering just how strong his psychic abilities were.

He watched the change come over my face, then stood up and walked away. "If Klenaya and Kyle are going with you, you need to leave information and coordinates," he threw back over his shoulders before exiting the room completely.

"Well then." I stood and tried to tell myself that the reason the council wanted to see me may have something to do with how I'd helped Yama and the others end a sickness that had contaminated the tacium and could have wiped out this whole universe.

I squared my shoulders, my head held high. If not, then I wouldn't be the first person to walk to their doom with a smile on their face.

Chapter 3

The light was low, the sun having slung off some time ago. The Isles were positioned on five hundred thousand square miles of land. Which meant it was big enough to hold millions. It wasn't always stationary though.

Although most of the time it simply floated in the waters of Tygren. Water taken from the Tygren could heal, as well as destroy, depending on the person who'd collected it and their will and intent.

On the Isles, everyone were pacifists, so that wasn't really a problem. Since night was setting in, the whole place was lit up, the Isles were not known for their early bedtimes.

Leon stood beside me, taking it all in, as he'd always wanted to know what the Isles really looked like. Klenaya and Kyle walked on in front of us talking a mile a minute as they pointed out different things.

I let out a puff of air, the vibe and tone of the Isles washing over me, telling me that this was my home. Something stirred deep in my chest, and I didn't recognize it enough to know if it was longing for home or the feeling of suffocation.

Plucking a large purple flower from the ground, I put it to my nose and smelled, thinking of days long ago in my yard, running through fields of these. The Isles looked the same, I noticed, as my eyes roamed over the triangular and oval-shaped buildings, all with small lightbulbs on the side ensuring that the place stayed lit up until the sun appeared again.

People walked by, some in jeans, others in business attire, some chatted to the person beside them, while others looked down at their phones or Devens, which were communication devices with about a million functions.

See, here's the thing, most people assumed that because people from the Isles were pacifists, that meant that there were never any disputes. That wasn't the case. People disagreed all the time here, it was how we solved said disputes that was different.

The Isles were filled with a very diverse mix of people and not everyone was nice, but that didn't make them violent either. People were as different here as they were anywhere else.

"Well," Leon said, throwing his hands out in front of him. "Where do we go next?"

The twins came back to where we stood and from the light in their eyes, they had about a million locations they wanted to check out.

I smiled at them, eager to show them whatever they wanted to see. "Let me just..."

"I'm glad you made it safely," a voice said in my head, and I frowned for a minute before I realized it was my mother.

"Mom, hi. I was just about to..."

"Don't move," she cut me off. "Just stay where you are and come quietly. None of that Kelm-like behavior while you are here."

The cage is open, the dog is loose.

"What?" My mom's voice sounded confused.

"That other voice, Mom, do you hear it?"

She didn't answer right away, and I could practically feel the tension. "Don't act up, Delia. Just go with them like a daughter of the Isles would."

Go with who? I turned around trying to get some clue as to who or what she was talking about. Because from where I stood, most people were just minding their own business, and not paying us any attention.

Kyle gave me a strange look. "Are you tripping? Did Yama slip you some Yun root before we left?"

I thought about what my mom had said, then closed my eyes and reached out to the water around me. It only took a second to get the full picture. Panic must have shown on my face, that or my friends could see my heart as it beat out of my chest because all three of them went on alert.

"Get away from me," I said. "I'm going down. Don't try to fight. We don't do that here."

As soon as I said it five men and four women all dressed in blue and silver appeared around me, hands out in front of them, to show me they were unarmed and not powered up.

Leon stepped closer to me, his eyes watching them intently. "How is this passive?"

"They won't hurt me," I said because I knew that to be true if nothing else. "My mom knows you're here. Just wait for her to find you." It wasn't the best solution, but at the moment it was all I had.

"No," Klenaya said, coming to stand beside me, and from the tremble in her voice, I could tell she was scared.

"It's okay," I said, hoping to alleviate her fears. I didn't want her frightened. She and Kyle were like family to me and I'd do anything to keep them safe. "Stay with Leon." I gave him a meaningful look and he nodded. "Just stay with Leon," I said again, my nerves playing a fast-paced game of hopscotch across my skin.

A man with short black hair, who I assumed was the leader, was the only one to speak, his voice short and matter-of-fact. "The council will meet with you first thing in the morning, until then, you are to be caged."

Chapter 4

B ile rose in my throat, my stomach clenched, my heart drummed, my soul ached, my eyes stung. I wanted to scream louder than I ever had before. My mouth filled with blood, as I bit my tongue.

No! No! I said over and over in my head. The walls got closer, the floor rose up, the ceiling came down, and then I just couldn't take it anymore. "Mama!" I said, my voice loud and broken. "Mama! I'm sorry!"

She hadn't come then, not when I'd been locked up before. The air left the room, and suddenly I couldn't breathe. I'd said they'd never put me in a cage again, said I'd never do anything to get locked down again. The walls got smaller and were they white?

My skin crawled, because they were white, they had been white before. White and padded, but sometimes they would turn red... when they came. When they did what they did. When they... when they hurt me. "Mama! Mama, please! I'm so sorry!"

Where they here? I looked around. The ceiling was on me now, the walls squishing me in. They'd come now. They always came. They'd come, and they'd hurt me, and no one would hear me scream. "Mama!"

Would they tie me down this time? Chain me? They liked the chain, that was their favorite, that and the cage. The celling kissed the floor. The walls ate into my skin. I curled into a ball, and I couldn't stop shaking, couldn't stop the tears.

Last time they'd kept me for five years. Maybe this time it would be ten. Maybe I'd never leave. Maybe this was my life from now on. I... I... can't! "Mama, I'm so sorry! Please come help me! Daddy! Where are you! Why didn't you come? You knew I was innocent, why did you leave me there? Daddy!"

I awoke on the cold floor and quickly pulled myself up, going still when I saw my sister Lena on the other side of the cage. She had the same bronze skin tone as me, but her hair was cut short down to her ears.

The style looked good on her, but that was nothing new. My sister never went out the front door unless she was one hundred percent. Most people thought her snobbish and stuck up, but to me, she'd always just been my big sister.

"Why didn't you come get me?" I said, my voice low and hard, as I asked the question that'd been gnawing at my gut for the past six years. "We are mentally connected." I pointed to my head. "You left me to rot. Never even reached out to say hello." Yes, we'd been over five hundred miles apart when I'd been locked away, but with her powers that was no excuse.

My sister nodded, not surprised at my words, then took a few steps back. That hurt, more than a knife to my back. Behind my sister were three white couches, a small bar, and an oval-shaped table.

It looked like a very nice living room. The walls were black, embroidered in gold, the floor the same. It was clean here and smelled of minty pine. I took a deep breath, holding on to the bars of the cage, and turned around.

My room had a bed, dresser, refrigerator, microwave, and a door that led to a separate bathroom. My eyes roamed around the walls, and I took a breath when I realized they were maroon and not white as I'd originally thought. I wasn't back in that hospital. I was home, on the Isles.

"Where are my people?" I asked, my focus going back to my sister.

She cleared her throat and stepped back some more, her hands tight at her sides, her face telling me she had secrets she'd yet to share. "You'll need them. They'll be here."

"What in the Isles does that mean?" I gripped the bars tighter, my hands starting to ache. "How long have I been here?"

Her eyes, like my own, were dark gold, with flecks of white. Right now, they stared at me in reprimand, the way a parent looked down on an errant child. "About three hours. You'll have your say in the morning. Your friends will be there."

I nodded, at least a bit relieved they hadn't sent them away.

"Are you hungry?" she asked, and I shook my head. My stomach was tied into a dozen knots, no way could I eat now.

She swallowed hard and her hands trembled. I blinked, not sure I was seeing right because there was naked terror on her face and I'd never seen her afraid of anything.

"They fear you," she said, looking around to make sure no one was watching, her voice full of emotions. "Don't let them win." She came forward and wrapped her hands around mine on the bars, then let out a sob, and ran from the room.

What in the Isles? I stared after her, nothing but confusion on my face. They feared me? Who? Surely not the council, because they were all-powerful, and I was, well, me.

Sweat dripped down my spine. People killed what they feared. We were a pacifist people, but I'd never once stopped to wonder if that also included the council.

Chapter 5

I was served a hearty breakfast the next morning after a night of wondering where my friends were and what in all the Isles my sister had been talking about. I didn't eat it though. My stomach was too full of knots.

The man from before with the short black hair unlocked my cell and then moved to the side so that I could walk through.

He didn't say anything, but the tension surrounding him was enough for me to choke on. I pulled arms around myself, feeling cold and empty inside. I didn't want to go back in that cage, and I wasn't sure what would happen if I was made to.

I was led down a long corridor to a set of large double doors. The black-haired guy pushed them open and held them, still not uttering a word. I swallowed hard. He was being really creepy, but I'd worry about that later.

I walked into the room and took a step back, my eyes going wide. There were five white couches in here. The floors were white marble as were the walls. It was a large space, but nothing else was in the room.

On one of the couches sat my mom, dad, and sister. None of them looked happy, in fact, they looked absolutely terrified. Why? Was it for me? Just what was going on here?

My brows furrowed, and I turned to see that on the second couch sat Leon, Klenaya, and Kyle. I let out a breath when I saw them, though I didn't think they should be here anymore, especially since I didn't know what was really going on.

On the third couch sat the Council of Langen. The couch had five spaces, and each sat on their own cushion.

First was Togen. By his skin tone and facial features, if I was back home, I would think him Japanese. He stared straight ahead, his face serious, his eyes ever watching. His left arm was made completely of fire, but I knew from growing up that it was solid and would only burn if he wanted it to.

Beside Togen was Legen, her right arm was brown sand, her skin tone the same color. Her arm too, I knew would be solid to the touch. She had high cheekbones, and the way she sat was like a queen on her throne.

Beside Legen was Hesen. She had an arm that looked to be constantly moving as if, it, itself, was a small windstorm. Her skin was pale like Leon's and her eyes showed nothing but intelligence and foresight.

Beside Hesen was Vicoun. His skin was a very dark black. His left arm was made of water, but like the other council members, I knew it would be solid to the touch. He gave me the impression that he was always thinking, looking for the best solution to any situation.

Beside Vicoun was Liisha, who had skin the color of pure platinum. One of her arms was fire, the other water. One of her legs was wind, the other sand. She had her head down, yet something told me she still saw every single thing that went on around here.

Together the five of them made up the Council of Langen. They were mother nature. Or, at least I sometimes thought they were. They probably weren't.

Togen was the first to speak. He pointed to one of the two empty couches left in the room. "Take your seat there and we will begin."

I pushed sweat-soaked hair out of my face and looked to where my family was. All three looked ready to fall apart. I then looked to where Leon and the twins were. For the most part, they just looked confused, but there was a bit of hope in each of their eyes, which did make my heart thump just a little.

Walking, one foot in front of the other, taking slow steps, I eased myself onto the couch, back straight, body erect, as I didn't want to get too comfortable.

"Delia," Togen said, eyes staring into mine in such a way that a lump formed in my throat. "You, a child of the Isles, have killed not just one, but numerous people as of late."

I blinked because technically that wasn't really true. "But they're not dead," I said, not even sounding convincing to my own ears. "The blue substance tacium makes sure their life will never truly end."

To my right, I heard my mom let out a gasp with a sob, and my heart turned on its head. I didn't want to hurt her. My hands started to tremble, and I wanted to reach out, tell her that this wasn't her fault, because she hadn't raised me to fight, I'd chosen it on my own.

Yes, we had our differences, but she was still my mother, and she'd never once made me feel unloved or unwanted. I did feel abandoned, but that was another matter altogether. Or was it?

This time it was Legen who spoke. "You slept and lived with a man for three years, then you picked up a gun and shot him six times through the heart. That is not the way of the Isles."

My fist clenched in my lap because they had to know the truth of what had really happened. "He mind-warped me! He used his powers to take over my mind! I didn't shoot him because I wanted to."

"It doesn't matter!" Togen's eyes blazed. "You still did it."

Legen's eyes turned to Klenaya and Kyle and fear leapt to my throat. Something about the way she looked at them.

"You stopped an illness from infecting Kelm and all of the countries in the universe Selptin. You and you alone did that."

I shook my head, "No I didn't. The people of the Isles all helped me to push that disease back."

Hesen was quick to speak and her words were fierce. "It was you and you alone who stood before everyone on Selptin. Yes, you called for help but had you not been there, every one of them would have died. You facilitated their cure, and that was you and you alone."

I gave her a confused look. Was that a bad thing? My mom let out a heart-wrenching sob, and yeah, I guessed it was.

I turned to look at her, my hand trembling with fear at her overreaction. Something else was going on here.

My mom was in my father's arms, her face hidden. He had his arm around her, as he looked straight ahead, but I didn't miss the quiver of his chin. My father's skin was a copper color, his eyes golden. He looked like a math professor, or maybe the dean of a college, and kind of acted that way too.

My mother was a tall, slim woman, with beautiful ebony skin, and hair that she wore all natural. Her eyes were dark silver, and like my sister, she never left the house with a hair out of place. To me, she looked like a fashion model, and maybe to others as well, though right now she couldn't stop crying.

My sister had her elbows on her knees, head in her hands, rocking back and forth. What in the Isles was wrong with them?

I turned back to Leon, Klenaya, and Kyle. I saw the hope dwindle from their eyes and it felt worse than a knife to the throat.

"Yes," Legen said, looking at me. "You saved them and that sealed your fate. There is nothing we can do to help you now."

Vicoun shook his head, and I noticed the sadness in his eyes. In fact, they all looked upset, none of them seemed pleased with what was going on. "I wish that I could save you. I've been trying to come up with something, but... Our hands are tied."

"Then untie them!" my mom said, though crying, her voice was hard and strong. "Please don't do this. You don't have to do this."

My sister grabbed ahold of my mom and pulled her back down beside her, while my father wrapped his arms back around her again. The look in his eyes was rage. Rage like I'd never seen on my father before, and I knew he'd been in his workshop for the rest of the night, letting that anger out.

Because despite all else, he was still a pacifist man, living in a pacifist society and that's how they dealt with those types of things around here.

The expression on Vicoun's face brooked no argument as he looked at my parents. "Charles and Deanna, both of your family lines go back to the beginning of the Isles, which is why I'm sure you understand why we have to do this."

Have to do what? I started to ask, but then Liisha raised her head, her eyes a rainbow of colors. "Put her back in chains, back in the cage. Now we wait for the Roken."

My mom let out a gasp. My father stared straight ahead, his jaw tight, eyes hard. My sister held her head high, defiance dancing across her features.

Kyle and Klenaya looked to Leon, and he nodded to tell them that everything would be fine, but I could tell that he knew it wouldn't.

My heart twisted in on itself, because suddenly I didn't want them here, didn't want them to witness whatever was about to happen.

Wait! My head snapped up. Did she say cage? Chains?

I took a deep breath. I would not show fear. Not in front of six of the people I loved most in the world. I looked at Kyle and Klenaya. "It's okay. I'm going to be okay. I want you to go back home to Kelm now. I'll be fine."

Klenaya's eyes flashed dangerously as she and her brother came to their feet. "Don't talk to us as if we're children because we're not."

Leon whispered something to them both, and they nodded and sat back down, staring straight ahead.

"Douglas," Togen said, and the dude with the black hair came forward, silver cuffs attached to a long chain already in his hand. Fear crawled down my spine doing the crypt walk as it danced to every part of my body, but I was determined to stay quiet and still.

My mom opened her mouth to object, but then looked at the twins and instead hung her head low. *Thank you.* I sent over mentally to her. *I don't want to scare them and I'm okay.*

"You're in chains like a dog!"

She hadn't cared before. Still, her voice was the most vicious I'd ever heard it and it did shake me to my core. I didn't want them to worry about me. Just take me back to my cell, I'd fall apart then, but for now, I needed her to calm down.

I'm okay, mama please don't make this harder than it has to be.

Delia! You don't even know what's coming, do you? The cage is open, the dog is loose.

I looked up shocked, but she was already walking away, my father and sister behind her. Had she been trying to warn me away all this time?

Yes! Her voice said into my head. *I could not defy the council.* Ah, so that had been her way of warning me away without coming out and saying it. If the cage is open, then the dog is loose, but it's not open, and I am in chains. My brows furrowed. Had she really expected me to figure that out? I really had been gone from home too long.

But my only question was, now that they had me in chains, what were they going to do with me?

Chapter 6

I sat down on my bed, my mind and everything else numb. A plate of food had been brought for me, all my favorites, but it sat cold in the corner untouched.

I wondered where Klenaya and Kyle were. I wanted them gone, wanted them and Leon to know that it was okay. Whatever happened was okay.

I think I must have sat in the same spot for hours, silently falling apart and putting myself back together again.

A hushed whisper had me looking up. "Delia, come on. Let's go." My sister pointed to her head. "The guards are sleeping, and the cameras are off. Come on."

Shocked that my sister would so brazenly do such a thing when she'd always been a follow the book kind of girl, I shook my head. "I don't want you getting in trouble for me." She'd had such a clean record up to this point, and heck, at least my parents had one child they could be proud of.

Her voice was urgent, boarding on incredulous. "You think they don't know about this?" Yup. She was reading my mind.

I didn't care if they knew about it or not, though it was a bit shocking. I didn't want anyone else getting into trouble because of me. "Where are my friends?" Because that's what I really wanted to know. "Did they get home okay?"

Lena's head turned, as she looked around. "I don't know when someone else might come here." She took a deep breath before she spoke again. "You have no idea what's in store for you. No idea what's really going on here."

Her eyes misted over, and she stared at me in disbelief, like she'd never seen me before. When she spoke this time, her voice was broken and pained, and it hurt me deep in my heart. "It's you... my little sister. It..." She shook her head looking as if she couldn't believe what she was saying. "No. No. Come on, Delia. This is the worst... just come on."

I stood, not able to take another second of my big strong sister breaking apart like this. "Where will we go?"

She let out a breath of relief that loosened her shoulders and made her features look a little less panicky. "Mount Town, under the cliffs. We used to play there sometimes as kids, remember? No one can see or connect with us once we're under the veil."

Which meant they wouldn't be able to find us, probably. The cliffs she talked about were a ten mile stretch of land. It was a place to go for privacy when you didn't want to be mentally connected with others, didn't want them to see what you were doing. It was a cooling-off spot, which was a good thing to have in a place like this, where privacy meant next to nothing.

"Well, we can't be there for long," I said, as she used a small key to both open the cage and remove the shackles from my hands and feet. The heavy chains hit the floor with a bang and took my heart right along with them.

I'd stayed in control this long by blocking everything out, but the loud echoing sound they made when they dropped sent shockwaves through my whole body, and suddenly I couldn't breathe, and the walls closed in on me once again.

My sister, seeing what was happening, grabbed me by the shoulders, and pulled me out of the cage. "Let's go."

We entered the hall where guards were curled up on the floor and on benches fast asleep, my sister putting her telepathy to work. Still, if someone just arriving came through that door, we'd be in trouble, so I knew we needed to hurry.

It'd been a while since I'd been here, so I could only imagine how I appeared to my sister with my hands out in front of me looking cluelessly up and down the street. "I can't remember which way to the cliffs."

She reached down and pulled out two black see-through rider boards. Rider boards were square, came in different colors, and were about twenty inches wide. If someone was watching, it would look like we'd stepped on an extra-large square.

I knew from when we played together as kids what she wanted, and the memory hit me dead in the chest. Thinking back to that time, I reached out my hand, pulled water from a nearby fountain, and made it my own, turning it into a large wave that we could ride out of there.

The water was in my control now, so it followed the path I laid out, rising high in the sky, as we rode it all the way to the cliffs. We passed many people on the way, and I noticed my sister with her hand on her head, lips mumbling.

The people often turned away after that or acted like they hadn't seen us at all, and I feared how much power she was using. She'd have to rest for a while after this.

The smell of salt, sand, and open air hit my nostrils, as miles of sand stretched out before us, and clear blue water crashed against the rocks. This was the water from the Trygren, which held a power of its own.

Once our feet hit ground again, my sister ran a quick hand through her hair, a clear sign that she was nervous.

"Hey," I said, putting a hand on her shoulders, making her turn big gold-speckled eyes my way. "You can go now. I can find my way from here. I don't want you to get in any more trouble than you have to."

She gave me a look that said 'whatever,' rolled her eyes, then pointed up ahead. I followed her line of sight and saw a large cliff: gray rock, jagged edges. It had small bits of white ingrained into it and water came down the side.

There was also plant life growing here, probably vegetables, as they'd grown wild down this way since I was a kid. I looked down and saw an opening at the bottom of the cliff that I was sure led to a cave.

"Delia!" Klenaya said as she came flying out of it, blue-green hair bouncing around her shoulders. She threw herself into my arms, squeezing me tight. "I'm so glad you're okay! But now we have to figure out how to handle this."

I gave her a stern look and cut my eye at my sister as Leon and Kyle joined us. "Handle what? There is no violence here. We enforce laws without it."

She waved her hand. "I know that. I respect your culture and all, but Lena said if you left they'd hunt you down and drag you back. She said the only place you can hide from them is here."

I raised a brow at my sister but had to admit it was true, though I was sure it wouldn't take them long to figure out where we were, especially if they weren't able to sense us anywhere else.

"Oh, don't worry about that," Lena said as we started toward the cave. "I hid your vehicle in there." She pointed toward the cliffs. "And I left clues that you were going somewhere deep underground. I don't think their first thought would be that you're still here on the Isles instead of as far away from here as you can get."

I nodded, thankful for all she'd done. Then I bent over and took off my shoes, letting out a contented sigh as my feet sunk into the warm sand. I wasn't out of the woods yet, not by a long shot, but at least now I had a little hope.

The cave we entered had a small fire going and piles of blankets set up all over the floor. Parts of the cave were sharp gray and had blue rocks hanging from the ceiling and on the sides.

It smelled like salt and earth in here, and I took a good whiff, happy for anything that didn't remind me of that cage. I took a better look around and noticed green and blue vines intertwined with the rocks. It looked like they'd been made that way and put on display, but I knew that wasn't the case.

Lena pointed to a pile of blankets, and I took a seat, pulling one around my shoulders and back. Klenaya and Kyle sat on my right, while Leon was on my left, and Lena was directly in front of me. All of us were in a circle around the fire.

"So, what we need to do is figure out how to get you out of here for real," Lena said. She put a hand on her stomach, and her mouth tightened just a second.

"You need to eat," I said, not even knowing how much power she'd used to pull all of this off. "You have to keep your strength up."

She waved a hand toward the entrance of the cave. "That's not a problem."

Leon came to his feet. His red hair was slicked back from his head, giving him a sleek cool look. "I'll take care of that."

I stood as well. "I'll help."

With his telekinesis and my power over the water, we could pretty much bring forward anything we wanted. On a normal day it would be more fun to throw a hook in the water, but time wasn't on our side.

I left my shoes inside the cave, still loving the feel of the sand against my feet. Birds flew up above, squawking and swooping by every few seconds, some dropping down to get drinks of water out of nearby ponds.

The sun was setting low, reflecting off the water, giving it a blue tinted glow. Around us were too many rock faces and cliffs to count. The serene sound of the waves crashing was almost enough to make me drop my guard, but not quite.

We walked in silence for a couple of seconds, before Leon stopped, and placed his hand on my arm, halting my steps as well. "What's really going on?" He had his cop face on now, and I felt compelled to answer.

"I don't know." I shrugged. "There's something my family's not telling me. Something that has them scared shitless."

He reached down and picked up a coral-le shell. It was blue, green, and yellow, and looked like a small part of a rainbow. "Put that to your ear and it'll tell you your future," I said, making him laugh.

It lit up his whole face and even reached his eyes, so I knew it was genuine, which made warmth spread over me. I didn't want him, or the twins wracked with worry over me.

"I don't believe you."

I gave him an amused grin. "It's true." I took the shell from his hand. "Put it on your eye and it'll show you where you're going."

I placed it on his left eye and he grabbed my hand, the skin on his fingers only a little rough. Our eyes met and locked. He looked scared. Scared for me, and I wished I could say something to make it better.

Before I could, he cleared his throat and pulled away. "If it's showing me where I'm going, isn't that like telling me my future?"

I gave him the shell back. "Try it and see, but be warned, they only work when they need to." He gave me a, 'yeah right' look, then reached down and picked up a few more.

We made it to the water still laughing and talking. In under a minute we had enough fish, shrimp, and crab legs, to feed all of us for at least tonight.

Up ahead, I pointed to a few cliffs. "Good vegetables grow there." He reached out a hand and brought down some grelen, broccoli, and zucchini. Grelen were shaped like carrots, except instead of orange and sweet, they were red, savory, and meaty. Because we didn't have any kind of net or bag, Leon used his telekinesis to float everything in front of us.

"Really!" Klenaya exclaimed when she saw us coming through the door with so much food. "I'll build another fire."

Kyle stood as well. "Good thing you came when you did, your sister and I were about to start slicing into Klenaya if we had to wait a second longer." Both women gave him a hollow look which he took with a big smile.

None of us talked as we ate, most of us just cramming food into our mouths, barely swallowing. Or maybe that was just me. I hadn't eaten my last few meals, and right now I was famished.

My sister too looked a lot better, and I was glad to see her gain some of her strength back.

I was just licking my fingers, finishing off the last of my fish when she stood and motioned for me to follow her outside. "We need to talk."

We stepped out of the cave, to see that night had fallen, but the glow from the moon was enough to keep everything around us lit up.

She took a deep breath, then nodded, and I got the impression she was giving herself a pep talk before she spoke. "The Roken are a group of fighters above even the council, and unlike them, the Roken are not pacifist. They will boil your skin, rip out your eyes, tear each of your fingers and toes off one at a time and make you eat them. They will put their meaty claws into your skin and pull it apart, shredding your gut." She stopped talking and gave me an expectant look, and what did she really think I had to say to something like that?

"Okay?"

"They're coming to kill you."

I choked out a cough and my eyes went big. "And you're joking right?" Please let her be joking.

Her lips got tight and she looked away. "Why do you think mom and dad are so worried? Why do you think I did all this?" Her voice broke and her breathing became labored. "I don't know how to protect you from this, but I'm trying."

My heart swelled with love at the same time it broke from the look on my sister's face. I knew something bad was going on here, so I was sure she'd embellished a bit in order to scare me so that I'd be quicker to leave.

I didn't want her or my parents to get in trouble for helping me, and she probably knew I'd leave the Isles if I thought they would. Truth be told, I'd never even heard of a Roken so...

I tried to pull her into a hug, tried to tell her I'd be fine, but she pushed me away with the shake of her head. "You've never heard of them because until now you've never had a reason to." She swallowed hard. "They've been training for the last thousand years. Every single day. All with one goal in mind... killing you."

Chapter 7

I stepped back, feeling like she'd smacked me, my breath coming a little faster now, my head spinning. "What?"

"Look, I only just learned all this six years ago when you first got locked up. They call you the destroyer, an end to all things, and the only way to stop you is to kill you."

"Stop me from what?" Honestly, the more she talked the less I understood. I had an ancient hoard of fighters after me because... "They fear me?" I asked, remembering what she'd said when I'd still been in that cell.

I looked toward the cave, and now more than ever I wanted Leon and the twins gone. I squared my shoulders. "Let me send my friends off, and then we'll deal with this."

Lena's eyes went wide. "No! You have to go with them, you have to hide. The Roken will show you no mercy! They will tear you limb from limb."

"Because they have me mistaken! I'm not some crazed destroyer, you know that."

"I do." She nodded slowly. "It's just that," her voice went low as she looked toward the ground, "you fit in that box, so they're sort of taking this and running with it. The council tried to shield you. We're a pacifist people, Delia, you know that, but this isn't something they could continue to hide.

The Roken would have found out anyway. There is nothing that slips by them for long."

I took a breath, still not sure if any of this was real, but staying alert enough in case it was. "Is that why I never heard from you guys the whole time I was in that mental hospital? Why you didn't get me out?"

A bit of shame crossed her face, and she looked over toward the gleam of the water. "After you killed Greg..."

"He's not dead, and do you have any idea what that man did to me, what he put me through?"

"After you killed him," she continued as if I hadn't said a word.

"He's sitting in a high-security jail right now on Kelm."

"After that..."

"He has a nice room, soft bed, plenty of room. Trust me, he's not hurting."

"It was his death that set all of this into motion. The council forbade us from having contact with you. After you got out, you continued on the path they said the destroyer would. Step by step."

She shook her head and put a hand to her chest. "Look, I know you're not the destroyer. You're my baby sister, and I'm going to do everything I can to protect you."

This eased some of the tension in my shoulders and I gave her a slight smile, even if I was sure this whole Roken thing was the product of someone's very vivid imagination. I still-

"Squawk!" I looked up and my jaw hit the sand as birds, black in color, and at least twenty feet long, flew over our heads, blocking out the moon and everything else. Their wings were at least ten feet long and they had yellow hawkish eyes and long crooked beaks. Their skin looked as tough as leather, and I had no problem believing that nothing could penetrate it.

All the color drained from my sister's face and her eyes went wide. "It's the Xenus! Beasts from the depths of Roken. They always appear first. The Roken will soon follow. Delia, you have to run!"

My heart started clawing to get out of my chest, as fear like I'd never felt slithered down my spine. "Not without you!" I grabbed her by the hand, and we took off running, away from the cave, anything to keep the three inside safe.

The beasts opened their mouths, however many hundreds of them, and out shot thousands of knives, all spiked and tipped with fire.

They rained down on us, as we ducked and dodged, barely escaping.

I held out my hand and called out to the water of the Tygren, forming a shield around us that I hoped with everything in me they couldn't penetrate.

One of the Xenus flew down in front of us and let out a loud squawking roar. We both fell, tumbling over each other, but thankfully the shield didn't break.

The Xenus opened his mouth again, but this time its shoulder jerked, and I assumed it'd been hit. Then blue light flew into its mouth, and down its chest.

The xenus shook it off, as a minor annoyance, and I turned in dread to see Leon, Kyle, and Klenaya standing just a few feet away, all three with their hands out.

Leon flicked his wrist, and the beast's head jerked back a little, but that was it. His telekinesis was not working. Neither were the twins' powers. They shot blue energy repeatedly at the Xenus in front of us, but it ate it as one did a tasty treat.

The flock of Xenus were focused on me now, but if Leon and the twins kept at it, they may turn on them. "Put your shields up and run!" I shouted. Klenaya sharing her shield with Leon as blue crackling light surrounded them.

They took off running and at first, I thought they'd go back toward a more populated area of the Isles, but with a sinking heart, I realized they were headed straight toward me. *Why wouldn't they save themselves?*

I made a separate shield for myself, still keeping one around my sister. Then I pulled from the water of the Tygren again, turning it into fog that blinded me from the Xenus' sight. It blinded the others too, but I quickly cleared a small bit away so that they could see me.

The Xenus had us surrounded, but the others couldn't see that. Only I could see through the fog that I created, so at least that was on our side.

"You guys have got to get out of here," I said, my voice strained. I was using too much power with the shields, and I knew soon my powers would fail me. "Hurry, while I'm still able to hold them off."

I got four blank stares in return.

"We're not leaving you." The look on Leon's face said he didn't even know why I'd suggested such a thing. "So instead of wasting time on that, let's figure out how to beat these things."

"Well we'd better figure it out fast," I said as my legs went weak. "Because I don't know how much longer I can keep this up."

I held out my hand to the Tygren, hoping the mystical waters would restore some of my strength. Then my knees buckled, the shields dropped, and the fog went away.

The one Xenus in front of us let out a blood-curdling scream, as about a hundred fire tipped knives flew out of its mouth, headed straight for my face.

Chapter 8

I rolled out of the way, reaching out for the water I'd called forth, letting it wash over me and through me, as I fell hard on my side.

I grunted with the pain, but it was only there for a second before the water started to work, and a bit of power surged through me. It didn't take me to one hundred percent, but it did restore enough of my strength that I could stand without feeling like I was ready to pass out.

I couldn't put the shields back up though, which left my sister and me unprotected.

Klenaya let out a groan and then the shield around herself and Leon disappeared. Her hair was in disarray, and her legs were trembling and I knew it took everything she had to remain standing.

Then I heard a grimace come from Kyle and his shield fell away too. His shoulders slumped, and he stumbled back but was able to keep himself from falling over.

Pulling from the Tygren, I let loose a hail of skin burning steam, away from where we were, but above the head and in the breathing air of the flock of Xenus.

They writhed and squirmed, clearly uncomfortable, maybe even in pain, but that still didn't stop them. More and more converged on where we were and now their eyes weren't just on me. They were on my sister and the others as well, making a fierce need to protect them and everyone else rise in my chest.

"We can't lead them into the city. Not if they're willing to strike down anyone they see. The people of the Isles are not at fault for this," I said.

I stood, and the one Xenus in front of me opened its mouth again. A crackling flash of blue hit him in his right pupil, and it turned quick eyes toward Klenaya, as did the rest of the Xenus.

They looked from her to Kyle, to Leon, to Lena, and then moved their bodies toward them. It was like they figured once they got them out of the way they could get on with doing me in.

The water in my veins heated up and steam came out of my mouth as I felt myself slipping, because if they thought I would stand and watch as they killed everyone I loved then they didn't know me very well.

My hair blew backward, and my eyes glowed. I looked at my sister and saw the same. Using and controlling the water inside of me, I rose in the air, taking my sister's hand as I did so.

"Nst, grul, mui, grol," we both said, speaking in the ancient language of the Isles. "Yia, nst, klm, grol, guuo!" The wind shook, the water rose and bubbled, the cliffs trembled, the sand erupted, the leaves on the trees fell to the ground, and still we stayed firm. "Nstee rol, klm, nst!"

The Xenus twisted and turned, letting out loud roars and hisses that let me know they were in pain. It was enough to keep them from attacking, but not enough to take them down completely. "Nstee, rol, klm, nst!"

The ancient waters of the Tygren flowed through me now, giving me strength and adding extra power to my words, but still, not one Xenus hit the ground.

Then from below, I heard a low chanting and I turned, shocked to see Iiann and Flynn, the brothers from Lamink. Lamink was in the same universe as Kelm, just a different country. They rose in the air with us, their eyes glowing brightly.

They'd helped me fight like this before, so I knew they had what it took. I looked down and saw that Bale and Yama were also with them, and when did they all get here? Something to worry about later, because right now...

We were at eye level now with the flock of Xenus, but it was still too many of them. Though some had cracks forming in their skin, and some even leaked a little blood, us four together still weren't strong enough to take them down, not after how they'd shaken off all my previous attacks.

The water inside me turned to fire as it raged over and through me. If we didn't do something fast, they would destroy us all, and I just wasn't about to let that happen. I reached deep inside myself and called forward more water.

I gathered it around me, boiling it, freezing it, turning it to hail and ice. Then I sent it out. I made it rain only on the flock of Xenus. Fire drops, icicles, rain so hot it went through the skin, hail so hard and cold it froze with one touch.

Then I focused on the Xenus themselves, taking the water inside of them and boiling it in some, freezing it in others. Smoke came from their ears, ice covered their bodies, rain froze and burned their skin. And soon they exploded like kettles left too long on the stove. They popped, bodies breaking into thousands of pieces and falling down around us.

Then I was falling because I couldn't breathe because I'd done too much. I reached out to the water as I went, taking more in and letting it heal me as I hit the ground. Falling into the blood and tissue of the Xenus, I turned, to see that Lena, Iiann, and Flynn had made it down as well.

I came shakily to my feet, my eyes going to the two brothers. Flynn was on the slim side, with purple hair, yellow eyes, and ebony skin. He looked every bit the stuck-up guy that he was, and I remembered that him and the twins didn't really get along.

Kyle and Klenaya didn't get along with his brother Iiann either. Iiann was tall, packed full of muscles, with long wavy black and silver hair, his skin just a shade lighter than his brothers.

"What are you guys doing here?" I asked. I knew I'd left our information with Yama, but I had no idea he'd called the brothers from Lamink to help us. Not that I was complaining, though I wasn't sure how Kyle and Klenaya would feel about it. The two sets of siblings hated each other, and I didn't see that changing anytime soon.

"Babe," Iiann said, pulling Kyle close as the other man walked up. The two shared a long hug, then a brief kiss, pressing their foreheads together.

"I'm okay," Klenaya said to Flynn, as he wrapped his arms around her and pulled her close, kissing her on the forehead, and looking like he dared even one person to try and touch her.

What! My head whipped to Leon, but he looked as shocked as I felt. "Guess they don't hate each other so much after all."

"Good job," Yama said to me, and I shook my head.

"Not going to ask if I'm okay?"

He gave me a curious look. "I would know it if you weren't."

My sister put a hand on my shoulder and then her face went green as she turned to the side and retched. I put a hand on her back and wiped hair out of her face because I knew exactly where she was.

I'd been there too when I'd first protected myself with violence. Her body trembled, and tears ran down her face. "I... can't... I'm not..."

I grabbed her by the shoulders and turned her around to face me. I wanted to tell her that I understood, that the soul-crushing feeling in her gut would one day become a small ache, that it'd be hard at first, but one day she'd accept that she'd fought to save herself and others.

I wanted to tell her all that, but in the end, I just pulled her to me and told her I was sorry.

She pulled away, wiping her face and shaking her head. "Not your fault. You're my baby sister. I've been trying to protect you your whole life. You didn't think I'd stop now, did you?"

"Not trying, have been," I said. "You have been protecting me my whole life." She gave me a slight smile and squeezed my hand, but I knew she had a lot to work out.

Leon stood with his hands out, his brows scrunched together. "What made you guys show up?" he asked Yama and the others.

"Klenaya called me," Flynn said, and I could almost see his nose up in the air. "Told me you guys were in trouble and needed our help. So, I got my brother, called her father, and here we are."

Leon nodded, his cop face firmly in place when he asked. "So, who's watching your throne, and how long has this," he pointed between Klenaya and Flynn, "been going on?"

"You know when we met," Flynn said, and somehow I got the feeling he was looking down on us all. "Or need I remind you?"

"You don't need to remind anybody of shit," Iiann said. "Stop being an asshole."

Looking at the two sets of couples, who last I knew hated the sight of each other, my head spun, either that, or I was just worn out from the fight.

I turned eyes to Bale and Yama who both gave me blank stares, though there was a bit of amusement in Yama's eyes. "You two knew about this?" I asked, because yeah, they most certainly did.

"It wasn't a secret," Kyle said, and I noticed that he and Iiann were still standing close, hands touching.

"Yeah," Iiann said, giving me a wry look. "Why are you focusing so much on that for anyway? You need to get laid or something?"

Kyle gave Iiann a cross look, making him shrug, and Flynn coughed out a laugh, which had Klenaya narrowing her eyes at him.

The brothers were both jerks, how had I forgotten that?

Yama walked toward me, his purple hair swaying with his every step. He looked regal, like the high ruler he was, and every move he made embodied that. "Anywhere you go, they will find you I'm told, so how do you want to handle this?"

I thought about it for a second, thought about how much damage the Xenus could have done to them and knew I had to end this now. Truth be told, with the exception of myself, Lena, and Leon, none of these people could die.

They could get hurt, though, and they'd definitely feel every ache, every pain, and there was still the trauma to their minds, something the tacium couldn't heal.

I looked up at Yama and his red eyes gave me the impression that he already knew what I was ready to say. "I don't think..."

"Get down!" Yama threw himself on top of me, then rolled to the side.

A large whip, as wide as ten belts, and as thick as a brick, came down where I'd been standing. It was laced with fire, and it dented the ground where I'd stood, setting it ablaze.

Heart doing the tango, I looked up to see about a hundred fighters of all different shapes, sizes, and colors. They wore the same black pants, shirts, shoes, and hats, made out of a rough material that looked like denim mixed with steel.

They floated high in the sky, looking down on me like they would love nothing more than to rip me apart. My mouth flung open, and my breath hitched because I could feel the magnificent power radiating off them, and everything in me said they wouldn't be as easy to take down as the Xenus.

One stepped forward, his skin and beard the color of rust, and he had murder in his eyes as he raised his whip up and looked down at me. "Destroyer! You will not escape me as easily as you did them."

Then the others raised their whips, and the air blurred with their movement. Then pain cut through my bones and straight to my soul. I let out an anguish-filled scream, then blackness took me away.

Chapter 9

When I came to, I was in a cage, outside, in the middle of town. My back ached like fire where they'd hit me, but I was slowly able to come to a sitting position, knowing that the water I'd used to heal myself earlier was the only reason I wasn't dead now.

I looked around, anxious for my sister and the others. I found them, standing beside my parents, concerned looks on their faces.

I could smell the waters of the Tygren behind me, and that's when it hit me, we were in Tambul Square, the biggest gathering place we had. This place could fit tens of thousands. Seemed these Roken were really into putting on a show.

What did it matter? Everyone on the Isles was mentally connected as long as they weren't in Mount Town, where we'd just come from, so if they wanted to know what was happening, they would.

My parents stood together holding each other, Lena on their right. Leon stood beside her, hands in his pockets and rage on his face. Beside him was Yama and Bale. Bale looked grave, while I noticed a jump in Yama's jaw.

Klenaya had fire in her eyes, and Flynn stood behind her, massaging her shoulders, trying to calm her down. Kyle too, looked like he was ready to erupt, and Iiann had an arm around his waist, whispering fiercely in his ear.

My shoulders slumped. I didn't want them here for this, not any of them. I would die today. I knew that now. The Roken were not only powerful, they also had the gift of super speed. There was no way I could fight that.

I stood, my back crying out in protest as the metallic smell of blood filled my nostrils, and hot liquid flowed down my back.

I cracked my neck from side to side. If this was to be my end, then I'd face it head-on. I wouldn't run, wouldn't cry, or plead for my life. I'd go down with honor because I still had that if nothing else.

The one with the rust-colored skin stood before us all, his fellow Roken behind him. Directly in front of them were the council of Langen, and I'd never seen them look so scared.

The air shifted and then I had cuffs on both my hands and my legs. I was now locked in place, as chains from the top and bottom of the cell kept me from touching the floor.

I was suspended in the air, literally being torn apart at the limbs and there wasn't anything I could do about it. The indignity of it all, being laid bare like this in front of all the people I loved and cared about. For them to have to see me like this hurt my heart down to its core.

The rust one, still in the air, with the other Roken behind him, banged a hand across his chest. His voice was loud, booming, and echoing when he spoke. "I am Ispen! And we have prepared over a thousand years for this!"

He pointed at me. "She is the destroyer, and unless we end her now, this land and many others will never know peace. She will tear through it all, ripping it apart with her bare hands and leaving nothing but blood and bodies in her wake. She will crumble worlds, destroy universes, and none will be left standing by the time she is done."

I watched him rant and rave, wondering if he was high or something. Did he really think me capable of all of that? Me, who was always the last to put her fist in the air? Me, who always tried to settle any disagreement before it turned into a fight? Me, still a pacifist at heart, even if I hadn't acted as such lately.

The air shifted and then he had a large white engraved plaque beside him, floating in the air. "We all know the destroyer will have pacifists' roots and that there are three things that will identify that person."

My wrists and ankles began to ache. He had the cuffs as tight as he could make them, I believed. Sill, my head snapped up for this, because now I would finally learn the reason for all of this nonsense.

"One, the destroyer will kill that which will still continue to speak." He turned to where, Yama, Bale, Kyle, Klenaya, Flynn, and Iiann stood. "She has killed many from their universe." The crowd gasped, either shocked or disgusted that a child of the Isles could do such a thing. "She's boiled their skin, torn out their eyes, bit off their faces, crushed them under her feet, yet all still breathe, all still speak."

Well, they were immortal. I mean come on, and boy didn't he make me sound a lot more violent than I was. Still, I could feel the shift in the crowd. Suddenly they were starting to wonder if I was the innocent little girl they'd watched growing up, and some of them had already made up their minds.

We were still connected mentally, so I felt it, every time I lost one of them, and that made something deep in my gut, in my soul, start to stir.

"One was a man she claimed to love for three years of her life. She ripped him apart with her bare hands, and then kicked him away like he was nothing, but the destroyer's heart is a dark abyss, so this is not surprising."

Anger tickled my skin and danced across my neck. Greg was an abusive asshole and he deserved everything he gotten. I let out a small growl before I could stop myself and the whole crowd tensed, along with the council and the Roken.

"Two!" Ispen held up his fingers. "The destroyer will be able to make it rain fire mixed with ice. She will use this on her rampages, decimating whole worlds with the flick of a hand, as she laughs and dances in the blood and waste of the slain."

Okay, this guy was really overdoing it, and really had he met me? Anyone who knew me, knew I could never, I just couldn't.

"Three!" He held up the plaque that'd been floating beside him, and I saw that it was a carving of a woman, with shoulder length hair, her hand held out to a horde of people, all who looked sick and dying. "The destroyer will single-handedly push back the illness of Elken." He turned to Iiann and Flynn. "She rid your land of this, surely you remember that it was her and her alone with the power to destroy this flesh-eating disease."

Ha! I had him there because I'd pulled on the strength of every single person on the Isles to rid Lamink of that disease.

"Now, all of you standing here know that she borrowed from you to defeat the illness of Elken, and who but the destroyer could hold all the power of the Isles in the palm of her hand, and escape without a scratch to her skin?"

My gut twisted as more and more agreed with him. People I'd known my whole life started to turn away, some even wished for my death. Only ten people seem to stay strong and that was my family and my friends.

My grandparents, aunts, uncles, and cousins, I had no idea where they were or what they thought because I couldn't feel them in the crowd. Maybe they feared me so much they'd left? The water inside me started to boil and I really hoped that wasn't the case.

Ispen looked down at the council. They seemed frozen in fear, like they were afraid to breathe. "You know what must be done! We the Roken are plenty in numbers and still, we may not be enough. I know you are a pacifist people, but we may need to borrow your strength, and even then, it may not be enough."

I could feel many of them were conflicted, but apparently, some had been told that this day would come, and they'd prepared and knew what they had to do. They would kill me.

I let out a gasp, my skin and heart turning cold.

One by one I felt them pledge their support to the Roken, and something dark and deadly inside of me rose to the surface.

These people who I'd known all my life, loved all my life, would really abandon me when I needed them the most?

Not only that, but they were willing to help the Roken kill me, because that's where we were now.

Nothing could stop this. My friends, my family, they were no match for the Roken, much less the Roken and the whole of the Isle. Then suddenly I realized why only three of my family members were here.

The rest had been sent away, banished until this was done, for fear that they, with my sister and parents, would rise up and try to protect me.

I held my head high. I'd said I would face my death with dignity and honor, but now all of that went out the window.

If these cowards really wanted to kill me, they'd have to use every bit of power they had. Water boiled in my body, as the Tygren bubbled and hissed, steam rising from it, and swirling around me.

My mouth pulled back from my teeth in a snarl, and my voice was deep, thick, and gruff when I spoke. "Do you think your chains can hold me?" I threw my head back and laughed, and it was evil, ugly, and everything that I was not, but for some reason, I couldn't seem to stop myself.

I rattled the chains holding me and threw my head back and screamed out a howl. In the crowd, I heard the sobs of my friends, my family, but I was too caught up to let it affect me.

The mystical waters from the Tygren circled me, and I heated it up, burning into the chains that held me captive. "Yia, nst, klm, Grol, guuo!" I screamed, and my hair blew back from my head, my body trembled, and the cage holding me shook uncontrollably.

"I will not yield! I will not stop! All life and death are in my hands now, and *I* am judge, jury, and executioner!" I let out another howl, shaking the wind, and breaking the cage apart, my arms and legs were freed, and I stood in front of them all at a crouch, wild and uncaged.

Chapter 10

I spen's eyes went wide, and there was nothing but stark terror on his face. "Get her! Get her now! She will destroy all if we let her escape!"

I held my hands up and the Tygren obeyed my command. The water twisted and turned as I created tsunamis and rip currents. Then it broke apart, still spinning and deadly, as large water monsters rose up around us.

I pointed to the Roken. "Rip them apart!"

The air rippled, but I already had a shield of water, heavy with the currents from my tsunami, protecting me from all harm.

The crowd stepped back, but it was not them I was after. I walked head high, water ripping straight into the horde of the Roken. One came toward me, and I boiled the water inside of him. He burned from the inside out, his skin peeling off him as he melted to the ground.

Three converged on me, and I froze the water inside of one and watched as he iced over and broke apart. "Nst, grul, mui, grol!" I screamed out, as I rose in the air, my hair blowing back from my face, my eyes glowing.

I opened my mouth and water shot out, straight into the eyes of the second Roken, burning them out, as he dropped to the ground. The third one tried to hit me, and I made a lasso of water and wrapped it around him, freezing and burning him at the same time, until he keeled over, half frozen, half melted.

"Yia, nst, klm, Grol, guuo!" I yelled out, my voice and the wind the same. They all came on me at once, super-fast, and my water monsters were just as fast as they were and began ripping into them. Just a touch from the tsunami that were my beast's hands had the Rokens' body splitting apart, their guts falling to the ground.

I shot out a mini cyclone of water and wrapped it around a Roken's neck, taking it off. Blood gushed out, but before the body could hit the ground, I'd already turned and sent water through another one's eyes, taking them out as well.

It went on like that for a while, me and my beasts, ripping apart and shredding everything in our path until only one Roken was left standing.

Ispen had his fire laced whip in his hand, and he brought it up, his teeth bared as he looked at me. "I will not let you destroy all life! I will-"

Water twirled around my hand with the power of a tsunami, and I reached into his chest and pulled out his heart. "You were saying," I asked, before squishing it in my hands.

He fell to his knees, one finger pointing at the council, as if telling them to continue his work. Then his head hit the ground, and I wiped my hands, stepping over him as I went.

The crowd looked terrified, but I wasn't finished yet. "Anybody else want to try it?" I asked, my voice thick and hard.

A figure walked toward me, and I held up my hands, ready to take the person apart piece by piece. My water monsters came to stand in front of me, and I sent them back to the Tygren, confident I could handle this myself.

"Delia!" the voice said, and I realized it was Yama. Energy whirled around him, and his red eyes glowed low and dark, making him look eerie, otherworldly even. "Stop this now! Your enemy has been defeated! There is no one left for you to destroy!"

I grunted, down to just my instincts, and I could hear the cries from my family, from my friends. Yama's eyes bored into mine, and suddenly I realized I was surrounded by blood, loads of it, all of my making.

I looked down at my hands and they were covered in it, that and Roken body tissue. My lips trembled, and I looked to Yama, still not comprehending all I'd done. "I didn't... mean... Didn't... want..."

I collapsed in his arms, and once again, darkness was my friend.

Chapter 11

I was given a room in Yama's mansion, as I was unwilling to move for the first few days after what I'd done. I was horrified by my actions, and even more scared that everything the Roken said had been true.

I really was this destroyer. How else was there to explain it?

"You're thinking too much again," two voices said in unison. Kyle and Klenaya walked into the room, one carrying a tray of food, the other a large drink. They'd stuck by me through this, saying they didn't care who I was, or what I'd done, only that I was still alive.

My parents and sister apparently felt the same because they'd been mentally checking in with me daily, to make sure that I was okay. I didn't sense any anger from them, only relief that I was alright, and that this was over.

I smiled at the twins, as the smell of pork and potatoes filtered to my nose. They smiled back, then exited the room, as they knew I wanted to be alone.

Leon came by every day, even if it was just for a few minutes. He'd bring a board game or a set of cards, and that would at least relieve some of the tension.

Yama too made frequent visits to my room, and I realized just how calm and unworried I was whenever he was here.

Still, I had terror-filled dreams about what I'd done. I couldn't escape it, and I wasn't okay with it... I just wasn't. I'd killed so many Roken, all with the flick of a wrist, and I hadn't felt a thing when I'd done it.

I picked at the food on my plate, not really having an appetite at the moment. My parents and sister may have thought this was over, but deep inside me something stirred, and I knew it was just beginning. I was, after all, the world eating, universe crumbling, destroyer.

Leah Untamed

Chapter 1

I threw down the ace of hearts and almost did a backflip when nothing but clubs and diamonds followed. I wrapped hands around my cold beer, then smiled at the two people frowning down at the table. "And that, ladies and gentlemen is how you win at spades," I said.

The guy, a man named Pugo, ran a slow hand under the scar under his right eye. He was supposed to be one of the best card players around, or so I'd been told.

His wife, Ralena pursed her lips, black hair pushed back from her head. Like him, she was the serious type, and since neither seemed much for showing emotions, their frowns were very telling.

My partner Xavier stood. His black hair was loose around his shoulders, his pale skin in direct contrast to my more mahogany tone. Xavier was well over six feet tall, cocky as heck, but man when he smiled... My knees went weak, no matter how much I tried to hide it.

"And this, ladies and gentlemen," he said, pulling me close, and lowering me into a dip, "is how you celebrate winning at spades." He kissed me hard and fast, his tongue an expert with my mouth, as we'd been doing this for the better part of a year now.

He tasted like beer and fried pork skins, which was quite a pleasant combination. I laughed and then pushed him away, standing back up in the process.

Pugo and Ralena got up, very careful not to touch each other or look our way, as heads held high, they walked out of the room.

"Well, darlin', that's twenty thousand apiece free and clear. You up for a little celebration?" I went through a mental check list of my bills.

At a different game we'd played, we'd each earned one hundred and twenty thousand. We'd both given twelve thousand to our friend Twist, so that'd left us with one hundred and eight thousand.

My plan had been to put a down payment on a house of my own, but I'd quickly learned that no one was eager to lend money to a professional gambler.

I chuckled when I thought about it because really, it hadn't been all that much of a surprise, but for some reason, I'd thought they'd work with me anyway. It was wishful thinking, and I knew better, but sometimes you got caught up in the dream.

I'd needed a co-signer. My parent's job description was the same as my own, so that was an immediate no. My brother owned a string of hotels and had thousands of employees.

He'd have done it had I asked, probably would have just bought the thing outright for me, but he'd always said he'd have to take care of me one day, so I sure as shit wasn't going to ask for his help, my price being what it was and all.

My sister now owned three fitness centers, but I'd always promised myself I'd make my own way, so I hadn't asked her either. What I'd done was win thirty more thousand at the card table and bought the house I wanted outright and paid up the first six months of my homeowner's insurance.

I'd gotten the utilities on the month after that, so now I just needed to furnish it. Also, the insurance was due again, as were my taxes. My car had broken down some time ago, so I was hoping to spend a little money on getting a second-hand one to tide me over.

None of the money I'd won tonight would go toward that though. I closed my eyes and thought about it. See, here's the thing, as a card player and gambler, my life was often hard and fast, and I was okay with that.

Still, sometimes I had to slow down and take a look around. I'd seen on the news that a lady I knew from around town had suffered a devastating blow. Her house had burned down with all her belongings in it. She and her husband hadn't had renter's insurance, so they'd been left with nothing.

They had a son of around five, and a daughter on the way, so I figured my next few wins would be going to them. I did that sometimes, reached out to give back when I could, and it always felt like the right thing to do.

"Leah! Xavier!" Twist walked up with a beer in his hand, his numerous piercings shining under the bright lights. "Did we win?" he asked, a big smile on his face.

I laughed and nodded. Twist was fifth-generation Chinese American, skinny to a fault, and his red hair, with the green tips, helped him pull off the perfect emo look with no problem at all.

"Good. Let's get something to eat," he said. I was down for that and from Xavier's nod, so was he.

I put a hand on Twist's back and gave him a smile. I was glad he was with us. Twist was a good friend to myself and Xavier and usually went with us to all our big games.

He actually worked as a floor runner in one of my favorite gambling houses, but always took time off to hang out with us, when the need arose.

We picked up our money from the table and I figured it'd been a good night so far.

The air was fresh and cool as we stepped outside, and since I was high off the win, and what I had planned for the money, I was feeling a little carefree.

"I want a burger this big." Twist made a motion with his hands. "And about a mountain of fries." Twist was twenty-six, only three years younger than myself. Xavier was... oh who knew how old he really was, early thirties if I had to guess.

Xavier wrapped an arm around my waist, smelling of cedar and lemon. I inhaled deeply, loving the natural scent of him and thinking of what we'd be doing later tonight.

We stayed like that for a second, before I detangled myself. "You can have your burger, Twist. I'm in the mood for a big ass steak. What about you, Xavier?"

"I think we better fight," he said, arms tight at his sides.

My head snapped up, as did Twist's. Making their way toward us, with static bats held tightly in their hands, were three men and two women.

Static bats were covered in barbed wires and carried a blue electric charge. If hit once with the bat, it could cause a break-down of the skin and muscles. Hit more than once, well...

The sword on my side trembled with the urge to come out, but I put a hand on it, not wanting to use it unless I had to because once unleashed...

One of the guys, tall with red hair, raised his bat up and pointed at me. "Don't move. We've got some business with you."

Chapter 2

I held my hands at my sides, ready in an instant. Twist whipped wind around his feet and used it to raise himself a few inches off the ground, face intent on those walking toward us. One of the reasons I loved Twist so much was he was always by my side when shit went down, ready. No questions asked.

Same for Xavier. He was telekinetic like me, but he also had the power of transformation. Which meant he could transform people or objects into anything he wanted. It only held for two hours, but that was more than enough time.

He stood, his hands up, looking like somebody waiting to fuck some shit up.

"Leah, my people tell me you won tonight," the red-haired guy spoke again. "Well, I'll be taking that and anything else you have."

My brows went up. So, this was a robbery? Hmmm. Something about it seemed off. "What are you up to? If you know my name, then you know that blood is about to flow. I ain't giving up shit without a fight."

A guy with short black hair spoke this time. "Then you'll never see Tisha and Speed again."

My heart stopped at his words, my skin crawling with fear and anger. Those were the names of my sister and brother. Just who the fuck were these guys? I cleared my throat but still kept my hands ready. "You have my attention."

"Good," one of the women said. She was of medium height and had dark brown hair. She came off as unassuming but looking deeper at her demeanor made me think that getting on her bad side would be a very dangerous thing to do. "They came to Tajan City last night, playing fast and loose. They lost over three hundred thousand dollars. Now they refuse to pay, saying they were cheated."

The other woman started to speak. She wore a hat that covered all of her hair, and her eyes were the color of crystal. She had a serious look about her, and from the way she stood, to the way her jaw stayed tight when she talked, I knew she meant business. "Well, you know Dragon doesn't take too kindly to that, so you're going to pay what they owe, and an extra two hundred thousand for wasting Mr. Dragon's time."

I wasn't paying shit and Dragon knew me well enough to know that. He'd just sent these five on a suicide mission, all just to deliver a message. Dragon was a tall man, with olive skin, and no eyebrows. He had a stocky build, I mean, even his muscles had muscles. Those who didn't know any better were often fooled by this and took him for a brainless hired thug.

Dragon was about as smart as they came and just as vicious. He was one of the biggest players in Tajan City, but not the only one. He mostly held down the north side of that town, and his rule there was law.

See, Tajan City was like a whole other world. It had its own rules and its own laws. Like Pear Town, another place me, Xavier and Twist had visited, police from here didn't go into Tajan City. They had their own law holders set up, and what could get you arrested here would likely get you a pat on the back there.

Tajan City was an all day, all night, gambling town. Nothing but casinos, gambling houses, gambling parks, gambling diners, etc....

As I said, Dragon held down the North side of town. The east, west, and south, were in the territories of three other bosses. These areas had been fought for and won with blood and bodies. So now they all respectably stayed out of each other's way.

I cracked the knuckles on both hands as I thought about it. Dragon was going to kill my brother and sister, either way, I knew that. If he felt they'd disrespected him, he'd make an example out of them. Oh, he'd take the money I gave him, and kill them anyway, very publicly so others would know he wasn't to be reckoned with. *Shit*! Why had they gone to Tajan city anyway? And why didn't they just pay? They had the money.

Also, where was Niche, my brother's best friend? I doubted very seriously my brother had gone to Tajan Town without him or was he already dead? This whole thing just left a sour taste in my mouth, and I needed to know what had happened. Just the thought of them being hurt...

Anger rose in me, lifting my hair, shaking the trees and rattling the windows of nearby buildings. Had Dragon really cheated them? I didn't know. He sometimes did that. Picked out those who looked rich and weak and took them for as much as he thought he could get away with.

Neither of my siblings were pushovers, which he'd found out when they'd refused to pay. Still, the question was, had he known who they were when he'd fucked with them?

Even if he hadn't then, he sure as fuck did now so he had to know I was coming for him. The sword on my side shook again, and I could see a small glow coming from it. I ran my hand across the hilt. Now wasn't the time.

Looking at the five in front of me, I threw my hands up, hoping I could reason with them. "My problem is not with you. You came here to deliver a message. I got it. End of discussion."

The one with the red hair wagged his finger at me, the way one does to a naughty child, but his eyes were hard, his words laced with acid. "I think we'll just take what we came for."

He swung his bat back and then advanced toward me.

Xavier took a step in front of me, something he knew I hated. "You don't want to do that, partner," he said to the dude with the red hair. "Pretty sure that bat doesn't do what you think it does."

Red ignored him, and Xavier's hands moved quick and fast. As the five of them rounded on us, their bats turned into small pebbles that fell from their hands.

"What the-" the woman with the dark brown hair said, but Red had already leaped my way. His skin was electric, just like the bats, and right now it crackled and glowed blue and white.

All of their skins did, which meant they'd been the ones to infuse the bats. I threw a hand out and used my telekinesis to pull at his chest, aiming for his heart.

He must have had telekinesis too, because when he held up his hand, I felt a blow to my face that sent me flying back. I fell hard against the side of a building, and he raised me up using his powers and slammed me to the ground.

I hit with a thump, blood, and scratches on my elbow and side. "Okay, then." I got back to my feet, just as the woman with the brown hair tried to hit me with an electric fist. I jumped back out of the way, then used my telekinesis to tear her tongue out.

She opened her mouth to scream, she couldn't do that anymore, and I ripped out her tonsils and whole esophagus just for good measure.

One of the other men advanced on me, this one was tall with a bald head. His fist crackled with energy, and I knew if he hit me with that, I wouldn't be getting back up.

I reached out my hands and used my telekinesis to pull his arms from his body, leaving nothing but blood and tissue. Then I did the same for his legs. He fell to the ground, a bloody torso, unable to cause harm anymore.

Twist was busy twisting and turning, making his own little hurricane. Someone was caught up in it with him, as arms and legs fell to the ground. Once the person's head hit, I saw that it was a guy with a close cut. He'd been standing beside Red when they'd walked up.

The lady with the hat came toward me and I waved a hand and squeezed. Her brows rose in surprise, then she grabbed her chest and fell to her knees, panting and looking at me as if seeing me for the first time. I yanked my hand backward, and her heart leaped from her chest, falling into tatters around her feet, while she crumbled completely.

Red who'd been fighting hand to hand, toe to toe, with Xavier looked around. All four of his buddies were dead, and when he turned back my way, I used my telekinesis in rapid-fire motion, pulling out his eyeballs, teeth, and gums, in under thirty seconds.

His eyes went big, then he joined the rest of his friends on the ground, all of their lives lost, just to deliver a message.

"Well," I said, wiping some of their splattered blood from my face. "We're going to Tajan City."

Chapter 3

Though it was night now, everything here was lit up from the streets to the trees, to the freaking grass and sides of buildings.

"Wow," Twist said, eyes shining as he took it all in. "Don't think I've ever come here."

"Probably not," Xavier agreed, with a nonchalant look on his face. "Tajan City is not something you easily forget."

I rolled my eyes at him. "Bet you've been here a million times. Is there any place that's new to you?"

He shrugged, then looked toward a large wheel that invited anyone walking by to take a chance and spin it.

Beside it was a large patch of grass, and three men were playing horseshoes. A few tables were spread out, with card games happening on every corner. To our left, dice were being played, and I noticed they lit up when thrown down.

We were on the east side of town. This was Kandy's territory, and I wondered if she or her gang had heard anything, specifically where Tisha and Speed where being held.

I mean, it's not like I could ask Dragon or any of his peeps, pretty sure I wouldn't live long if I did.

A guy with blue hair walked up and patted Xavier on the back. "Been a long time. What's been going on?"

"I've been around," Xavier said, and then he gave the man a curious look, his wide shoulders closing the guy in.

I turned to Twist, hoping that Xavier would be able to get a little information out of the man, especially if the dude thought I wasn't paying attention.

Twist, at the moment, was keeping himself a few feet off the ground, so he could see a little better than Xavier and me.

"Anything?" I asked, scared to wonder what was being done to my brother and sister at this very moment. Images of them being hurt, tortured, and beaten to death, played havoc on my mind.

Panic had my fingers curling, as fear wrapped itself firmly around me. I tried to focus on a positive outcome in an effort to control myself but saw that I was failing when the large wheel to our right, started to shake and rattle.

Blood raced to my head, and my hands trembled with the urge to hunt down Dragon and take his whole fucking head off. "He's not getting away with this," I said, my voice shaky and tense. "I'm going to crack his chest open and pull his lungs, out, that way the next person will think twice before they even try it."

Twist came to the ground as the grass waved back and forward, and the glowed-up dice rolled down the street. "Calm down." He put an arm around my shoulder. "You know we're not leaving here without Tisha and Speed."

"He didn't know much." Xavier walked back toward us. "Haven't seen Kandy today, but said her enforcers were all through here." Because they had to keep everything on point and make sure the money count stayed right, I figured.

Xavier's brown eyes looked around. "I recognize a few of them."

Sweat dripped down my face, and I wondered if there were known spots that Dragon held people he kidnapped.

Wind flew around Twist as he spoke, and because there was so much light bearing down on us, some of his piercings sparkled and shined. "Do we want to tip our hand this early?"

I wanted my brother and sister back, but I knew acting like a brute wouldn't help anything. We had to be smart about this. Both of their phones had gone straight to voicemail when I'd tried calling them, which meant they were probably cut off and couldn't be tracked.

The cheers and groans of people winning and losing assaulted my ears. Also, the smell of beer, hot dogs, and chicken was heavy in the air. People here never stayed in one spot long. Often times they'd play games and get food in one place, before quickly moving on to the next hot spot. "Gamblers in Tajan City tend to stumble from one part of the city to the other. If we ask too many questions, it's going to get back to Dragon."

Xavier's hands came out in a way that told me he was just waiting for someone to make a move. "Now see, that's a good thing, Darlin'. It'd cause him to show his hand a little sooner, and maybe we can get some information."

True, but there was no guarantee he'd be alone. When he wanted to make a move on someone he usually had at least three hundred of his crew with him, and that was only a small fraction of his people.

"I want to talk to Kandy," I said. "See what she knows."

Xavier rocked back on the balls of his feet, his thumbs hooking through the belt loops of his black jeans. "Sure that's a good idea?"

I walked forward. "Only one way to find out."

We passed by a strong-arm contest for those with super strength only, lined with people placing bets on their favorite competitors. From there we saw telekinetics lined up, all trying to move objects as big as mountains. Red lines were drawn on the ground and people placed bets on how far each telekinetic would make it and who the overall victor would be.

Excitement buzzed in the air as people yelled and called out their bets. The whole place jumped and popped with energy and I understood where it came from. I'd been here many times before and had always enjoyed myself. Today, though, everything depended on my sister and brother being alive. Nothing else mattered.

Kandy had many houses, and we went to three before coming to the one we were at now. She owned the whole east side. All money made there went through her hands. So, every house she had was a big ass mansion.

This one was no different. Looking at it, it was three levels and probably had over two hundred rooms. The brown bricks mixed with the white bricks were a nice design and extended to her yard furniture and porch fixings.

Eight guards stood on the front porch, four on one side of the door, four on the other. But there was no need. she stepped out of the house before we'd made it up the steps. "They're free to come in," was all she said before closing the screen door behind her.

I took a breath and then sighed in relief. She hadn't turned us away, nor had she seemed all that surprised to see us, which I took to mean she at least knew something. I hoped she did anyway.

Xavier motioned for Twist, who was hovering a few feet off the ground, to come closer. "Could be a trap, ya'll. I say we stay alert."

Twist nodded, and I gave Xavier's hand a squeeze thanking him for thinking when I couldn't.

The house was a nice contrast from the heat outside. A short guy with blond hair pointed to a room down the hall. The door was open, and Kandy sat in a chair, legs crossed, holding a yatena smoke in her hand. Yatena was a powerful drug. Its potency was about a thousand times stronger than weed, and if you were puffing on it you'd better be sure your body could handle it, or you'd be sick and high for days.

Kandy didn't seem to be having a problem as she blew the foul smoke our way. It curled around her dark ebony skin and filtered through the loose curls hanging down her back.

Kandy was tall and slim, a serious businesswoman but known to have a good laugh every now and then. Still, there was nothing soft about her. She'd fought tooth and nail to get where she was, leaving a hail of bodies in her wake and not turning back.

She looked like an empress now, sitting in judgement of those beneath her. Honestly, watching her sometimes you got the feeling that even the walls and refrigerators would start talking if she commanded them to.

The room she led us to was small, with a white shaggy, rug covering the entire floor. The walls and couches were a light blue, as was the big desk she sat behind. The place felt warm, intimate even. Shit, she even had blue and white candles lit throughout the room, as no other lights were on.

She made a motion for us to sit, and we all fell onto the couch directly in front of her. There were no guards in here, which meant she didn't think we'd come to do her harm.

She took another puff of her yatena and the smoke curled around us. I coughed in disgust. "Put that shit out, Kandy," I said. "You know I hate the smell."

She laughed and kept holding it in her hand, though she didn't puff on it anymore. "We need to hang out again." She pointed the yatena my way. "Always have fun, when we girls just let our hair down."

She turned to Xavier. "Nice to see you back here. Though I'd prefer you gamble on another side of town. You win too much for my liking." She sounded serious, and why wasn't I surprised that she and Xavier knew each other? The man knew everyone, though how he'd never tell.

She pointed to Twist, waiting for one of us to fill her in on him. I gave her his name and then steered the conversation back where it needed to be. "You know why we're here. What do you know?"

She opened her hands in front of her, her yatena tipping to the side. "Your brother and sister were taken by Dragon, and you want information about their whereabouts."

I nodded.

She exhaled through her nose. "I did hear some ramblings from a few of my people. You know how Dragon is. If they'd just paid everything would have been fine. Why cause all of this? Now he has no choice but to kill them."

Her words made it sound as simple as knocking flies from one's shoulders, and her desk shook as my anger rose.

She gave me a tired look that said I should know better, but at this point, I couldn't really stop it. This was confirmation. Before now I'd been holding on to the belief that maybe Red and his friends had it wrong or maybe had just been trying to rob us. But hearing Kandy speak it out loud hit me like a thunderbolt and made me want to scream.

The couch rumbled and shook, then Xavier put a hand on my knee trying to calm me down.

"All I know," Kandy said, looking around as the walls started to tremble. "Is that Dragon wants to expand, find some spots in your city, he wanted your brother to help him with that."

I frowned as I thought it all over. If he wanted my brother to help him expand then why did he pull this stunt?

Also, if my brother was here to do a business deal, what made him and my sister start playing cards? I ran a slow hand under my chin. The smell of rot was everywhere, and I meant to get to the bottom of it.

"Do you know where they are?" I asked, my eyes narrowing as I looked her way. "Was Niche with them? Is he okay?" Niche really was like a second brother to me and my sister, always had been.

"Don't know about Niche." She leaned back in her chair, her eyes dead set on mine. "I don't have information on your siblings, but Banjo in the west might. Maybe check him out."

Anxiety wrapped itself around my body. I wasn't sure if it was what she'd said or how she'd said it, but the smell of rot intensified.

I didn't say anything as she walked us to the door, but once we were on the front porch, I turned around to see that her eyes had gone hard as stone, and there was nothing but pure fury on her face.

I quickly turned back around, not wanting her to know I'd seen, but wondering if we'd inevitably stepped into the middle of another turf war, because if so, I couldn't guarantee that any of us would make it out alive.

Chapter 4

B anjo was a tall guy, lanky, even. His hair was dark blue, and his mind sharp as a tack.

Really the south side of town was no different than the east. The streets were loud with the sound of gambling, the smell of corndogs and liquor permeated the air, and even a lot of the houses had games and lottos set up in their front yard.

"I know of two more locations he could be if we strike out here, Darlin'," Xavier said to me. We were standing across from a group playing air basketball. They were about ten feet off the ground, as were some of the spectators, taking bets on how many points each player would make, and which team would come out on top.

Twist floated about five feet off the ground, his piercings still shining. "By now he has to know we're looking for him. We've been here for over two hours."

I checked the time on my phone, wondering what part of the country my parents were in. Like me, they paid their bills through games of spades. They traveled all around the world, only stopping in for a brief visit with me, my brother and sister every now and then.

In contrast, me, Tisha, Speed, and Niche got together at least twice a week, just to hang out and have a good time.

Whenever I was with them, I always finished the evening feeling good.

The basketball rim the players were using started to tremble, as I wondered if I'd ever have those times again. "Well, hopefully, he's at this next place," I said, surging ahead.

I tossed it over a few times in my mind whether I should call my parents or not. On the one hand, they would be here, guns blazing, and they wouldn't stop until they'd set the whole of Tajan City on fire. Many would die, and I just didn't want to take it there if we didn't have to.

On the other hand, if Speed and Tisha lost their lives, all because I didn't pick up that phone, I didn't think I'd ever forgive myself.

Also, I still didn't know where the fuck Niche was. He hadn't answered his phone the numerous times I'd called, and right now I was at a loss.

Xavier's warm breath tickled my ear, as he leaned over to whisper. "Don't be so hard on yourself. You'll do the right thing when the time comes." My shoulders relaxed at his words, and I moved a bit closer to him.

We walked until we came to a large open park set up with pools and tennis courts. Everyone was taking a bet on the competitors, this place no different than the rest in the city.

Picnic tables were set up throughout the park, some under tents and canopies, others resting on open grass. One was under a blue canopy and had well over twenty guards in front of it. "Bingo," I said, my heart speeding up.

Me, Twist, and Xavier walked up and at least six guards came to stand in front of us before we could get within three feet of Banjo. "He doesn't want to be bothered."

My veins boiled as images of Speed and Tisha flashed before me. "Get the fuck out of my face and tell your boss that Leah the gambler is here."

He pointed his finger at me. "I ain't telling him-"

I used my telekinesis to pick him up and toss him into the other guards standing in front of the table. The other five who'd walked over with him jumped, but Xavier turned two of them into frogs, and then they just hopped away.

Twist caught two up in his whirlwind, twisting and turning them so much that when he let them go, their eyes were rolling to the backs of their heads, as they shook nonstop. The last, I tossed behind us, as Twist, Xavier, and I walked forward.

The fifteen bodyguards left weren't moving, which meant their boss had told them not to. They parted as we got closer to reveal Banjo's lengthy frame sitting on top of the table. His dark blue hair was cut short, and he looked delighted to see us. "Always love it when she makes an entrance," he said to a guard on his right.

I stood stock still, not at all fooled by his candor. Banjo was as vicious as they came, and if there was a way to fuck us over he'd do it.

"I heard you know something about my brother and sister being taken by Dragon. Would you care to share that information?"

He ran a hand down his face and leered at me. "That depends."

Xavier bristled, and I could see him raising his hand. I gave my head a slow shake to let him know I could handle myself. My mind went to what Dragon could be doing to them now, and my voice was a little choked when I spoke. "I'm asking, man." I held my hands up in front of me in a non-threatening manner. "I'm just asking."

"I know you are, but I don't like the color of your hair, so..."

One of the guards kicked my legs, and I fell hard to my knees, a ripple of pain going through my whole body. A knife was put to Twist's throat, and Xavier's hands were tied behind his back, all the while, one of the guards held a static bat to his head.

I gritted my teeth, wishing like the stars we had some verve pills. Verve pills not only gave you enough energy to run well over a mile a minute, they also healed your wounds and kept you from getting hurt as long as they were in your system.

Xavier and I had taken our last one hours ago, while still playing spades, and I'd been in too much of a rush to get more so this was all on me.

"Bring a card table over," Banjo said, as he rose from his spot. "And get the new deck I just bought. And more bats! We're going to need more bats!" He laughed, clapping his hands together.

Oh, right, that was the other thing about Banjo; as smart as he was, he was still batshit crazy, and a force to be reckoned with.

The sword on my waist buzzed with the urge to protect me, and I put my hand on it, willing it to calm down. Now wasn't the time to show our hand.

A wooden square table was placed in front of us, and three chairs were placed around it. Two arms grabbed me, and lifted me up, sitting me in one of the chairs, the same for Twist and Xavier.

Two guards stood on either side of all three of us, each with static bats in their hands. A deck of cards were thrown on the table, accompanied by a squeal from Banjo.

My hair started to lift from my head, and I bit my lip, trying my best to control my telekinesis. I'd never been out of control like this before, my telekinesis usually only reacted when I wanted it to, but with my brother and sister missing, everything was out of whack.

Still, the two barbed-wire electric bats aimed at my head was excellent motivation for me to get my act together.

"Now," Banjo said, walking around the table, grinning from ear to ear like a lunatic. "You're going to play for your lives. Whoever loses..." He pointed to the bats, a big smile on his face, and I could practically see him coming all over himself in his excitement.

My eyes went dark as nothing but pure rage washed over me. Did he think I was his monkey, ready to do fucking tricks at his whim? Nah, fam, didn't work that way.

The card table shook, and I looked at Xavier and Twist letting them know I was going for broke. Apparently that's all the confirmation my sword needed because it leaped in the air, crackling with life as it took the heads off the two men currently holding bats over top of me in one long swipe.

I used my telekinesis to slam the table into one of the ones on Twist, while my sword cut the binding holding Xavier's hands back.

Xavier tackled me out of the way, as Twist started a windstorm, whipping the second man who'd been over top him, and the two who'd held bats on Xavier up in it.

At the same time, my sword took out two more. I stood and held out my hand, and my sword flew into it. Xavier's arm went up, and a guard to our right lost his toes, then his feet.

I used my telekinesis to pull the nose and lips off a female guard's face while willing my sword to cut the head off another.

Body parts fell all around us as Twist's windstorm turned into a full-on hurricane.

There were four left, but suddenly two of them exploded. Shocked, I looked up to see Niche standing there. My heart sped up at the sight of him. I didn't know what he was doing here, or how he'd found us, but I'd never been so happy to see someone in my life.

His leg kicked out and one of the other guards went to the ground. Xavier waved his hand, and the second guard turned into a mouse, while the one Niche had kicked lost his eyes.

Twist came back to the ground, and the four of us stood in front of Banjo. We couldn't kill him. To do that would start a war I didn't think any of us could handle, and from the cocky smile on his face, he knew it.

My anger grew as I watched him grinning at us, and suddenly I didn't care. Oh, I wouldn't kill him, but if he thought he wasn't about to get a smack for all the havoc he'd just caused, well he was about to find out who I really was.

If you crossed me, then I made sure you knew it, and once I made it known to you, you took care to never do it again. I lived in a tough world, and in my profession, if you didn't make it known that you weren't to be fucked with, you'd be robbed every time you left the gambling table.

I walked forward, ignoring Xavier as he called my name. Banjo flicked his wrist and a ball of fire appeared in his hand. I scoffed at his little display. Both my brother and father had that power, I grew up around it, he couldn't scare me with that shit.

I kicked him hard in the face twice, then grabbed him by the neck, raising him in the air. His fireball dropped away, and someone threw water on it, putting it out. I didn't care, I was too pissed off at this point.

I slammed Banjo hard to the ground, his head making a sickening sound as it hit. "If you ever test me like that again, I'll run you through with my sword, cut your body up into tiny pieces, and serve it to your guards for dinner."

I let him go, knowing that it wasn't over, knowing that his pride and his ego wouldn't let it end that way. He'd gather more of his crew and come for us again. Which meant as well as dealing with Dragon, we'd have to take on him and his people now too.

I flexed my hands. Things were about to get a lot bloodier, but at this point, I'd decided if I wanted Tisha and Speed back, it was all or nothing, so I wasn't holding back anymore.

Chapter 5

"Hey, dude. Where did you come from?" I asked Niche.

Niche's family was originally from Thailand. He was a little taller than Twist with a slightly stocky build.

With piercing silver eyes and black hair, he had a confidence and swagger about him that only someone who owned one of the hottest nightclubs around could pull off.

We were under a tree, not quite in the west part of town yet. We sat by the water on some large rocks, trying to keep out of sight and cool off. "Here." Niche took off his backpack, and reached inside, handing each of us a bottle a water, then he pulled out a bag of verve and I almost wanted to kiss him.

He gave one to me, one to Xavier, and swallowed his own. Then he took out another, put it on his tongue and motioned for Twist to come and get it. I gave him a hard stare. His best friend was missing, and he thought it was a good time to try and get laid?

Twist shook his head and held his hand out. "Later for that. Come on, Niche." The other man let out a large sigh then pulled Twist close, flicking it from his own tongue to Twist's.

Twist's hands trembled a little as he opened his water bottle, and I blinked. That they knew each other and had been fooling around was now obvious. One of my best friends with my brother's best friend, how had I missed that?

"None of your business," Xavier said, from behind me.

I nodded. I knew that, but Twist looked shaken. Niche had affected him and as Twist usually just wanted to have a good time for the night and never see the person again, this really was surprising.

"I was with Speed and Tisha when they came," Niche let me know. "We just didn't arrive together and hadn't planned on leaving together. I was supposed to watch in case things turned sour. Which they did."

He ran a hand through his dark hair. "Speed gave me a list of people to call if things went blast." He made a blowing up motion with his hands, then pointed at me. "Your name was not on that list."

I blinked, wondering where all these other people were because we could sure use their help right about now. "So, he told you not to call me, no matter how bad things got?"

Niche took a swig of his water. "Since we were kids, he always did everything he could to protect you and Tisha. You know that. The only reason she was here in the first place was because she was named in the deal too."

"What deal?" He kept talking about it like he thought I knew.

"Dragon wanted to set up casinos and gambling spots in all of your brother's hotels. He even wanted to set up a small room in one of your sister's gyms, to see how it went."

I sorted through everything I knew, and it still wasn't adding up. "So, if Speed and Tisha came here for business, why were they gambling?"

Niche's brows furrowed. "They didn't gamble while there were here. They just rejected Dragon's offer, and this was his retaliation. By him saying they owe him money and putting it out there, he made it so now something has to be done. His pride and rep will take nothing less than their deaths, but he's hoping to get a few dollars out of you and anyone else foolish enough to believe him before then."

"What about the people Speed told you to call?"

Niche pulled out his phone and looked at it. "Haven't heard back from any of them. We're on our own." Ah, so this was why he hadn't answered when I'd called, Speed had told him not to. How dumb.

I picked up a rock and tossed it back and forward in my hand because there was no way the four of us were enough to take on both Dragon's and Banjo's gang. Heck, we weren't enough to take on just one of them.

Then there was Kandy. What was her deal? I asked Niche about it and he waved a hand. "Kandy is a whole other matter. Let's not talk about her until later. She won't be a problem as far as this goes."

I let out a grunt. If he said so, but I was still keeping my guard up. By now the verve had made its way into my system and I figured I could probably do about three hundred jumping jacks before a minute was up.

I wanted to try it too, so much so that I stood and hopped from leg to leg. Twist was busy doing spins and turns in the air, while Xavier walked back and forward, and Niche started blowing things up.

Okay, we needed to move, because with verve, it was impossible to stay inactive. We could probably all run full speed across town right now and not even be out of breath, because, well, that's what the verve did to you.

"Well, seems like everyone knows something. I say we check out the Rebels, see if they've heard anything," I said.

The Rebels were the brother and sister pair who ran the west side of town. They'd been called that for so long that I'd forgotten what had first made the name stick.

What I did know was that they were protective as shit of each other, and while many had first thought them weak, they quickly learned they were anything but.

I was still hopping from foot to foot and now Xavier was circling around me. Twist was still flipping around in the air, and Niche had his hand out to him, motioning him to come closer.

"So, you want to talk to Baker and Reef. It's a good idea," Xavier said.

"We still need to be on our guard." Niche had Twist by the hand now, but instead of pulling him down, Twist was bringing him up. "You know that man doesn't take rejection well. He'll send out his boys," Niche said. He was talking about Banjo, and I'd already figured the same thing.

We had verve running through us, and I kind of wished they would find us, so I could expel some of this energy. "You got more pills?" I asked Niche. He was up in the air with Twist now, and Twist was holding him by the waist as he swayed back and forward. "Got enough," he answered.

"Enough for what?" I asked.

He looked at me like he used to when we were kids and I wouldn't leave the room so that he and my brother could talk about stuff they didn't want me to know about. "Enough for us to get another hit and enough for Speed and Tisha."

"Okay." I didn't know if Dragon had put his hands on my brother and sister. If they were hurt, really hurt, all the power of the verve would go toward healing them, but there might not be enough of it left over after that to give them extra strength or protect them from future harm. Verve did have its limits.

If we were to fight right now, the verve, what was left in our system anyway, would keep us from getting hurt, but that would pretty much use it up and we'd be back at zero again.

Still, we speed walked to the west side of town, and at some point, we decided to just outright run. It felt good, like I was doing something at least. Here, just like everywhere else, games, lotto's, and slot machines were set up everywhere.

We passed by a group playing chess in the air, where no hands were allowed to touch the table, and everything was moved with the mind. Of course, people were gathered around, taking bets on who would win.

Large slot machines lined the roads, and if you won, instant cash came out. If you tried to rob the machine, then the rebels had people set up that would put your face through the street. Most knew this and didn't try it.

It was as crowded here as everywhere else in town, and over the dings of the machines, we could hear crowds of people calling out bets, celebrating, or loudly wondering when they'd have their next hot streak.

On our way to one of the places we thought the rebels may be, we even passed by a dating game, where spectators bet on who would be sent away first and who would be the last one standing.

The first two places we went to look for the rebels were a bust, but on the way to the third, they found us. We were walking past a group playing flip the card. That's where telekinetics threw the cards up in the air, lined them up, and you had to guess which card was where before they flipped them over.

The rebel's family were originally from Mexico, but they'd been here a few generations now. At twenty-nine they were the youngest holding down their own territory, but it hadn't come easily to them. They'd had to prove themselves more than any of the other turf owners, and I knew they'd lost a lot on the way.

But they were quick, learned fast, and were as ruthless as they came when it was time to protect themselves or their territory.

They walked up to us, about fifty people behind them. Baker stood, arms cocked out and I knew he had enough muscles to lend out a few and still not miss any. He always reminded me of the guy who'd give you just enough rope to hang yourself, then maybe reel you back in, if he felt like it.

His stare was cold and hard as he watched us, black hair cut close to his head. To me, the look in his eyes was all knowing, and I remembered one of his powers was telepathy.

I had a small trace of it, which I suspected is what helped me communicate with my sword, one of the things that bound me and my sword together. There were a few other things as well, like my blood being inside the sword. Still, my telepathy was child's play compared to his.

I wasn't strong enough and I knew it. Heck, I never even really used the small bit of telepathy I had. I didn't need to, my telekinesis never let me down, and I didn't have a good enough handle on the telepathy to try it.

Still, even with my limited use of it, I slammed down the walls in my head, and in the other three members of my group, the verve in me giving me the extra power I needed to do that.

He smirked at me but didn't say anything. I actually liked Baker. He and his sister came to a few of the houses I gambled at sometimes and we always had a good time.

Reef, like her brother, had dark black hair and eyes. She looked sweet, innocent even, but I knew her to be a nose to the grinstone type who didn't take shit from anybody.

"What do you want, Leah?" she asked, like she didn't already know the answer.

"Give me some verve," I said, as a way to test her.

She and her brother shared a look and I didn't doubt for a second there were some silent communications going on.

It was Baker who answered. "We're not getting into your shit with Dragon. We're all good right here."

Xavier stepped forward, his black hair was loose around his shoulders, and he had his thumbs through his belt loops again. "Now, come on, Baker. She didn't ask you to get involved in anything. She just asked for some verve, you really gonna refuse?"

"We sure are," Reef said. "Giving you verve will be us taking a side in this whole thing and we're not ready to do that."

"But we have cookies," Niche said, walking forward. Though he sounded like he was joking, his eyes were hard as steel. "Dragon is looking to expand. He's not happy with what he has. How long before he comes for your territory? Why not snap his knees in half before that can happen?"

Baker and Reef looked at each other and burst out laughing.

The windows on a few nearby windows rattled and my voice was low as I spoke the truth. "If... if they're not breathing... if he hurt them in any way, I'm not sure what I'll do."

This stopped their laughter and Baker pointed to the North. "You'll keep that shit over there because as me and my sister already told you, we're not getting involved."

Reef gave Twist a strange look, and then his wind whipped around her feet. Like my sister, Reef was an empath, but tapping into Twist's powers without his permission, nope, wasn't going down like that.

I was already pissed, so I probably couldn't have stopped myself even if I'd wanted to. Not thinking of the consequences, I punched her in the face twice, making her let go of his wind.

She fell backward and her people, as well as my own, surged forward. Reef held up her hands to stop her people before they, you know, slaughtered us. "My bad," she said. "My bad. Only..."

She did a spin and kicked me hard in the face three times. My head snapped back, but since I had verve in my system, I didn't feel the pain and no blood shot out, as the verve had already healed anything that could have been broken.

"Okay," I said, wiping a hand down my face. "Sorry, I hit you."

She narrowed her eye. "Yeah, well, it felt good kicking you in the face so I'm not apologizing."

We both let out a laugh, which eased some of the tension, but that only lasted for a second. "I'm serious, Reef. Don't ever try that shit with a member of my crew again."

She nodded, and we let the matter drop.

Baker threw up his hands. "We can't help you, Leah. Things are finally good here. Telling you that we believe Dragon is holding your brother and sister in a warehouse on Brookden Street, and have well over a hundred guards on them, would definitely put us in some shit we don't want any part of. So, I'm not telling you anything."

"Yup," Reef nodded at her brother. "We don't know anything about Dragon and Banjo thinking that Tajan City split two ways instead of four, sounds better to them, but first they need to expand to places outside of Tajan City to build up their revenue and crew. Don't look at me like that. I don't care what you say. I ain't telling you shit."

I took all of this in, my mind fitting it all together. I figured Tisha and Speed were probably one of many they'd approached. Either that or being that they came from a family of gamblers they thought they'd start with them first. Maybe to test the waters.

Baker and Reef were still standing in front of me, neither saying another word. "Yeah, well, thanks for nothing," I said as I turned to walk away. "I'll just inquire elsewhere next time I have a question."

"So, what now?" Twist asked once we were out of hearing distance.

I looked toward the north of the city and flexed my hands. "Now we go and get my brother and sister back."

Chapter 6

"**I**s this what you guys normally do?" Niche asked, eyes shifting from myself to Xavier and Twist. "Just barge into places outnumbered with no game plan at all?"

Xavier sniffed the air, his shoulders rolling. "Serves us well."

Twist laughed and then wind whipped from his hand and brushed lightly through Niche's hair. "Yeah, and it's fun."

Niche scoffed, but I noticed his hand lingered in his hair for a bit as he looked at Twist. "Fun is what we did Saturday night. This right here is..." he stopped talking and his eyes went hard. "You know what, I don't even care. If it helps us get Speed and Tisha back I'm down for whatever."

We walked past a guy trying to get us to come under his tent, for the 'biggest bet we'd ever place,' as the loud cheers and roars from the crowds surrounded us. "You're not wrong," I said, looking at Niche. "If the rebels heard they have a hundred guards, then they probably have twice that many maybe even more. No way we can beat them all."

Small black strands of hair fell onto Xavier's face and he used his whole hand to push them back. "We could negotiate, though I don't believe any of us are good in that department."

"Thought we'd already decided he was going to kill them no matter what we did. Do you think that's changed?" I asked.

"No," Twist did a backflip in the air, "But if we make him believe we have something he wants... The question is what?"

"Well, we know he wants all of Tajan City to himself, Banjo notwithstanding, but to use that knowledge is to sell out the rebels, and I'm not willing to do that."

Niche ran a tongue over his perfect white teeth, looking deep in thought. "I could just walk through the front door. I took special care to stay out of his line of vision last night. I could just say I was looking for my best friend and the last place he'd been seen was here."

Twist leveled him with a stare. "Are you inviting him to kill you or..."

Niche let out a chuckle. "I'm a little more resourceful than you know." He tilted his head to the side as he looked at Twist. "Have to say I'm a little disappointed that you *don't* know."

Twist shot a quick glance at Xavier and myself, looking like he wished the ground would open up and swallow him whole. "I know exactly how resourceful you are, but that's not what I'm talking about and you know it."

The smell of popcorn hit me square in the nose, and I looked up to see a machine betting you'd never had popcorn this good. I shook my head and then turned back to the others. "How do we know that the information we have is correct? It could still all be a trap. Truth is, I don't know who to trust. I just want my family back."

My mind went back to my eighth birthday. My parents had luckily already purchased the stuff for my party because they'd lost all their money at the card table the night before.

Fred, one of our neighbors from down the street had tripped over his own feet and smashed my cake. I'd cried like my life was over and my brother, who'd been ten at the time, had reached into the top of his closet and pulled down the jar where he kept the money from all the little odd jobs he did around the neighborhood.

He and Niche had pooled their cash and ran down the street to the local grocery store. He'd begged Mr. Hangins to write 'Happy Birthday Leah' on the cake and then the two of them had walked carefully back home.

I still remember the look on Speed's face when he'd come through the door with it, hoping that I'd like it, but scared that I wouldn't.

I'd jumped into his arms after he'd set the cake on the table, and he'd used his fingers to light the candles. Me and Tisha, who'd been seven at the time, had laughed as we blew them out together.

The street under our feet rumbled, the air shook, buildings started to tremble, and a few trees cracked apart. I angrily swiped at my face, telling myself that now wasn't the time to break down.

A warm arm around my waist pulled me closer and I fell into Xavier's embrace knowing there was a real possibility that Tisha and Speed were no longer alive. "We'll find them," he said, squeezing me tight, his voice both fierce and comforting at the same time. "No matter what it takes, we'll find them."

I clung to him, letting my guard drop for just one minute, one second. Then I wiped my eyes again, straightened my shoulders and felt a whole lot of steel go down my spine. "Give me another verve pill."

We made it about ten miles from the edge of Dragon's territory before my sword started to hum, and then it leaped from my side. It blazed red and silver, just waiting to take a head off. Which it only did when... "Incoming!" I yelled then ducked low as hundreds of Banjo's men surrounded us, jumping from trees and off buildings.

Banjo himself was nowhere to be seen, but I had no doubt he was somewhere watching, waiting.

A guy with a head full of silver hair slung a hand my way, probably trying to use his telekinesis on me, and my sword chopped off both his arms before I could react. A woman came at me from up high, having either jumped off a building or out of a tree. I held up my hand, got her in my telekinesis hold so that she couldn't move, and slammed her hard to the ground, before pulling her eyes out of her head.

Something hard hit me in the neck, but I had the verve in me so even though I stumbled, I didn't feel the pain. Instead, I turned around and elbowed the man who'd hit me.

His head snapped back, but no blood came out, and from the way he smiled, I figured he was feeling the effects of verve same as me. Quick as a blink, he grabbed me by the throat and lifted me in the air. Panic rose in my gut, but before I could react he'd slammed me hard to the ground, putting his boot to my throat.

Then his shirt turned red, and I saw my sword coming through his chest. He opened his mouth wide, and no blood came from it, but still, the verve in his system wasn't fast enough to protect him from the tip of my blade.

My eyes popped as I heard explosion after explosion going off, and I looked up to see Niche put his hand on one guy's face blowing it away, while swinging the other hand behind his back, and making the guy behind him explode.

Someone tried to use their telekinesis on him, but he blew their hands off, then their legs.

Wind whipped all around us, but Twist was always in complete control. He had a small hurricane going now, and as he twisted and turned, arms, legs, and heads dropped to the ground.

It took a lot out of Xavier when it was people he was transforming, but still, I saw more than enough frogs and mice hopping around. A man grabbed him from behind, wrapping his hand around Xavier's neck, and Xavier used his telekinesis to split the man's body in half.

Then he kicked the guy in front of him with the static bat, in the face, while turning the bat into a small coin, to be tossed aside.

I stood, and ducked as a hand came toward my face, then kicked the guy's feet out from under him, then said fuck it and used my telekinesis to rip his legs off.

The longer we fought the more the verve wore off, and I knew soon there'd be nothing that we could do to stop the slaughter. I was already growing weak, and I was sure the rest of my group were as well.

Twist was a few feet off the ground, and he grabbed Niche by the hand, pulling him up with him. "Leah, Xavier, we have to get out of here. Use your telekinesis to raise yourself, and I'll send wind your way to keep you moving."

As he said it more and more of Banjo's men were coming, some of them high in the sky. I shook my head as they surrounded us, my heart doing backflips out of my chest, my sword at the ready in front of me. "It won't work. We have to find another way."

A guy with a long black beard and mustache began spinning his hands in rapid-fire motion, the way Xavier did when he was ready to transform something.

Not willing to end my life in the form of a frog, I held up my hand. Then drew it back, as the man's whole body froze over and shattered to the ground. Behind him stood Kandy, hand outstretched, eyes completely iced over.

I looked around her and saw that she'd bought hundreds of her gang, fresh fighters who were ripping Banjo's people apart.

"I'll hold it down here," she said, sending a shard of ice through a guy's eye, then freezing a woman to the ground and icing her over until she broke apart. "Go and get your family back. Tell 'em Kandy said hi."

I nodded my thanks to her as Xavier, Twist, Niche, and myself fought our way through the crowd, her people helping to clear a path. I had no idea what was going on inside her mind, and at the moment, I didn't care.

Had she not come when she had, there was no way we would have made it out of there alive and that wasn't a debt easily repaid.

I held out my hand and my sword came flying into it, dripping with blood, body tissue, and guts. I smiled at it, glad that I could always depend on it in a fight.

The verve in my system was waning and I looked at Niche. He shook his head. "Only have two left."

"Save them," I said, as we finally came out on the other side of the battle. "Tisha and Speed might need them."

I had no idea where Banjo was, but he hadn't shown up for this fight, just sent his people in to destroy us. Now though, I understood that his attack on us earlier had been because he was working with Dragon. Who knew what these two were really up to?

As we surged forward, I realized that we'd moved locations doing the fighting and now we were only five minutes away. I wiped sweat and blood from my face, not sure if it was mine or someone else's.

The ground rumbled under my feet, and the trees shook as I went past. Dragon had picked the wrong family to fuck with, and he was ready to find that out.

Chapter 7

The warehouse where they were said to be held was covered with guards, and about the size of a football stadium. *Just how many people did Dragon have in there with him.*

I wondered at our chances, then the rebels came from trees, bushes, and thin air when we were still at least twenty feet away.

Reef and Baker stood before us, hundreds of their rebels behind them. Reef's words were hard when she spoke, her tone showing nothing but disdain. "You didn't really think Kandy, myself, and Baker would let those two fuckers take over all of Tajan without putting up a fight, did you?"

Her brother held up a hand, directing a few of their people to come in from different angles. "We've known for weeks what they were planning. Just had no idea they'd pull Tisha and Speed into it. Would have let you know ahead of time, if we'd had a clue."

I nodded, not really caring if they'd truly known or not. They were here now, and that's all I cared about.

Reef held out her hands then turned to look at me, Xavier and the others. "Can I tap into your powers, if I need to?"

She was helping us, so why not? I gave my approval, as did the others and we all rushed forward.

When we were about ten feet away, Dragon's men descended. We fought through them as quick as we could, removing arms and legs, catching them in windstorms, turning them into insects, and blowing them up.

Our main focus was getting through that front door, so Baker and Reef's rebels did most of the heavy lifting.

Standing in front of the door, was a man who looked like he could probably bench press a thousand pounds and not break a sweat. Not having time to fool with him, I used my telekinesis to yank the door off its hinges, hitting him hard in the back of the head and sending him flying.

Before we entered, Baker put a hand to his head and closed his eyes. "I got the four waiting by the door with static bats. They're all asleep now."

Reef leaned her head to the side and squinted. "I've got the four after them, influencing their emotions. Right now, they think they're on a beach drinking beer and watching the sunset." She let out a disgusted chuckle. "They have the silliest grins on their faces."

Right, because telepaths and empaths could fuck with your mind and emotions like that, which is one of the things that made her and her brother so dangerous.

With the door open, I wasted no time busting inside, since the rebels had already cleared away the men guarding the front, we walked unbothered for at least twenty seconds, before Dragon's people started to jump out.

"Halt!" a voice said, and just like that, they all cleared away and gathered behind two men. Dragon and Banjo stood side by side, looking like they already had the whole of

Tajan City under their thumbs. They certainly had the north and south.

Dragon stood, back erect, arms out. The muscles in his arms were thick and protruding, making him look even more threatening. His bald head shone from the large overhead lights in the ceiling, and I remembered that he'd gotten to where he was by being quick-witted and thinking on his feet.

He looked like a typical hired bodyguard, but he was anything but. He was in direct contrast to Banjo's tall and lanky frame. Though Banjo sometimes acted outlandishly, I kept in mind that both these men were thinkers, planners.

Who knew how long they'd had this in the works. Tajan city was huge, and both Banjo and Dragon had thousands under their command, but who knew what others they'd called in.

It was a perfect plan when I thought about it because at the moment I realized it hadn't all been about Tisha and Speed. That Dragon had wanted to expand and felt insulted by their rejection I didn't doubt. But he'd had to have known it was a possibility they wouldn't throw in with him, and I think he and Banjo had already set a lot of this in motion.

They'd probably known that me or maybe even my parents would charge in here head first. They knew that we had a relationship with Kandy and the Rebels as we did with all the bosses here. No doubt it was Dragon and Banjo who'd made it known ahead of time that they wanted to take over the east and west.

How else would they draw Kandy and the rebels into a fight? Also, this way they could say that Kandy and the rebels had brought the battle to them, attacked them first, because they had, but it wasn't that simple.

Still, if Kandy and the rebels fell here today, it would be easier to bring both their gangs under control, if they toted the line, that it had been Kandy and the rebels who'd been the aggressors.

Because that's where we were. Kandy's people were at this moment going toe to toe with Banjo's people. The rebels were here ready to do battle, not only with more of Banjo's people but Dragon's people as well.

Now the top members of Kandy and the rebels' gang would know that Dragon and Banjo had been planning to take over, but it was sensitive information and not something you let leak out and trickle down to everyone beneath you, especially if you were secretly planning to do something about it.

All the rest of Kandy and the rebels' people probably knew was that they'd attacked Banjo and Dragon. This way, if Dragon and Banjo killed them, it wouldn't sour the stomach of their crews so much to join the opposition, because hey, they hadn't been the ones who'd started this fight, right? Shit, they'd probably even tell them that it was Kandy and the rebels trying to take over and this is what they got.

It should have been an equal fight, but Dragon had three times the number of people as Banjo, The rebels, and Kandy. He'd started amassing them after they'd first divided the territories and hadn't stopped yet.

They all stood behind him now, thousands of men and women, each popping with power. Some hovered in the air, others had skin that was lit up blue with electric power, some had balls of fire in their hand, and I was sure he had telekinetic, transformers, and even more powerful people standing strong by his side.

Fear came, trying to get in. It crawled up my back, and around my chest, but I pushed it away, because I still hadn't found my brother and sister yet, and until I did, I had to stand tall for them. I had to.

As we walked closer, the air blinked, and in an instant, the rebels were on the ground, a boot to Baker's throat, and a sword pointing at Reef's. Dragon had the power of super speed, and he'd just shown us exactly what we were up against.

He looked back at the rebels' squad, a sneer on his face. "Back off. We'll get to all that, but you haven't seen the main part yet." He let them go, and they both stood.

Reef had blood coming out of her arm where he'd cut her, and Baker had it coming out of his side. I didn't doubt that they had verve in their system, but they'd probably used it all getting here.

The rebels being hurt, and concentrating on their wounds, meant they wouldn't be able to fuck with the mind or emotions of Dragon, Banjo, or any of their crew.

It was a smart move going for them first, plus any extra power the rebels had right now was probably being used to keep whatever telepaths and empaths Dragon and Banjo had out of their heads.

The rebels had hundreds of men and women here to protect, though I didn't doubt that some of their squad had the same power and were helping to keep Dragon and Banjo's people out of their heads.

I was doing what I could for myself, Xavier, Twist, and Niche, but I was peanuts compared to the rest, and I knew I wouldn't be able to protect us for long.

Dragon looked at me, a sick grin on his face, and everything in me froze because I knew. Even before he and his gang parted, and I saw the two bloody heaps laying there I knew.

My body started to tremble, and my hair flipped and turned, as something powerful and vicious stirred in my gut, lashing out to the rest of my body. One of the rebels grabbed my hand, sticking a bag in it, and from the feel, I knew it was verve pills.

I walked forward, the windows rattling as I did so. Around me I could hear Dragon and Banjo laughing, taunting, still not aware of how much danger they were in.

I dropped to my knees in front of the broken bodies of Tisha and Speed. Their faces had been beaten in, their limbs broken, their necks cut. I let out a low groan, a wail, as thousands of images went through my mind. Us running and playing together as kids, sitting at the dinner table talking about what we'd done that day, hiding under the covers together as we watched yet another frightening movie.

Tears ran down my face, and I felt for a pulse on both of them, my hands trembling. Something hit me in the chest, a wound, a scar so painful that I just wanted to curl up in a ball and lay there with them.

Instead, I pulled them closer. They were still breathing, but not for much longer. I didn't have any water to give them with the verve pills I stuck down their throats, but I knew even the ones that I couldn't get to go down would dissolve in their mouths and still get into their system.

I held them close to my chest, not wanting Dragon or Banjo to know what I was doing. After the bag was empty, after I'd given them ten pills a piece, I came shakily to my feet.

My sister's face was beaten in. These motherfuckers had hit her repeatedly until they'd bashed her face in. My breath came short and I felt my control slipping. Every finger on my brother's hand was broken, his eyes gouged.

The windows blew out, and I used my telekinesis to send my brother and sister behind Niche. I knew he'd protect them until they healed, if they healed. He'd protect them with his life, but they... they were broken... and...

I let out a guttural scream and it came from a place deep inside of me. They'd beat my little sister's face in. They'd laid hands on her and beat...

Rage like I'd never known before wrapped around me, as I felt every ounce of control I had slip away. "Get the fuck out of here!" I said to Xavier and the others because I wasn't responsible for my actions from this point forward.

The air blinked, and then Dragon went flying, my telekinesis having blown him back before he could get close. His squad was gathered together, his and Banjo's, and I walked toward them, rage and hate guiding my every step.

"Who did it?" I yelled, as the walls fell away, and the ceiling started to crumble. "Who put hands on my sister?" Bones shattered as I went through them, my telekinesis and my sword taking out anyone who got close.

I ripped out eyes, tore bodies in half, broke apart spines, crushed hearts, and ground bones under my feet. I removed heads from their bodies, crumbling them to dust when I did so.

Blood, bones, and body parts flew all around me, as I went, knocking down anything in my way. Some had the good sense to run, but others, well they weren't so lucky.

In the end, I had a pile of bodies at my feet and two motherfuckers standing in front of me, looks of sheer terror on their faces. Dragon and Banjo, and neither of them were laughing now.

Banjo tried to throw a ball of fire at me, but the force of my telekinesis knocked it back and then I held out my hand and my sword flew into it. In one swipe, I took off his head, then split his body down the middle, using my telekinesis to rip his arms and legs off, then grind his bones until they were nothing but dust.

Dragon had been coming at me this whole time, but my telekinesis kept throwing him back. He'd hurt... maybe even killed... Tisha and Speed, all for profit and gain.

The floor crumbled and broke away. I gripped my sword tight in my hand and started at his ankles. I sliced through them, then worked my way up to his legs, his knees, his thighs, his middle. Blood splattered on my face, tissue and skin flew through the air and still I kept going.

I sliced into his stomach, his chest, and his shoulders. Then I went to work on his face, slicing and dicing until it was nothing but mangled meat, unrecognizable.

He crumbled to the ground, his body nothing but random pieces scattered about. I held up my hand and used my telekinesis to shatter every bone he had left, grinding them down to dust.

Then I took a deep breath, wiped my mouth, and turned to see the shocked faces of all those behind me.

Chapter 8

I didn't feel an ounce of remorse as I walked over to Xavier and the others. My body was still popping with energy, and the only thing I wanted was to know if my brother and sister were okay.

Xavier grabbed me as I went by and pulled me close, his heart beating fast, his breath ragged. "What do you need?" he asked me. "Tell me what you need?"

I shook my head and removed myself from his arms. Kandy and her gang had arrived, and Speed lay in her lap. He was breathing, his hands and limbs were no longer broken, and his cuts and wounds were gone.

Kandy was rubbing fingers through his hair, and I could see the tear marks on her face. Were Kandy and my brother an item? Wow! How had I not known that?

Niche had my sister on his lap and I fell to my knees in front of her. She was okay, she was breathing, like Speed, her wounds were no more, her face slowly coming back to normal.

I let out a laugh and a cry as relief washed over me. "I cannot lose you," I said pulling her close. "I need you guys like I need air. I cannot lose you, you hear?"

She nodded, and I knew she was still getting her strength back, so I let her go and stood. Tears rolled down my face and my body started to tremble from the shock of it all. Xavier wrapped an arm around my shoulders, while Twist wrapped one around my waist.

Kandy was still holding onto Speed, while Niche was brushing hair out of Tisha's face. I closed my eyes, trying to catch my breath, leaning heavily on Xavier and Twist for support. "Dragon and Banjo are gone," I said, making all eyes in the room fall on me.

Tisha coughed, then sat up, her eyes taking in everything around her. I figured Kandy and the others had been pouring even more pills down her and Speed's throats and pretty soon they'd probably be bouncing off the walls.

Speed wrapped a hand around Kandy's neck and gave her a quick kiss on the lips, then rose to his feet, Tisha and Niche doing the same. Neither of my siblings were shocked to see me, and I figured they'd witnessed that little display I'd just put on.

Tisha, Niche, and Speed came to stand beside myself, Twist, and Xavier. "Dragon and Banjo are gone," I repeated, stepping forward a little. "They're gone, and their territories now belong to me, Speed, Tisha, Niche, Twist, and Xavier, and honestly after what they did to my brother and sister it's the least they could do."

"Does anyone have a problem with that?" Tisha asked, and she closed her eyes, and I knew she was using her empath powers to check for any malice in the room. After a few seconds, she opened them and nodded at me.

Speed leaned over and kissed me on the cheek. "Glad you never knew it was me who'd stolen your roller blades that time." He smirked at me, and my face softened, not caring about something that happened fifteen years ago. He was here, he was safe, and that's all that mattered to me now.

I looked at Kandy and then back at Speed, wondering how long the two had been an item, but figuring that was a conversation for another day.

The rebels were no longer bleeding, and I figured they'd probably taken some verve the moment I'd stepped forward after they'd handed me a whole bag of the stuff.

They had their own reasons for being here, as did Kandy, but I didn't care. Without their help, none of us would have made it out of here, and that was a debt I could never repay. "Thank you," I said, my voice breaking a little. "Thank you."

Now that everything had calmed down, the smell of blood, urine, and human feces was filtering to my nose, making me gag. "Okay," I said, looking at the others beside me. "We can go now."

Chapter 9

I sat in my new office in Tajan City going over a few notes. All the houses that Banjo and Dragon had personally lived in we'd converted to big ass game and gambling centers. We'd upped the pay fifteen percent of all their people and that had brought them under control.

I'd given the twenty thousand I'd won over to the couple who'd lost their home in the fire, as had Xavier, plus we'd been able to give them a little extra, and that had felt good.

We were still in the middle of setting everything up, but it had been decided, unanimously, I might add, that I would simply draw a monthly check from all of the properties, gambling houses, casinos, gambling machines, and real estate we now owned.

Also, no matter how much I begged and pleaded, no matter if my bills were eating me alive and all I had in the fridge was a stick of butter, I wouldn't be given more money until my next monthly payment.

I was a gambler, and no matter how you cut it, this was needed to keep me in check. So, I'd signed papers agreeing to this, as had Xavier, because well, he was a gambler too, wasn't he?

Speed and Tisha were doing okay, and turns out, they'd just gone to see Dragon for a meeting, and the minute they'd refused to work with him, he'd ambushed them.

My blood raced when I thought about it because I'd really lost control there, but I'd do it again in a heartbeat to anyone who threatened the lives of my brother and sister.

Speed, Tisha, and Niche were the ones with the business experience, so they kept things here moving along nicely. They all still had their own businesses to deal with, so it was a bit of a juggling act.

Speed and Kandy had apparently been fooling around for a while, and since they both seemed happy, I had no words to say.

Xavier popped in and out like usual, nothing much really changed there, but that was one of the reasons I liked being with him so much. He was so freaking unpredictable and something about that really spoke to me.

Twist was the one really running things on a day to day basis. He'd quit his job as a floor runner in Jinx's gambling house. He now owned a part of the North and South of Tajan City, so he didn't feel the need to keep working for someone else.

Like the rest of us, he had a whole floor for his office, and by my observance he really appeared to enjoy what he was doing. He also appeared to really enjoy whatever he had going on with Niche. Neither of them was known to keep a boyfriend for long, but for now, they seemed to like being with each other.

I'd taken my first check and furnished my house exactly the way I wanted it. I'd also paid up my taxes, insurance, and purchased a brand-new car.

I'd taken ten percent of my check and put it in a retirement fund for my parents. Speed and Tisha had added ten percent of theirs as well. We figured we'd do this every month, that way when their last hands were played, they'd still have something to fall back on.

The account was in Speed's name, and I expected he added a little more than ten percent to it, and that was okay too.

I picked up the deck of cards on my desk, shuffling them, as I thought of Xavier and my next big game. The pot was at two hundred thousand and I was itching to play my next hand.

Kerry Unrestrained

Chapter 1

"**E**veryone we've sent there has disappeared. Once people portal into Hansack, they never portal back out," Lia, the head of our team, said.

Gerell squinted, a curious look on his face. He was a muscular guy of twenty-six who looked like he'd be more at home on a skateboard than anywhere else.

He had skin the color of walnut, maybe a shade lighter, not that much different than my own, and he had an incurable habit of saying the first thing that popped into his mind, no matter the consequences. "You mean they like it so much they want to stay, or they fall away into the deep, dark abyss? The optics are important you know." Sitting beside him, his boyfriend Lincoln let out a bark of laughter while rolling his eyes.

Lincoln's skin was a dark chestnut color, he was the same age as Gerell but the two couldn't be more different in temperament. Unlike Gerell, who like me, stood about five-six, Lincoln was around five eight. He had a bald head, except for a small blueish brown patch in the front.

"I think you know what she means. Now pay attention," Lincoln's brother, Andrew said. Andrew usually came off as the stern schoolmaster who kept the other two in line. He and I were both twenty-seven though we'd figured he was three months older than me. His skin was a dark ebony, and he was completely bald, though I could tell from his brows that his hair too was blueish brown.

Andrew stood six feet, which meant he usually towered over me when we talked, but I didn't mind, I always liked to be as close to him as I could get.

"How soon will we have to pull out?" I asked. We were all in one of the conference rooms of the Coalition of Interplanetary Crimes building, where we worked as agents. Instead of a festive red or blue, the place was a sterile white, which put you in the mood for work and nothing more. Something done on purpose by the coalition no doubt.

Our job was to investigate other universes, that may be guilty of breaking the interworld treaty. For our team, we mostly dealt with human rights violations, though there were a lot of other teams here at our agency. There were also coalitions set up in alternate universes and we communicated with them on the regular.

Lia looked at us all, making sure she had our full attention. She was my height and had short, spiked, pink hair. Actually, her eyes and skin were also the same color. We'd did a test run once to see where she'd be sent if entering my homeworld and the machine had spit out Puerto Rico.

To Lia, nothing came before the mission, and she usually kept the rest of us in check. "Good question, Kerry," she said, her heels clicking as she walked across the floor. "We'll be leaving as soon as we can get prepped. This is serious."

We all lived on Plex, which was Lia's homeworld. The rest of us were from an assortment of other worlds, though of course Andrew and Lincoln were from the same place.

I ran a hand down my face, wondering about the world we would soon enter. I'd admit, I was always excitedly curious when entering a new land. I'd seen worlds that had people eight feet tall, worlds that fed strictly off energy, worlds that had people with beaks and wings, fur and tails.

They rarely spoke in the same tongue as us, but our brains had been fitted to hold over three thousand languages, so that wasn't a problem.

Gerell got up on the table and sat down, his legs hanging off the side. "So how many worlds have reported people missing due to this one place?"

Lia gave him a stern look. "Read the report. Twenty worlds that we know of, but we're talking about thousands of people here, so I'm sure the number is higher than that."

What? I looked over my Icater, a small oval-shaped device that held such information. "So, none of their people ever searched for them?"

Andrew, who was beside me, turned my way, the sparkle in his eyes whenever he looked at me, making me weak as always. "They disappeared too. Whole teams."

"Oh, fireblaster! No!" Gerell jumped off the table, a look of grievance on his face. "Whole teams disappeared, never to be seen again, and you're just going to send us in there as if it's nothing. Does Xetin know about this little suicide mission you've signed us up for?" Xetin was Lia's girlfriend.

"Stop being dramatic." Lincoln pulled Gerell into the seat beside him. "If you'd bothered to read the report, you'd see that they'd all went in as agents. We're going undercover."

Oh. I hadn't gotten that far in my own reading, but it still didn't make me happy. Undercover or not, it really didn't seem like a good idea. "And it's just our little team. No others will join us?"

Lia let out a huff of air, and that usually meant she was done with our shit, though this time I believed a little more explaining was needed. "Look, I've lost three friends to Hansack. You guys are trained agents. This is your job, or have your spines started to crack under the pressure?"

I blinked, having never seen her this mad, but then I remembered she said she'd lost three friends to this world and I realized how important it was to her. Still... "There are obvious risks to our lives going there. You can't just expect us to not have questions."

She closed her eyes and then exhaled. "You're right. I'm sorry." She held up her Icater. "Familiarize yourself with the world, the people, their customs, and beliefs. It's easy to go undercover because they look no different than you or I. We start going over a plan in two hours." She walked toward the door. "Oh, and one more thing. We don't know if it's something that has to do with their atmosphere or what, but going there affects your brain in a peculiar way."

I pushed my Icater away, frustrated that she just kept piling it on. "In what way?" I asked, only slightly peeved. I mean, I loved my job, loved what we did, helping others and bringing down the bad guys. I'd been taken advantage of once and I still wore those scars every day.

I pulled the Icater back toward me. I was usually gung-ho to start a new assignment, but now all I felt was growing unease. I knew the coalition would monitor our every move while there, but at the moment that wasn't making me feel better.

Lia held her hand up, and the door slid open. "The people of Hansack speak mostly in rhyme, and so does anyone who enters there until they come back home. As I said, going there does something to your brain.

Chapter 2

We'd discovered a long time ago that when going over material for a new mission it was less distracting to do it alone, as that way we soaked up more information.

Sitting in one of the rooms of the Coalition, I pulled up pictures and information about Hansack. Apparently, it was ruled by a family called Zin Zin. From reading, I saw that they'd never been nice, but until one brother had challenged another for control about ten years ago, they hadn't been all-out vicious either.

Other agents had been there before and transmitted pictures and information back before they'd lost contact altogether. I looked in horror at the many images of Zeke, the leader of the Zin Zin family, cutting off peoples' heads, gutting them, burning them alive, and doing so many other messed up things.

I put a hand over my mouth and gagged when I saw that age didn't matter, if you didn't follow the rules as he'd set forth, he'd kill your whole family, babies and the elderly alike.

In fact, I noticed as my stomach exploded with disgust, that this Zeke took special pleasure in hurting those who couldn't defend themselves, if the smile on his face was any indication.

Why was he like this? From what I could understand it was so that he held all the power, and all money went through his hands. A greedy, egotistical, power-hungry man, that's how he read to me.

I read through more material and saw that the rest of his family were complicit in his acts of violence, and the smiles on their faces as they helped to murder and kill told me all I needed to know about him and his siblings.

I looked at more pictures as I continued to read. The man had thousands, no hundreds of thousands of followers, and just like him, they didn't care the age as they hunted down and sliced apart anyone who didn't respect his name as they felt they ought.

Disgusting, I thought as I pushed my Icater away, not able to look at it anymore but knowing that I needed to. Worship, that's what this Zeke liked, for all those around him to worship him. He really did get off on it.

After going over all the material, it took me an hour to calm down enough to come out of the room I was in. This Zeke was a sick man, and all those who followed him were just as insane.

"THINK YOU'RE READY for this?" Andrew stood in front of me, his eyes so intent that I felt myself shiver a bit inside.

I pulled out my guidtag, the device we used to open portals to other worlds and ran my fingers over the small cylinder-shaped design. "Can't say I'm not terrified, but we've all been through some hellafied stuff before this and still survived it."

Andrew moved in closer, his hand going up my arm, a guarded look on his face. "I didn't tell you, but when Lincoln and I went to our home world the other day, my mom was convinced if we left, she'd never see us again. Took us a whole hour to convince her we'd be okay."

I reached out, lacing his fingers with my own. Andrew and I had been doing this dance for about a year now. Heck, he slept at my house a least three times a week, though nothing ever happened.

I cared about him, more than cared about him, but right before I'd met him and the others, I'd been living on the streets for the past two years and hadn't been in a relationship or had sex in five.

Andrew knew and understood all of that, so he never tried to push me. He accepted me, just the way I was. I moved even closer, breathing in the spice and musk scent that was him.

The thing about Andrew was, I never got the feeling that he was standing off the side, frustrated with me, waiting to pounce. No, he understood my situation and only ever made me feel comfortable and loved.

Filled with an overwhelming need to show him how I felt, I pulled him closer and brought our lips together. His lips were hard and chapped but were still the most delicious thing I'd ever tasted.

Feeling something stirring deep inside me, I threw my arms around him, only to pull back when I heard Gerell and Lincoln talking loudly as they entered the transfer room with us. The transfer room was where we normally gathered right before opening a portal to a new mission.

"If we see someone from Siana then we'll deal with them, but I'm not going out looking for them," Lincoln said as he and Gerell walked over to transfer agents who would make sure they had all the gadgets and supplies they needed. Andrew and I had just finished doing that.

Gerell stood with his arms out as transfer agents checked him over and loaded him up with necessities. "I'm just saying, some of them got away, and look what happened to Kerry."

I blinked and looked away. Andrew's face went soft and he placed a hand on my shoulder. Thinking of that whole ordeal always caused me to tense a little, as it marked one of the most horrific things I'd ever been through but taking it day by day and going to therapy, I'd learned to deal with it on a healthier level, at least I thought I had anyway.

I looked over to where the guys continued to talk about it. We'd all met on Siana, including Lia who'd been undercover for the coalition at the time. The Siana were a people who spread out to different worlds and kidnapped a bunch of people in order to sell them to a host of different beings from other universes.

They'd caught us all, but together we'd fought back, and together with the help of the coalition, we'd brought them down. Only one had come back to claim me as his prize, but he was now locked away, and all those he'd collected over the years were now back where they belonged.

Which is why I fought so hard for human rights now, and why even though I was a bit uneasy, I would not turn my back on this assignment.

Andrew looked at Lincoln and Gerell bickering back and forth and shook his head. "This is what my home life looks like all day and night."

I let the tension in my shoulders go and laughed a little at his words. Andrew, Lincoln, and Gerell all lived under one roof and constantly drove each other up the wall.

I lived by myself, and honestly, I preferred it that way. Living on the streets, like I had, meant that there was never any privacy. I'd felt naked and exposed every second of the day, and now that I had my own four walls that no one could enter unless I wanted them to, well, let's just say that the feeling was close to euphoria.

"Hey," Andrew said, calling over to his brother and Gerell. "How about we focus on this mission, okay? Leave Siana to another time."

Gerell gave him a sour look, while Lincoln told him to mind his business.

"Look," Andrew said, and I put a hand on his arm before he could go further. "We all have our ways of dealing with what happened to us. This is theirs. What is it hurting?"

The Sianas' had held us captive for weeks, pampering us, feeding us good and hearty meals, morning, noon, and night, treating us to the best hair and nail stylists, dressing us up in pretty clothes, and killing any one of us who dared question why or step out of line.

A shiver went through me as I thought about it because until the very second, it'd happened, we'd had no idea that one by one we were about to be auctioned off to the highest bidder.

What we had known, was that if we didn't comply with the Sianas' every word, then with the point of a single finger we would be killed; fire would erupt inside of us and then we would be no more.

Which meant for weeks we'd lived in utter fear that one wrong move or word would see one of us dead. We'd watched it happen to those around us, sometimes to the person standing right beside us, and that alone was enough to play on your mind for years to come.

I felt two hands on my arms, slowly caressing them, and I let out a breath, his touch a welcoming distraction. "We are not there anymore. You're safe. They can't hurt you here."

His breath was warm on my ear, and I hadn't realized until it started to slow down, just how fast my heart had been beating. Taking a look at my surroundings and feeling a little better, I reached out and twined our fingers together.

I didn't believe I could have made it while on Siana had Andrew not been there as a voice of reason through the bad times. No matter what had happened he'd always tried to make the best of it, and I thanked him for that more than he'd probably ever know.

"Okay," Lia said, walking into the room, a look of determination on her face. "If you read your guidtags then you know there will be a lot of rhythmic, rhyming words. Maybe not every word, but there will be a pattern to how we speak." She stopped talking for a minute, her eyes going to each of us to make sure we understood.

I listened carefully, knowing that she needed to reemphasize this because we were going in undercover and couldn't appear surprised at ourselves or each other as we began to talk.

Gerell waved a hand, a no-nonsense look on his face. "Well I rhyme all the time anyway, so this won't be a problem."

Lincoln slipped a few supplies into one of the pockets on his coat and snorted out a laugh. "What, in the shower when you're trying to sing?"

Andrew laughed as well. "How about in the kitchen when he's watching us cook, but complaining that we're not going fast enough?"

Lia looked at all three of them and smiled, having become used to these types of interactions by now. "So, you sit back and let the brothers do all the cooking?" she asked Gerell.

He gave her an exaggerated look of outrage. "And in return, I'm forced to clean all three bathrooms by myself, every single day. How is that fair?"

I rolled my eyes at his put-upon expression, trying hard not to chuckle. "I have to clean my bathroom and cook for myself, you don't see me complaining," I said.

Lincoln's brows rose to the top of his head. "That's because no one else wants to eat that red noodle mess you call food."

"It's called spaghetti."

"Ha!" Gerell said in that tone of voice he used when he thought he'd discovered something only he alone knew. "Remember when she forced us to eat it that day? She claimed it was called lasagna then. She can't even keep the name straight."

Andrew looked at me, a twinkle in his eye. "You did say it was lasagna that day. How did it suddenly turn into this spaghetti you speak of?" He turned to Lincoln and Gerell. "A little more investigation is needed on our parts, I do believe."

Lia walked to the back of the room where we would leave from. "I don't seem to remember any of you complaining as you stuffed your faces and begged for seconds. If you're going to investigate anything, how about starting with that?"

While I smiled, they all tried to talk at once and she held up a hand, cutting them off. "Playtime is over. I need each of you to prepare yourself, for I fear you won't like what you're about to see."

Anxiety made my palms wet, as she pushed the side of the guidtag and we all stepped through the portal.

Chapter 3

The place was dark, the smell was horrendous, I looked at my teammates to see if they were seeing this. Bodies hung from poles every few feet, too many to count, though this shit looked deep.

I took a breath, trying to center my emotions, the scent of decay threatening to choke me. People walked by as if they didn't see a thing, like they were used to it, oh man, what a shame.

The buildings were large, yet none of them were crumbling, so somebody worked hard to keep this place from going under.

Andrew shook his head, his eyes big as saucers, I guess he couldn't rectify this shit as we saw it. "Never been to a place quite like this. Don't want to misstep and get put on a list. We need to find the culprits and make them pay, round them up in front of us and see what they have to say."

I gave him a smile to show my compliance, because like always he was ever reliant.

Gerell stood tall, his fists at his sides, right now, he looked like he was ready to start a riot. "If they come for me, they better do it quick, cause I'm taking out as many as I can get. This is disgusting on so many levels. It makes me wonder, where are all the rebels?"

Lincoln pointed up, his face in a grimace, "You see what they got, always to be remembered. They're hanging there now for others to see, this is what you get when you fuck with authority."

I looked to the decaying bodies and knew it was true, those who spoke up they'd pretty much shoot.

Lia turned toward a noise, and we all looked that way, hordes of people were coming and I wondered what they'd have to say. "Remember now, that we're undercover, let's wait and see what we discover."

We backed away as more people came, so many that it looked like a football game. They were dressed from stylish to trashy, some had on shoes, while others looked like they'd just hit the snooze.

They all stared ahead, a gleam in their eyes, they looked kind of fanatical, and I couldn't help but wonder why.

Then I heard it, a scream and a shout, I started looking around, to see what it was about. Andrew raised his hand to one of the corpses; on the body was a sign that read 'did not respect authority.'

I swallowed hard, wondering how so little could offend, then from the corner of my eye, I saw a group of men. They were walking slow, didn't want to give themselves away, though I could tell that something nefarious was happening here today.

Lincoln moved closer, like he wished they would try us, these people did seem off, but maybe this was their survival, living in a place like this, I ain't seen nothing to rival it.

Lia stayed alert as the crowd continued to grow; "If it gets to be too much, we might just go. But we'll stay as long as we can, to get in the know and find a talking man."

The people kept coming and soon we were squished together, no one cared, as of now the crowd was yelling. Then I saw the platform raised high in the sky, while all around us people started to cry.

Then the name Zeke came off their lips, and I remembered from the Icater that he was in charge of this. He stood tall, about six or seven feet, I wish I could be more accurate, but that was all I could see.

Dressed in all white, he had about twenty people behind him, though he was the one who stood out, maybe because he was trying to. His features were hard, though his face had no scars, I wondered how he'd lived before making these people enthralled.

Then I remembered he was one of the Zin Zin, he'd fought his brother for power, and this was his win. From my Icater, I knew he'd skinned his brother alive, he'd wanted absolute power, at least that's what I surmised.

I started to say something, but the crowd got loud, then the yells from above, I couldn't tune them out. Somebody was in pain, that much I knew, but at the time just didn't know who.

The crowd, they went up in a frenzy, the yells were making them giddy. They loved it, somebody else's pain, but why, what did they have to gain?

The man Zeke and the many behind him, had to be his family the ones he hadn't yet demolished. He raised his hands high in the air, then the crowd did the same, like puppeteers. "Good people, here today, you're about to witness the death of one who got in my way. I'll strike down anyone trying to stop us, we didn't ask for the rebels, but I know how to block them."

Standing there, right beside me, Andrew's face got hard and I wondered what his thoughts were. "Are we really going to stand here and do nothing, as he executes people right in front of us?"

We all turned to Lia, eager for the answer, to see just how she wanted to handle this. Her head shook from side to side, so we were supposed to let this one slide. "The crowd is worked up in a frenzy, if we attack now, they're likely to skin us."

I shook my head, and no one was pleased, this shit wasn't right, and I didn't want to leave. "I don't know how long I can listen to him holler, all of you, don't it bother you?"

Gerell threw a hand in the air but the look on his face told me how much he cared. "So, when's our assignment, how soon till we get started, because I'm really not trying to be a part of this mobbing?"

Lincoln was quiet, only for a second, then he turned toward the stage, his fists clenched tightly. "I got a clear shot, Lia what you want to do, tell me how can so many worship this dude?"

In his anger, Lincoln spoke too loud, because now we were the center of the whole freaking crowd. The men I'd seen before were moving fast our way, and I wondered just how this would play.

The crowd moved closer and I felt myself gulp, just what was it they wanted from us?

"You better get out of here while you still can, if not they'll take you apart and there'll be a sin." The men had reached us but there was no malice on their faces, maybe they'd come to try and save the day then. "The man they caught, he's a friend of ours," said the same dude who stood five nine. He had light red hair, cut short on the sides, and I'll admit a little murder in his eyes.

It was five of them gathered, but they didn't do a thing, like they were willing to let their friend lose his brains. I looked up on stage and saw they'd brought him out, who would have thought, he'd be bleeding from his mouth?

He was a tall man, slim as can be, and I wondered how long they'd had him in captivity. His hair was long, way past his shoulders, and his neck was so swollen it looked like a boulder.

I turned to the man, the one with red hair, and said: "What did he do, why'd they put him up there?"

By this time the crowd was paying us no mind, they'd gotten their fix because their eyes began to shine. The man with red hair turned my way again, he said his name was Lanster and he couldn't save his friend.

I gave him a look, because he hadn't even tried, had it been one of my team, they never would have taken me alive.

Lanster looked toward the stage, a grimace on his face, then an older grey woman turned our way. "Melact, Melact! I think we got us one! Melact, Melact! Let's create a swarm."

All around us the crowd buzzed, then Lanster looked at us, his eyes big as bugs. "They're going to flank us, we have to get away, I have a place not far from here, we'll go that way."

The crowd got closer, menace on their faces, and me and my team we ran in opposite spaces. This world was wild, I didn't know what I was doing, but the crowd, they just kept on pursuing.

Who would have thought it would end this way, man I thought I'd live to see another day? At the last second self-preservation kicked in, and I held out my hands, and that was the end.

Chapter 4

I took their energy, drained them each dry, it was only about twenty, but none of them survived.

Lanster looked at me, his face full of anger. "They're going to come harder now, so we're all in danger."

The rest of the crowd must have stayed back, because after that we walked without any slack. We went down a curb, around a corner, then we started to go down under.

A dude with Lanster, who stood five six, had black hair around his ears with a nice little clip, he turned to us, his face alarmed, "You're in it with us now, welcome to our home."

I swallowed hard, because this was what we'd wanted, to gather information without being found phony. We were still undercover no need to address, that we didn't belong here like all the rest.

The room they led us to was inside a cave, they looked like they'd been living here for days. The place was big, holding over five hundred, couches and beds, and many people looked pummeled.

Some were recovering, other wounds were severe, and I wondered what in the world was going on in here.

Lanster looked around, but there was no dirt to be found, not even on the ground. Someone had put tiles onto the walls and under our feet, I didn't know how they'd done it but man what a feat.

Taking it all in, it was as clean as can be, the smell though, told me there were too many bodies. All crammed together, it would never stay fresh, especially with the sick and wounded, I wondered how they got any rest.

Lanster must have seen our faces because then he commented. "It's not just the Zins that's in it to win, we have five fractions, don't know when this shit will end. They keep coming after every one of us, we can't get along so when we see each other we bust. Killing each other, taking the enemy out, I don't want to fight 'em but not sure what to do about it."

Andrew's brows furrowed, his eyes going narrow. "Why don't you five work together, you can't keep fighting each other forever. I know Zeke and his followers control all Hansack, but if you band together you could attack."

I looked at Andrew, what he said was correct, if they worked together and started being more direct, then they could take out those holding them back, and since we were here, we'd pick up any slack.

"So instead of working together and getting shit done, you doing their job, taking out everyone." Lincoln looked confused like this shit didn't compute, especially since Lanster seemed like a reasonable dude.

Gerell looked at them all, over five hundred sets of eyes staring back, it was enough to give even the strongest person a slight heart attack. "So when they come for you, what are you going to do? Going to let them take out you and all your crew? Why don't you fight together, I don't understand, what could have happened to make you want to kill your fellow man?"

A guy with black hair, done up in spikes, stepped up to us and he wasn't looking right. He had rage on his face, and a couple things to say, so I paid attention, because you could learn a lot from listening. "I got hit over twenty times with bursts of fire, they trying to take me out, but see I'm still riding. Hit twenty times and I'm still standing tall, hit twenty times, and I'm coming for ya'll. Ain't no peace to be had, ain't nothing left to say, them motherfuckers will rue the day they dared to throw their bullshit powers my way. I won't back down, I won't be stopped, they trying to take me out, but I won't drop."

"Then you'll be dead before your body hits the ground, if you don't work together then every one of you will go down." My voice rose a bit, but I was tired of this shit. Fighting each other was weak, when they had a common enemy named Zeke.

He ain't taking no prisoners, he's ripping their throats, he's coming for them and he and his followers don't choke.

Lia cracked her neck from side to side, and I could tell from her face she was ready to riot. "Are any of you at least willing to listen, to what the others have to say, because then maybe we can end this?"

A woman who stood about six feet tall, walked up to us, her stride confident as all. "Hear a mother's pain, hear a mother's rage, them bitches keep trying to put my son in his grave. I won't let him fall, not as long as I stand tall. If they're coming after him then they better bring it all. My son won't duck, he won't dodge, and them motherfuckers better know

I'm coming after 'em hard. They ain't seen nothing like the fury of a mother. I don't think that they're ready, but I'll pull out my machete."

"Yo, you don't need it," said a voice from the crowd. "Hit them with your solar blast and take every one of them out. They coming at us, every chance that they get, every time that we move, they find out where we're at. Walking these streets is as dangerous as can be, we in a war zone now, and not just from the Zin Zin and their people."

A man who said his name was Scott, looked like he'd been hit with loads of buckshot, he held up his arm, and I saw many spots. "I told them a long time ago, when this shit first started to grow, that if we didn't work together they'd kill us in droves. I said: Hold them bitches account-able, make them bitches pay, when we become desensitized it's every citizens' grave. But they didn't listen, and that's why we're in this, really don't see a good way to finish this."

It was easy to sit back and tell them what they're sup-posed to do, but these people had been through stuff that wasn't easy to work through. "People are dying, don't you want it to end, I know you'll never be friends, but at least try not to offend."

Andrew walked over, to me he got closer, "If we can bring them all together, then maybe Zeke and his followers can be taken down forever."

Lia shook her head, the look on her face filled with dread. "Have you not been paying attention, these people hold grudges, they're not going to listen. If there's really five fractions, then we better expect immediate reactions."

"But they're doing their job for 'em, why they fighting each other, instead of working together, taking out these zealots?" Lincoln seemed confused as I was, and all of this, it gave my heart a little tug.

I couldn't see straight to the core of the problem, but if these people didn't get it together then the Zin Zin would destroy them.

Lia turned my way, and I knew she had something to say, but then the walls burst open, and about a hundred people started choking.

Chapter 5

Me and my team we stepped out of the way, we didn't want to kill any of these people, not today. But powers were flying, people were dying, if we didn't stop it there'd be more rioting.

I held up my hands, no time to surmise, I held up my hands, and tried to save our allies. We needed these people, to help stop their own suffering, if they didn't listen, they'd be the ones in trouble.

I begin to drain the energy of all those around me, as many as I could, it was kinda outstanding. They dropped to their knees, starting to become husks, and I pulled back, because I didn't want to turn them to dust.

With their energy weakened, they couldn't do nothing, so I had the room and I went ahead and confronted 'em. "The Zin Zin want your life, are you really not tired of this strife? If we work together we can overcome them, get the other three fractions, and channel that passion."

One guy who had gray hair, stepped away from a pair, and started to share. "The Zin Zin came in the middle of the night, they pulled me out of the light, and I did try to fight. My kids now they are no more, the Zealots killed them in front of me then waved their blood under my nose."

The man's eyes glazed over, then he fought it back, but he still looked like he just might crack. "They hung my kids, with others from the poles, said it was our fault, for sticking our noses where they didn't belong, up in their business, I don't know how they found out, but a lot of people went missing."

"They came for my sister, she was only thirteen," said a woman who was dressed all in green. "They pulled her by her hair, slammed her head in the street, broke her back, and then cut off her feet."

With everyone talking, Lanster came to a stand, and started conversing with another man. I hoped they were coming to some type of agreement, so that we could end this now, and focus on Zeke and his people.

Lia turned to us, and I couldn't read her face, just listened closely to what she had to say. "This is only two fractions, we need the other three, let's take a few of them with us, surely they know where they'll be."

I looked around the room, these people were still weakened, I hadn't taken much, just enough to make them sleepy. "I'll go and see who I can gather, maybe we can cut through all the preconceived chatter."

Andrew stepped up, by my side, like always, he was ready to ride. "I'll go with you, to see what they say, if they agree, maybe we can finish this today."

We walked up to Lanster, he was still in conversation, but stopped when he saw us, looking out of patience.

"We got two fractions here, we need the other three, then maybe we can end this amicably." Andrew stood tall as he said the words, the man beside Lanster also heard. The two men looked at each other, but neither said a word, then they both nodded, neither using their vocal cords.

They walked over to find people to join us, and I turned back toward Lia to let her know we were on it. They came back with two women and three men, and told us they would help us best as they can.

One of the ladies had pale skin, her hair short and black, the other had dark skin, hair hanging down her back. Two of the men stood, shoulder to shoulder, they looked like they could be brothers. Both had red hair, cut close to their heads, though one had a beard that was starting to spread.

The last man had black hair up in a bun, the look on his face said, he'd kill anyone.

They led us outside, away from the cave, Lia asked them many questions, to see what they'd say. They didn't all get along, that much was evident, but they'd been picked for a reason, and it wasn't their etiquette.

Still the bickering and fighting got old after a while, but here that was their style.

Andrew walked right beside me, his brother and Gerell in the back, Lia behind them. The five from here they walked up front, and every now and then, I heard one of them grunt. They would never get along, and that was cool, but we were trying to accomplish something so we needed to school 'em.

The air here was hot and stuffy, making me feel just a little bit huffy. Andrew turned to me, his face a little grim. "Do you think these guys will ever be friends?"

I looked up front, to where their voices got louder, and knew it was a lost cause, the sooner we got this over the better. "I think it's years of hate, built up over time, and Zeke strokes the flames, messing with their minds."

Andrew nodded, and opened his mouth to speak, then one of Zeke's followers came flying right at me. I went low as did the others, we were surrounded; they were trying to destroy us.

It was about twenty of them, against us ten, they must have called that an easy win. Except we never went down, not without a fight, I shot energy out my hand, and that was enough to smite. One went down and then another.

I turned to Andrew, in time to see his power; he produced a rope of energy and then wrapped it around a prowler. The man choked, all his air gone, then Andrew squeezed it tighter and the man was no more.

Gerell was dipping and dodging, as he read the energy signal of those that were on him. Then he held up his hand and directed his energy, straight through the eyes of one man, and then to his kidneys.

Lincoln had balls of energy; he hit one man in the face, and that did spin him. The man turned in a circle, then fell to the ground, and Lincoln kept going ready for the next round.

Lia had a sword, made completely of her energy, and the way she fought, was perfect synergy. She cut down a woman with light blonde hair, then a man who was trying to stab her anywhere.

The five up front were also doing their jobs, holding their own but I could tell it was getting hard. Then the woman with black hair fell to her knees, and then I saw her head over near some trees.

As quick as lightning she'd been taken out, there were more coming now, and this caused doubt. The other woman, who'd been with us, a knife went through her heart, and then she too was dust. One of the men, the one with the black hair, his head exploded, and then he was no longer there.

I stood and watched, horrified, and then the last two men with us, took off to hide. Cowards, they didn't have the stomach, but Zeke's people, they were still coming.

There were about fifty of them now; they had us surrounded, and if we made it out alive, I'd be astounded. Me and my team, we huddled backs together, ready to fight to the end, never surrender.

Then they parted and Zeke stepped through, the look on his face said, 'I got you.'

Adrenaline ran down my fingers to their tips, this arrogant guy, I wanted to bust him in the lip. He strolled up, as cool as can be, fists clenched by his sides, but he still looked happy.

He turned to his followers, a smile on his face, then he raised his hands and waved them around the place. "What do we have here, what are their names, did they really think, I would fall for their games? On their knees, why are they still standing, I want to know everything that they're planning."

Someone knocked my feet from under me, then a fist went to my face and another was coming at me.

Chapter 6

I went down, as did my team, when I looked up, Zeke's eyes held a strange gleam. "I have to teach you just like the others, don't come here, trying to report us. This is my world, your interference is not needed, you came here, trying to stop us but you're the ones defeated."

I felt a boot to my face; I hadn't seen it coming, my head snapped back, and my nose started running. The smell of blood filled the air, and I knew if we didn't stop this my whole face would tear.

Again, and again, the boot beat my face in, I tried to look around and saw that it was also happening to my friends. Pain rippled through me, but I tried to stay strong, in order to do that, I raised up my arm.

Up above me, I could hear Zeke laugh, he thought this was fun, but I was coming for his ass. My whole body turned to straight energy, hitting the guy who was currently trying to finish me.

The boot kicker fell back, and I tried to keep track, as I got to my feet and my energy went whack. It spread out all around us, and I held out hands, trying to compound.

My energy sucked the life from people, when applied like I wanted, the shit was lethal. Five of his followers fell to the ground, the ones who'd attack my people went down.

My body was buzzing, silver energy humming, if you tried to touch me you'd be expunging. The pain in my face lessened a little bit, and I knew my energy was taking care of all the slits.

My team stood, bloodied and bruised, but we still had work, to finish this dude. My energy shot out, in all directions, and five more went down, maybe it was reckless.

But I wanted to take out as many as I could, because they'd still try to kill us, I knew they would. Then a loud boom sounded and smoke filled the air, when it cleared Zeke and his followers were no longer there.

I looked around not sure what had happened, but that's when I saw Andrew had been captured. He was no longer with us, he'd been standing right there, I closed my eyes, trying not to despair.

Then my mind went back to the bodies we'd seen hanging; that wouldn't be his fate, I wouldn't let them arrange it.

Lincoln's eyes looked ready to pop, I saw a vein jump and wondered if he could be stopped. "We are now going to get him, if they hurt my brother, all of them I'm killing."

Gerell put his hands on his boyfriend's back, while Lia talked into her com, but we didn't have time for that.

We needed to find them right freaking now, as soon as I thought this, I heard a slight creaking sound.

I looked up, but first I couldn't see, then I watched as two multiplied to three. The ones who'd left, came right back, they must have gotten the fractions because behind them was a pack.

It looked to be more than a few thousand, so much for them being cowards. They'd gone to get help, and for that I was grateful, we'd need all we could get, because Zeke's face I was breaking.

Anger coursed through every part of me, if they harmed one hair on his head, they'd have to call in the infantry. I wasn't just going to let this go, they'd fucked up big time, and they didn't even know.

I thought back to the first time I'd saw him, I'd been scared out of my mind and only he'd been able to calm me. He stood tall right by my side, if they thought this shit would go unanswered they were out of their minds.

My energy shook, and I became unstable, their day was coming now, no more of that waiting. My hands trembled with the urge to do something, if I did get this out, someone was going under.

Lincoln's eyes went completely dark, I knew this shit was hard. I looked to Lia, to see what she'd discovered, because fuck all of that about being undercover.

One of our own had been taken, and if we didn't attack now they'd be no saving him. Gerell had a look of rage on his face, to him Andrew was like a brother who couldn't be re-placed.

The two guys with the red hair came our way, and the one with the beard stepped up like he had something to say. "These here are the other three fractions, they too are tired of Zeke and his thrashings. Each group has been personally hurt, if we band together we should have a little luck."

A woman with black curls all around her face, got straight to the point with optimal haste. "My brother went out, his wife was dying, he needed medicine to keep her from expiring. They caught him in the middle of the street, told him to pledge his allegiance, or he'd be defeated. He tried to fight them off, but that didn't work, they used their powers and hit him right in the gut. They beat his face in, I could barely recognize him, though the ring on his finger told me it was Isaac."

She stopped talking and her breath came short, like she had a lot of feelings she needed to sort.

A man spoke up, his hair bald as can be, he said: "Let me tell you, what happened to me. I was with a few others, we weren't bothering nobody, then Zeke's followers came out and surprised us. One they set right on fire, another one they used a tight wire. The third and fourth they ripped to shreds, I only got away because I fell and hit my head. Blood leaked out, and that was all they needed, they probably thought I was finished because of all the bleeding."

Another person stepped up and then another, each telling a story about this murderer. Anger and energy coursed through my veins, if I found Zeke now, I'd bash in his brains.

I turned to Lia, because we needed to get the others, no more playing around, Andrew was depending on us. Once all the fractions got together we'd storm his home, I hoped it wouldn't take forever.

Because something dark was happening to me, my energy was now black, for all to see. This was something new, but my rage was too. I'd never felt like taking my bare hands and popping someone's neck, if I didn't get Andrew back there'd be a lot of that.

Energy flowed to my eyes, and if anybody touched me they'd surely be dying. Right now I only had one agenda, get

Andrew back, and make sure Zeke surrendered. I guess you could say I was going rogue, because I didn't care how it happened, fuck doing what I was told.

My energy lifted me up in the air, and I was just staying there. I didn't want to strike out at someone who didn't deserve it, but Zeke and his followers needed to be worried.

I wouldn't back down, I wouldn't be stopped, until Andrew was by my side I was fucking shit up.

Chapter 7

We got back to the cave, but I was inconsolable, I didn't want to talk to anyone, my anger was uncontrollable. Lia and the others told Lanster what had happened, and he called everybody together, 'cause now was time for action.

I saw Lincoln off to the side, he had murderous rage right there in his eyes. Gerell stood directly behind him, arm around his neck, looking like what's next. He was being protective as I'd ever seen him, I pitied the dude who ran up on them, 'cause they'd be bleeding.

Lia's face was hard as a rock, but she was the leader so she had to stay on top.

Lanster talked to a few people, all seemed more than eager. Not everyone could fit in the cave, so we spilled outside, the situation more than grave.

One man, tall and lean, stepped up to talk, hand on his spleen. "Zeke's people number in the hundreds of thousands, that's a lot for us to rival. I've been waiting on this for a while, but we have to make it count. no kidding around."

As he said it, something occurred to me, and I looked up, hoping for clarity. "Where are the others, they're not all in fractions, they're not Zealots, so who are they backing?"

"They keep their heads down, they don't make trouble, if a Zealot comes, they try not to be discovered. But sometimes they can't avoid them, and then they sink to one knee, and pledge allegiance to Zeke and his people."

I listened off to the side, sitting against a big rock, ready to round the corner and go up the block. I didn't like all of this waiting, too much talking was circulating. Yes, I understood we needed a plan, but at the moment I just wanted my man.

My fingers shook, my fists wrapped in rage, I wondered if he'd tried to put Andrew on the stage. The one where he'd committed so many murders, the thought burned my eyes and made me shudder.

Once again on my feet, I saw Lincoln looking at me, he was as angry as I was, that was easy to see. Gerell stood beside him, his jaw tight, fists clenched like he was ready to fight.

Lia kept talking, but her shoulders were tense, we all wanted to help, but at what expense?

A tall guy I hadn't seen before stepped up, then he started to flow. "We have to be smart about what we do, Zeke will be waiting, he's no fool. We spent so much time fighting each other, that Zeke and his followers never went under. We all stood by while it happened, every single day it was more and more maddening. We thought one of the other Zin Zin's would help us, we really got it twisted because they yelped us. They wanted the power as much as he did, or maybe they're like the zealots, unable to see past his grin."

I ran a hand down my face, wiping away the sweat that had gathered in one place. We needed to get this going, every second that we stayed here was more than annoying.

Though these people had been going through this for a while, seeing the ones they loved, rounded up and reviled. I was freaking out about one person, but here there were many who were worse.

"Don't you dare feel one ounce of guilt, cause if you do that shit'll bury you to the hilt." Lincoln wiped sweat from his head, and to me his eyes looked full of dread. "What am I supposed to tell my mother, that I let my brother get taken while we were undercover?"

Lia answered before I could, so maybe she was done with her conversation for good. "You tell her nothing because we're going to get him back, pick up that jaw, I don't want to see it slack. Look, we have to work together, these people can help us I say we let 'em."

A bitter chuckle escaped from my mouth; we were supposed to be the ones helping them, what was this about?

A woman, short in height, whistled really loud, but said she promised not to bite. "We need a plan, we can't just stumble, if we run in there half-cocked they'll take us under."

I cracked my neck from side to side, because fuck this, I was ready to ride. "So what's your plan, what do you suggest, Zeke and his followers still think they're the best. If maybe we can make them think they'll win, then use our powers to take out all the Zin's."

She thought about it for a second, flipped it around, and when she looked back at me it was with a big frown, "it might not be an act, Zeke and his followers really know how to throw down."

I had listened to all I could take, these people were making excuses while Andrew's life was at stake. I walked forward just a few feet, told them I'd see them in the street.

I wasn't waiting a second longer, staying together, it made us stronger. But what happened to Andrew while we discussed, his head got taken off and thrown to greet us.

My mind was going to all kinds of places, I just kept picturing all them broken faces. So many had been hurt, by this Zeke, and trust me I knew, that was no small feat.

It took a special kind of dedication, to hurt and kill all that wouldn't obey you.

"We'll be seeing each other," I turned to Lincoln, "time to go get your brother."

Chapter 8

We walked back the way we'd come, Zeke and his people had already begun. The zealots were out in full force, yelling so loud their voices were hoarse.

We came from all sides, we didn't all walk together, trying to get the best advantage, we thought it would be better. We surrounded him and his people, but no way was this fight equal.

They outnumbered us two to one, and there'd probably be still more to come. I didn't care, none of that mattered, only getting Andrew back, untattered. I didn't see him at first, such was my rage, I didn't see him until he exited the cage.

His clothes were torn, his face caved in, he was barely standing, holding him up were two men. Beside him were three more that looked like him, one was a woman who was missing her skin.

Lia gasped, and Gerell blew out, Lincoln looked like he was ready to shout. My eyes went dark, as my vision turned lethal, and I knew without a doubt I was killing these people.

Zeke stood on the stage, a smile on his face, the crowd below engaged, I couldn't wait to leave this place. "Once again, we witness justice in action, these people, they called themselves fractions. Trying to destroy everything we've built, coming here with foolish notions, plotting to the hilt. We will not let them take us over, we'll fight to the end, off this exposure."

Then he turned and looked at the stage, Andrew and the others looked very grave. Then Zeke raised his hand, and out shot fire, the woman with no skin, she was burned with no pyre.

Her screams erupted, this shit was corrupted, the sound disrupted, but the crowd, they loved it. Then Zeke turned again, this time he grabbed a man. He tore his body limb from limb, then threw the pieces out, like he'd done it on a whim.

The zealots loved it, their faces repugnant.

Disgusting beast, looking for a feast, wanna pig out on the bones of those who got the least.

Zeke went to the next person, and my eyes shot to Andrew, they'd really hurt him.

His shoulders looked, like they'd been cooked. That bastard had burned him, now my hands shook. His eyes were swollen, one slipping out, looking at that I tried not to shout. His face was hanging, his fingers dangling.

Fury, anger, complete destruction, nobody, right now, better not touch me. Silver energy ripped through my body, my vision got clouded, for a second I was astounded.

Just pulling up an image of his face, and what they'd done here was a disgrace.

Whenever he looked at me, I saw through to eternity. I'd never felt like that in my life, and now I knew, they were in for a fight.

I cracked my fingers, my head went side to side, I felt my anger, it was on the rise. Zeke went to Andrew, and raised his hand, and that's when I diverted from the plan.

I threw my head back, and the scream was tremendous, I would not watch as they killed him. Energy sparked, energy flowed, I felt myself, as I lost control.

There was no running, there was no retreat, the only thing left, was Zeke's defeat. Energy shot out to the crowd, the zealots fell down and I was just getting riled.

I took them out, one after the other, I couldn't stop it, no way to recover. Energy tore one body apart, it took a man's eyes, another one's heart. They all dropped like flies at my feet, as I stepped forward, my eyes on Zeke.

One person ran up, it was bad luck. My energy wrapped him up and shredded him like a duck. Another one tried it, he didn't survive it, they kept coming, but my energy was wilding.

Heads started to roll, feet became detached, eerie screams sounded, I didn't care about that. I was taking them out, one after the other, as I went through the crowd, nobody above me.

I didn't know how many I laid at my feet, the only thing I wanted right now was Zeke. His zealots were crawling, my team was brawling, this wasn't over yet, not 'til I called it.

He tried to say something, the rest of the Zin Zin's flaunted. All of them looked my way, but not today, I didn't come here to play, my rage was here to stay. It knocked them back, it cut off their crowns, it ripped through their bodies, then they all hit the ground.

The fractions also took action, letting them know, we weren't backing.

I knew my team were doing their thing, they wouldn't just stand around and let the zealots reign.

Zeke turned his attention to me, my energy lifted me in the air for all to see. He wanted to talk, but I wouldn't let 'em, instead I raised my hands, and made his face spaghetti.

Ripping and shredding, I tore him to pieces, I don't know why he thought this would be easy. My energy shot out, in all directions, taking out anyone at my discretion.

My mind was chaotic, it felt hypnotic. Then I started to shake, and I couldn't awake, caught up in this nightmare I couldn't escape.

My body seized, my breath wheezed, nothing eased, I was more than displeased. I couldn't get a handle on my emotions, I'd let the dragon out, and now I was eroding.

The smell of blood filled the air, but right now, I really didn't care.

Zeke and his people were no more, so after everything, we'd evened the score.

We'd done what we'd come to do, to help these people, now I was through. I felt myself as I started to slip, my body itself started to rip.

I could hear them calling my name, but my team knew the game, we all played it the same. We all risked our lives to help others, I had no regrets, no thoughts undercover.

Then everything turned black, and I couldn't see, maybe this was the end of it all for me.

Chapter 9

I awoke to a dark room with white walls and immediately knew I was in the decontamination department back on Plex. I blinked, my eyes blurry, my throat dry and my thoughts no longer in rhyme. I took a deep breath, because it was kind of jarring going back to regular thoughts again.

My mind went over what'd happened, and then my pulse picked up as alarm shot through me. "Andr- Andrew," I croaked out, my mouth feeling like a desert.

"He's not here," Lia said, and I sat up a bit to see her in a chair by my bed. "He's okay, a bit sore, Lincoln took him to heal. He took him to their mother."

Relief washed over me, and I blinked a little more, as Lia was looking kind of hazy. "Good, a familiar setting will help." I ran a hand down my legs and across my arms, trying to work out the joints. Every muscle I had ached, and I still wasn't sure what in the world had come over me.

I'd never exploded like that, hadn't even known I could. The loss of complete control wasn't something I liked, and I hoped never to be confronted with it again.

"How was he?" I asked, looking at Lia's tired face. "How was he when he left?" I thought back to his broken hands and beaten face, and then took a deep breath, as a wave of rage tried to overtake me.

Now wasn't the time for that. I was safe, Andrew was safe, the people of Hansack— "What happened?" I asked.

Lia took a breath and got up, moving like someone who'd been sitting long enough to cause their muscles to get stiff. "We called in some healers from Banylen, for both of you. After you fell, and it was safe to touch you, we opened a portal and got you both here."

She looked off to the side for a moment, and I figured she was reliving the whole thing. "Andrew is okay. He's been healed, he just needs to rest, and the healers thought it was better to keep him under, he'll come out of it in a few days."

My brows furrowed. "Was he okay to go through the portal like that?" It didn't seem like he would be. So much got shook up doing a portal jump, that I couldn't help but be a little concerned.

Lia nodded and leaned back against the small dresser in my room, arms folded, her short pink hair spiked up on her head. "The healers said he was, and our people checked him over and agreed. Gerell went with them."

My eyes went wide. "To meet the parents?" I whispered.

Lia nodded, a lopsided smile on her face. "Yes, to meet the parents, Lincoln insisted."

I smiled back at Lia, happy that the guys were moving forward with things, but knowing it'd be a while before I was ready to go to that world and meet Andrew and Lincoln's mom and dad. "What happened to me?" I asked, pushing those other thoughts away.

It was something to think about later, something to talk about later, whenever Andrew came back.

"We don't know," Lia said, leaning forward. "Usually your body just becomes covered in energy, this time you actually became the energy." Her voice was filled with wonderment, and she looked like someone who'd just seen a pig fly and couldn't make sense of it. "We're going to monitor you closely for a while."

Both my thighs seized up, and I let out a yell, as I ran my hands over them, trying to breathe through the pain.

"Hey," Lia said, dashing for the door. "We need some help in here."

"It's okay, it's okay," I said taking long breaths, not yet ready to face anyone else. My legs, or more accurately, my thighs felt like they were being crushed by boulders and I finally relented, and waved a hand, letting her know I needed some help.

A tall lady with blond hair came in, looking straight ahead. She didn't ask me how I was doing, or have any smiles to give, and I'd forgotten that those who worked in this unit were about business more than anything.

She applied a shot to both of my legs, and instantly I felt better and was able to breathe again. Once she saw me lean back in the bed, no doubt looking relieved, she turned and walked out the door, never uttering a word.

"That's been happening a lot in the past two weeks," Lia said, coming to sit on the bed beside me. "This is the first time you're actually aware of it though. You've been out for a while."

Two weeks? "Has Andrew been gone the whole time?" Panic set my heart to racing. Not that I would blame him if he decided this was too much and he didn't want to do it anymore, but man, I didn't want to see him go, to leave me, to leave here.

I let out a sigh, my heart twisting and turning. If this was what he thought best, I'd support him, but man would it be hard. Still, his happiness and well-being meant more to me than anything else.

"You're thinking too much," Lia said, looking down at me. "He's coming back. He's not gone forever. He just needs time to rest around family."

"Okay," I said, shrugging, though my skin was starting to turn warm.

"He's coming back," she said, a little firmer this time. "I talked to Gerell today. They are all three definitely coming back."

"Okay," I said, not wanting to talk about it anymore. My emotions were a private affair, and I figured I'd deal with them more when I was home, alone. "What happened to the fractions? Lanster?"

Lia nodded, in a way that told me she knew I was trying to change the subject and was just going to roll with it. "Lanster made it out okay because you killed so many Zealots at one time, it was easy for us to fight off the rest."

I winced at her words, thinking back to how I'd taken out five and ten at a time, not caring one bit as they'd fallen by my feet. It was a strange feeling, and I felt more embarrassed than anything. They'd supported a monster who killed and mutilated people in front of them, never raising a hand to help them, so no, I'd save my sorrow for all those who'd lost their live under Zeke's command.

"You killed Zeke and the rest of the Zin Zin. Right now, Lanster and the members of the four opposite fractions are in the process of setting up their government in a way that gives all of them a voice." I kind of got the feeling she wanted to throw a 'good job' toward me but figured it was just a tad inappropriate, so didn't.

She went on talking, and I closed my eyes letting sleep take me away, still not sure when, or if, I'd ever see Andrew again.

Chapter 10

Andrew came back a week later. "You know, you could have portaled in to see me," he said, sitting beside me in my living room, his arm wrapped tightly around me, holding me close.

He'd only just arrived, and I was just too overwhelmed with emotion to speak. I'd missed him, boy had I missed him, and now that he was here I didn't know what to say.

I realized now, just how much he meant to me, how far I was willing to go to keep him safe, to keep that smile on his face. I could never put it in context before, but now, well now I knew exactly how I felt.

I turned to him, not sure how to get it out. "Andrew... I... Just..."

He put a warm hand on my neck, turning my face toward him, causing my emotions to explode. "I love you too," he said, then he kissed me, and all other talking went out the window.

Kia Unleashed

Chapter 1

If I didn't have sex soon I'd probably end up in a shallow grave with my friends bringing me flowers every six months. Succubi needed sex every night, but I'd screwed up with the fifth soulbar, one of the most powerful runes in known existence, and the First Families had punished me severely.

The First Families were the powerful ancient families who ruled over all magical and mystical beings. Their word was law, and any who tried to go against them found just how formidable they were.

With a few whispered words, you could have a large house with three cars, or be a beggar on the streets for the rest of your life. That, or they'd just kill you, they liked doing that too. The whole killing and torture thing gave them a special kind of joy.

I took a deep breath, my pulse racing with anger and indignation as I thought about it. The First Families had punished me by decreeing I could only have sex every three weeks, and this was to carry on for three months. I shook my head, remembering the gloating look on my grandmother's face as she'd handed down the sentence, no doubt something she and my mother had come up with together.

The sounds of the club wrapped around me, as I settled back in my chair. My grandmother was one of the head rulers of the First Families and she made no allowance for anyone, especially me.

The incubus on stage rocked his half-naked body to the ground, and I realized that being bitter when such a delicious treat was in front of me was a complete waste of time.

Resolving to enjoy the show, since that was all I could do, it wasn't like I could have sex or anything, I picked up the small shot of Curltoe in front of me and downed the whole thing in one go, the hot, sour liquid making my chest burn.

Curltoe was a powerful drink, too potent for humans as it often left them dead, insane, or dazed for weeks.

The incubus on stage spread his legs wide, and the women around me went wild, as I licked my lips. I could feel it building, could feel the need spreading over my whole body and man it'd been too long. I was on the last week of my third month and couldn't wait for this to end.

My body was weaker than it'd ever been, my reflexes slow, my powers diminished, my energy mostly drained. In fact, I believed the only reason I was even able to get out of bed and function at all was because when I'd messed up with the soulbar, some of its powers had seeped into my bloodstream.

The soulbar held the power of all magical beings, so for a while there I'd had the fire of the dragon, the wings of the Phoenix, the cry of the banshee, and so on. I'd gotten my wizard friend Drem to take the powers out of me and put them back where they belonged, but he'd warned there'd be some lasting effects.

Another shot of Curltoe was placed in front of me, and I drank that down, as the incubus was carried off stage by a horde of women. "To good times," I said, raising my empty glass.

My hand shook with the glass still high in the air, and I hurried to put it down before it crashed to the floor. Drinking Curltoe while I was already in a weakened state, was not a very smart thing to do, but I hadn't exactly been thinking clearly lately.

Two more incubi came onto the stage and the words, *one more week*, passed through my mind as I got up and slowly made my way to the door. My phone rang as soon as I stepped out into the cool spring air. Sweat dripped down my face and as I felt myself grow even weaker, I knew I'd overdone it.

"What," I said as I answered the phone, not sure the caller would get much more out of me at the moment.

My chief's grouchy voice came over the line, making me cringe inside because I knew what was coming. "Kia, got a case. Get with your partner. He has the details." With that he hung up, his part of the job done.

A wave of dizziness hit me, and I swerved a bit, bumping into the person next to me.

"Hey, you all right, Kia?" a voice I vaguely recognized asked me.

Strong arms wrapped around me, steadying my stance and I looked up to see Guyess staring down at me, his eyes drawn together in concern. His six-foot frame towered over me, and I blinked bringing him into focus.

Guyess had beautiful ebony skin, and the glowing tattoos marking him as a member of the Glecics clan only made it that much more illuminating. Like me, Guyess was also descended directly from one of the First Families.

There were five First Families and to actually be descended from one meant you were looked on with esteem and pride. "Pftt," I said, thinking about how much harsher I was treated by them because, hey, nothing like living up to expectations.

"Never known you to not be able to hold your liquor," Guyess said, his arms still around me.

Shame washed over me in an instant. He was right, I'd never needed anyone's help to stand on my own two feet, and since I was sure my grandmother and the other members of the First Families were just waiting for me to fail, I refused to give them that.

"You're right," I said, trying to slip out of his embrace, but, oh, still couldn't stand up straight on my own.

Guyess gnawed on his lips, weighing his options. "Don't you have to get to work?" I asked him, pointing at the club I'd just come out of. Guyess worked as a stripper there, and man was he good.

He let out a small chuckle as he put a firm hand on my elbow. "Think I want Lin coming after me because I let you walk home alone? I don't think so." With that, he guided me toward the parking lot, not saying another word.

Lin was my incubus boyfriend. I had another boyfriend too, Boya, my partner on the job, but he and Lin were also boyfriends, so it worked out well for the three of us. Boya had dragon DNA, and he and Lin would probably spend the night together, as they often did when I was out for the count.

Incubi and succubi could only have sex together once a month. More than that and both our bodies would begin to spark, crackle, and break down.

Two high voltage entities coming together often canceled each other out and our bodies needed time to build back up before we could have sex again, hence the one a month thing.

We arrived at Klemn in less than ten minutes. Klemn was a huge house shared by many agents such as myself, Boya, and Lin. Everyone who resided here was in law enforcement, just some of us were in different branches, though we all worked for the government, and the First Families, because everybody worked for the First Families.

Boya and I mostly dealt with magical creatures out of control, especially when it came to them doing something that could expose us to the humans, like killing, or robbing a place, that would leave behind a clue that the person who'd done it had a little something extra.

Me and Boya, along with Lin, worked for the agency Xelone, which dealt with human and mystical affairs.

Though they lived right beside us in Morse Town, most humans didn't know we existed and we figured it was better for all if it stayed that way.

Guyess helped me out of the car and guided me up the steps to the front door. A few agents passed us on the way, but they were so caught up in their own conversation, they barely spared us a glance.

"What the—" Ninia said as soon as she saw me. We were in the living room now, and the only thing holding me up was my friend Guyess.

I shook my head, trying to clear it. Since I'd started downing the Curltoe, my thoughts had been a little disjointed.

Ninia folded her arms and hit me with her 'the fuck you do now?' look I was convinced she saved just for me. Ninia was also a succubus, and worked for Xelone, as well. Like Guyess, she had dark ebony skin, my own being a more brown color. She also had spiked red hair that matched the red in her eyes.

Ninia was a good agent, one of my best friends, and a force to be reckoned with on any day. "Thank you Guyess. I owe you one."

He leaned his head to the side. "You don't. Gotta get to work."

And of course, that was the moment Iscca walked into the room. "Bet you need a ride after bringing miss 'I can't have sex, so I'm going to cry about it all night' here home." Like, Boya, Iscca also was descended from dragons.

Iscca looked at me, a smile on his face, as he tossed his keys in the air, his brows raised at Guyess. Iscca wore his black hair cut short to his head as he thought it looked better that way. His skin was pale, and he stood just about six feet. Iscca always wore that same bright, sparkling earring in his nose, and it fit his personality perfectly if you asked me.

Ninia leveled him with a hard stare. "Stop being an asshole. How is this helping?"

He leaned over and placed a small kiss on her cheek and the corner of her lips. "Yes, dear." Then he turned to Guyess. "Let's go."

Ninia watched them leave then turned to me, her eyes still as hard as they'd been when I'd first walked in. "Kia, this has got to—"

Before she could finish the sentence, my eyes rolled into the back of my head and then there was only darkness.

Chapter 2

I awoke on the couch, two people in front of me. Lin stood to one side, Boya the other, looking like complete opposites. Where Lin was over six feet, with light brown skin, a shaved head, and enough muscles to make one think he lived in the gym, Boya was pale, with curly brown hair that reached just below his chin. Also, Boya stood about five eight.

Right now, neither looked pleased as they stared me down like one would someone who'd gotten drunk and threw up everywhere.

"I'm better now." I came to a sitting position, leaning back against the couch cushions. Man, that felt good. "I thought I could handle Curltoe in my condition, found out that I couldn't. Gonna rag on me about it?" I really hoped they didn't rag on me about it.

Lin's voice was gruff when he spoke. "I'll tell the chief you can't work. Give the case to someone else." He looked to where Ninia and Steva sat together on the couch.

Steva was of black panther descent. He was about the same complexion as myself and had jet black hair that reached his ears, and emerald green eyes that sparkled whenever he looked at Ninia or Iscca.

"You take the case," Lin said, looking at Ninia and Steva.

"No," I said, holding my hand out. I actually did feel a little better, and besides, I'd sworn when I'd been hit with this punishment that I wouldn't let it hold me down, that I wouldn't let anything the First Families did stop me from living my life the way I wanted to live it.

I looked from Lin to Boya, both who seemed skeptical. "Tell me the deets. I can do this."

From behind them I could hear Ninia scoff, and I knew she was just concerned about me, but she really wasn't helping right now. Steva stood, pulling Nina up with him, his long claws wrapping around her hand. "Out of here with you."

I leaned my head to the side. "Why do you have your claws out, Steva? Are you expecting danger?"

He looked at me and shook his head as he and Ninia filed out the door, and I figured maybe my brain still was just a bit fuzzy.

Lin's brows drew tighter together. I knew he didn't like the idea of me taking a case in my condition, but he also knew how much my independence meant to me. Also, I would never let my stubbornness put myself or Boya at risk, and he knew that too. "I'm okay," I said softly, once we were alone in the room.

Around us, I could hear the sounds of agents moving about, and since almost thirty of us lived here, that was to be expected.

Lin narrowed his eyes at me and turned to Boya. "She's not okay."

Boya shook his head, his usual playful grin gone. "Oh, I know, but I got her."

Lin nodded, then pulled Boya close for a kiss, before leaning over and pecking me quickly on the lips. No sparks, no crackling, which meant my body really was coming apart at the seams.

The sooner this no sex thing was over the better. Honestly, if not for the power of the soulbar I was sure I'd be dead by now.

My grandmother had said, if I wasn't succubus enough to handle it, then that's what I deserved. In her eyes, I'd brought shame onto the Wyaque Clan by my mishandling of the soulbar, so the stricter my punishment the better.

Knowing that both Boya and Lin knew me well enough not to offer a hand, I stood on my own, my head only slightly dizzy now.

"What are we looking at?" I asked Boya, trying to take attention off the fact that I was leaning a bit to the right. I really did feel better, though, and I figured once I got moving, that'd do me a world of good.

Lin nodded at us both and left the room, his shoulders wide and broad, every inch of him something I craved on a daily basis. I looked over to see Boya's hungry eyes watching him as well, and this was nothing new. Boya was the life of the party on most days, but whenever Lin was around, he turned into a different person, always looking for the other man's approval.

I gave Boya a small smile as he peered at the device in his hand, going over the details. I never pried into his relationship with Boya. Whatever went on between the two of them when I wasn't around... was... well, between the two of them.

"A body was found right here in Spray Town." Our city, Dupoint, was broken up into four halves. There was Morse Town which was all human. Then there was Spray Town, where those with a little something extra like myself and Boya lived.

Winn Town was a little different as both magical beings and humans lived there. Over the years there had been a few humans who'd found out our secrets. Those the First Families judged as a threat were killed immediately. The others were giving a choice, go back to Morse Town and never breathe a word, or live freely among us in Winn Town.

Those who didn't want humans living beside them chose to stay in Spray Town, and only went into Winn Town when they had to. Almost all Samg families lived in Winn Town.

Samgs were human families that'd aided and supported us since ancient times. Each supernatural family had at least three Samg families assigned to it, and they were paid very well for their continued help and support.

Then there was Riverwalk, that's where the First Families lived. Try going there unannounced and you'd never be heard from again.

"What else do we know?" I asked Boya as his eyes grazed over the screen. "It's a man of frog descent," his voice got low as he read on, and I wondered if he hadn't looked this over before I'd arrived. "Kind of heavy-set, dressed in expensive clothing."

All the color drained from Boya's face, while nervous energy took up residence in my stomach. Boya's top informant was a man of frog descent who fit this description. Boya had been dealing with Gull so long that we'd watched his two daughters go from being toddlers to teenagers.

Gull and his family held a special place in my heart, and I knew Boya felt the same, even if we did normally give Gull a hard time. "We don't know that it's him," I told Boya. "There are many men in Spray that fit that description."

Boya nodded, but he didn't feel it, and I could tell from the way he refused to look me in the eye. Gull's family had gotten hurt three months ago when we'd been working on the soulbar case. Gull's wife, Chupli was of cheetah and bear descent, which meant his kids were part frog, bear, and cheetah. They'd defended themselves well, but neither I or Boya had forgotten what It'd felt like to have them hurt as a way to get back at us.

I walked toward him, and wrapped my arms around his back, pulling him close to me. I loved Boya, loved everything about him, and sometimes just the smell of him was enough to calm me down.

We'd been together for years, too many for me to count, not as long as Lin and me, but still long enough that we knew each other inside out. "Let's not jump to conclusions," I said, even though my insides had pretty much turned to mush by now. "Let's just go and check it out."

He took a deep breath, and I could visibly see as he pushed the worry and doubt away. "Okay, probably not him anyway. I think most lawbreakers know to stay clear of Gull by now."

I leaned over and placed a small kiss on his lips, wanting for just one second to get lost in the touch of him. "Come on. We won't know anything until we get there."

What neither of us bothered to voice was that Gull was a snitch who often turned in his fellow criminals when they pissed him off, or he felt like they were moving in on his territory. For this, he had a target on his back at all times.

Boya and I left the house. Not sure what he was thinking, but the one thing going through my head was if I'd be able to look Chupli and the girls in the eye and deliver the news because I honestly didn't think I was strong enough to do it.

Chapter 3

B y now it was well after two in the morning, but we were in an upscale part of Spray Town, and there were lights everywhere to guide our way. The area was cordoned off, and the officers already on the scene were doing an excellent job of keeping onlookers away.

"Should have known it'd be these two," a voice said, and I looked up to see detectives Rosen and Mason standing side by side.

Oh great, I thought, holding in a groan. These two were never nice. They were both from Samg families, but since neither of them were associated with myself or Boya, they held no loyalties to us.

Rosen was a tall black woman, skin only a shade lighter than my own. In her early thirties, she wore a natural do, that was short, curled on one side, slick on the other. She reminded me of an asshole cop who didn't know when to keep her mouth shut, because, well, that's what she was.

As was her partner, Mason, a tall slim white guy who stood about five feet eight. He had blond hair that didn't quite reach his shoulders, blue eyes, and an attitude that made me want to strangle him every time I saw him.

Whatever Boya felt about Gull and his family, he pushed it down, because dealing with these two, you had to be on your A game. He swaggered up to them, a crooked grin on his face. "Since when have you two started taking cases in Spray Town?"

Rosen and Mason usually worked in Morse Town, running interference whenever a supernatural being went over there and wreaked havoc. They were two of many Samg officers who put their lives on the line protecting our secret on a daily basis.

Mason came to stand in front of Boya, looking him up and down. "I go where I'm needed. Got a problem with that?"

Rosen walked up to stand beside her partner, her steps strong and full of confidence. "Take care of it for you if you do."

Okay, I may have been weakened, but I'd be damned if I'd continued to stand here while these two got off at our expense. "Either tell us what you know or get the fuck out of the way." I went to stand beside Boya, who was casually bouncing a fireball in his hand.

I gave him a sidelong look. He wouldn't harm them, no one fucked with someone else's Samgs, but I think he wanted them to know that he could, and since I was sure he was still scared that it was Gull laying over there, I think he just wanted them to do their job or get out of the way.

Mason swallowed hard. "We get called to Spray and Winn sometimes when things are light in Morse Town."

I looked over toward the other officers on the scene. They were all Samg. "Get them out of here," I said to Rosen. This was going to be hard enough, without onlookers gawking about.

Rosen leaned her head to the side, giving me a frank look. "You don't need our help?"

I held up my phone. "Call you if we do."

Boya turned to me, his eyes saying *thank you,* as we stood in silence until it was just us and the body under the sheet left.

For extra support, I laced my fingers with his, and together we walked toward what we hoped wasn't the last remains of Gull.

Because this was another night of me going without sex, my body shook just a little, but I fought it back, determined to stand strong by my partner. "I'll look," I said, going to one knee.

"No," Boya said, dropping to the ground beside me. "We'll do this together."

Taking a deep breath, we put our hands on the sheet and pulled it back, letting out a sigh of relief when we saw the unfamiliar face staring up at us.

"It's not him," Boya said, wiping the back of his hand across his mouth. "It's not him, but it's still somebody."

"I know," I said, looking down at the man, hoping he had identification on him. Reaching into the pocket on my shirt, I was ready to change out my gloves, when I heard a growl, and turned around to see three men, all of wolf descent coming on us fast.

I jumped to my feet, as quick as I could in my condition, and Boya also rose, his wings flapping out in the process. Then I heard another growl and turned to see two women of wolf descent and one of phoenix.

Had I been in top fighting condition, we could have dusted the floor with them, of that I had no doubt, but I wasn't at peak form, and it didn't take the three coming from my left, and the four from my right to tell me we were in trouble.

Boya put his arm around my waist and pulled me close. "I'm going to get us out of here." I didn't like running from a fight. I never liked running, it just wasn't who I was, but now?

Now it was about survival.

I held on tight, trying to ignore the twisting in my gut, but before we'd even made it an inch off the ground they were on us. Eight went for Boya, five for me.

I punched one of the wolves in the mouth, then kicked another in the face. One of the phoenixes elbowed me in the nose, and I tried to use my power to rip her throat out, but the only thing that happened was my hand started shaking midair.

Then one of the female wolves released her claws and slashed me hard across the face, making me fall back. I stumbled and had almost found my footing when a blow to my jaw sent me tumbling.

I landed right beside the frog under the sheet, my body on fire, but fuck that, I wasn't giving up yet. Beside me, I saw three burnt bodies, and the smell was enough to make me gag.

Fists were flying everywhere, and it took me a moment to realized that there were still five on Boya, pounding away.

"Nooo!" I said, determined more than ever to get to my feet. We'd been set up, that much was clear, but by who, and why?

I came up to my knees, and then I felt claws digging into my throat, trying to rip it out, after that, nothing.

Chapter 4

I don't know how long I lay there before I came to. I blinked my eyes as I looked around, trying to remember what'd happened. We'd been in a fight, Boya and I, ambushed.

Boya! With panic, I looked around, but the only thing I saw was the frog body under the sheet, and the three burnt lumps from earlier. Boya! Fear and trepidation took up equal parts of my brain, and for one full second I was frozen with fear.

After gathering myself, I tried to move, and that's when the smell of blood hit me, and I realized I was wet all over. Not only that, but when I opened my mouth to call out, all I felt was intense pain, and no sound came.

Slowly I tried to raise my hand to reach toward my throat, but that alone was making me dizzy, and then nothing but blackness again.

When I came to this time, I smelled lemon and all I could see was the color orange. Drem. I had to be at Drem, the wizard's house.

"I don't like bothering with you people," I heard him say from right beside me. "Need to start locking the doors whenever I sense you're on the way here."

I let out a small exhale of breath, my body feeling a lot better than it had before. "And... she's fine," Drem said, picking up his supplies.

Drem was a man of medium height and build. To most he looked around thirty, but in truth, like a lot of us, Drem had lived for thousands of years. His skin was olive, his hair jet black and hanging down past his butt.

Like always, he was dressed completely in orange, that being his favorite color and all. "Seems like every time you come here you want me to heal your damnable throat. Stop getting it torn out. I have better stuff to do, you know."

He was a grouchy ass man. "I didn't come here—Boya!" I said, now that I could talk again. "Did you find Boya?"

I looked around the room and saw Lin, Ninia, Steva, and Iscca, all standing above me, all looking pissed and worried at the same time. Kind of like how I was feeling.

Drem let out a grunt. "Now that you're fine, get out. Whelm and I have guests coming over." Whelm was always here. I hadn't figured out yet what he did, only that he was always around.

My mind went back to the way those thugs had pounded on Boya in the alley, and my fists curled at my sides as I stood. "We have to find Boya now!"

I refused to say *before it was too late*, because it wasn't too late, nor was it going to be fucking too late, because that just wasn't fucking possible.

"Ugh," Ninia said, hands going to her head. "Say that F word one more time and I'm going to stick you. I'm not playing. You standing here repeating the same word over and over is not helping. What the fuck happened?"

I raised a brow at her. "It was a setup. We were ambushed."

Lin wrapped his hands around my waist and pulled me closer, planting a kiss on my forehead. "Where were the officers?"

I swallowed hard, feeling nothing but at home in the crook of his arm. "Rosen and Mason were there, them and a few others. We thought... we thought it might be Gull under the sheet, so we asked them all to leave."

Iscca had whips of fire raging all around him, and I was sure that Drem or Whelm would pop up at any moment and tell him to put that shit out. "What were two Samgs doing at a crime scene in Spray Town?"

I shrugged. "They said they had to be there. We need to find out who told them that."

I removed myself from Lin, and stood on my own, amazed at how much better I felt. I wasn't back to a hundred percent yet, as only sex could bring me there, but I did feel healthier than I had in months.

"Boya," I said, my mind going back to my partner, my lover, my friend. The only thing giving me hope was that they'd taken him. They hadn't left him for dead like they'd done me, so that had to mean something, at least I hoped it did.

"We're going to find him," Lin said, his jaw working hard to keep his anger in check. Lin loved Boya as much as I did, and we... he... Where the fuck was he?

Anger hit me like a whiplash, and my claws shot out, while fire danced around my fingertips. My mouth hung open as I looked at it, as did everyone else's in the room.

"Drem told you there could be some lasting effects of you having the power of the soulbar, why do you all look so surprised?" Whelm said, popping up out of thin air, making us all give him wary looks. He did that shit all the time, and I was used to it by now.

Iscca narrowed his eyes at me, and I let out a huff of air. "Look, dude, I didn't steal your power. It's the dragon power from the soulbar, you know that."

"I think you mean dranghum," Iscca said, because those who were descended from dragons were actually dranghums. "Anyway, I was just wondering where all that power and fire was when my boy got taken?"

"Hey," Ninia said, popping him on the arm. "Wanna try that again?"

Fire swirled around Iscca as he walked to the other side of the room, kicking an orange crate filled with small items out of his way. "Pick it up or pay for it," Whelm said, popping back in.

Lin went deathly still and nothing, but his head turned to look at Iscca. "Not needed. Focus." A chill went down my spine. I watched his eyes bore into Iscca's, but he never said another word. For most that would mean they were trying to cool off, but Lin's silence was his fury, and everyone in the room knew it.

Iscca threw his hands up. "Sorry... I'm just..." he let the rest trail off, and with Ninia's help started picking up the items he'd knocked over.

I didn't pay any attention to Iscca. He hadn't upset me. He had a right to his feelings just like everyone else here. "Someone was killed tonight, someone who fit the description of Gull. This thing was planned from the ground up," I said.

Every criminal in Spray knew that Gull was a snitch and that Boya was the number one agent he talked to. Boya had taken a lot of people down this way, and something told me either them or one of their loved ones, wanted revenge.

My mind went back to how they'd beaten him, and I heard the scream of the banshee working its way up my throat. "No," I said, taking a deep breath, and pushing it down. I'd learned when I'd had the power of the soulbar how to control these other powers, and this was nothing more than lingering after effects, so I wouldn't let it take me under.

"We start with Gull," I said, then thought of something. "How did you guys find me? Did the chief call because Boya and I hadn't checked in for a while?"

Lin pointed to his head. "Forget who's in there with you? Your grandmother gave us a call."

My eyes went toward the ceiling. I'd forgotten that she and a few other First Family members were mentally connected with me for every second of my punishment, just in case I went into the bathroom and accidentally got myself off or something.

"She called you?" I asked Lin, giving him a blank stare. I was startled, hopeful...?

Before he could answer, Ninia, Steva, and Iscca walked up. Ninia had her phone in her hand, and she looked from me to Lin, dread on her face. "The uniforms we left to protect the scene just called. Said they don't know how they missed it, or how they'd gotten by them, but there's something on the side of one of the buildings you need to see."

My body went cold, and I felt my legs give out from under me. Lin wrapped his arm around my waist to pull me up and I could sense the furious rage emitting off him.

"Okay," I said, because that was all I could say. Because if the violent image I had in my mind of Boya being gutted and hung up as a sign for others not to snitch became a reality then nothing and no one was safe. I'd burn all of Spray to the ground if I had to, in order to find the motherfuckers who'd dared lay hands on him.

Chapter 5

I was out of the car before it stopped, Lin and the others right behind me. Iscca was already there. He'd said it would be faster if he flew. When I saw him, he was standing still, looking up, fire flying around him in angry wisps.

My breath stopped as I watched him, and I took a moment to compose myself. By the time I was walking again, Lin and the others had caught up, and we all arrived on the scene together.

"Motherfucker!" Steva said, and once I saw what was in front of me I echoed his sentiments but felt downright foolish for not realizing sooner.

On the side of the building, in large glowing letters was the phrase, '*Boya was here, signed Rome and Kriste.*'

My hands trembled, and for a moment everything went red. My claws came out, my teeth grew, becoming thick and sharp as knives, my skin buzzed, and my eyes blazed with fire. Rome! Fucking Rome and his sister Kriste. Which meant the whole Rosen and Mason thing was probably just a coincidence, because Boya and I would have cleared the scene no matter who was here.

I shook my head, so tired of dealing with Rome and his shit.

Rome was an incubus, his sister a succubus. They were both absorbers as well. Absorbers were rare and very sought after. They could actually transfer powers from one being to another. Rome had powered up a bunch of Samgs to go after the First Families not too long ago. We'd stopped him then, but two of the people who'd been caught in his net were the twins, Misha and Mitch. The twins whom Lin had loved and looked after for years.

He'd once dated their father Kevin and had taken on a fatherly role toward them doing that time. They were in their twenties now, but Lin still took on an active role in their lives.

"Should have known," Ninia said, and I didn't have to see the hard set of her jaw to sense the anger coming off her. "It's him. It's always fucking him."

I nodded because this had gone on long enough. We'd fought him twice before and barely survived. The twins had left with him that first time, as he'd used his absorber power to give them abilities. There was that, and the fact that they'd been caught up in his allure.

The First Families had murdered his cousin, so I got that he was pissed, but he'd hurt too many innocent people in his quest for revenge and this needed to stop.

Iscca was still burning bright. "We should have ended his ass when he tried to steal the soulbar. That's what we should have done."

I looked back on the wall again, my eyes going dark as I thought of what those sick fucks could be doing to Boya right now because Iscca was right.

The whole soulbar thing had been Rome and Kriste trying to take that power for themselves, and once again they'd used the twins, and they'd also hurt Gull, his wife, and kids.

They'd battled with us, until realizing they were going to lose, then they'd made their escape, this time leaving the twins behind. We'd taken Mitch and Misha to Drem, and he'd healed them both, making it so Rome would never be able to put them under his spell again. He'd also let them keep a few of their powers, but the less said about that the better.

"He's not getting away with it this time," Ninia said, running a finger through her short red hair. "We're calling in everyone on this. He touched one of our own. I say we take him out for good."

Boya. The only thing on my mind was Boya. In front of me, Lin didn't make a peep, and I wondered how long Rome and Kriste would live after we found them. He stood, shoulders wide, back straight, legs slightly apart, his eyes not moving from that brick wall.

Cat and mouse. They wanted to play games with us, but they'd crossed the line in a way that they couldn't come back from. "The bottoms," I said, looking at the others. "Let's see what they know at the bottoms."

The bottoms was a place deep in Spray Town. Magical and mystical creatures of all kinds could hang out there, drinking, gambling, getting high, and doing whatever else they wanted without fear of law enforcement or the First Families.

We were on strict orders to never police the bottoms, and I'd always figured it was the First Families way of saying, 'we know we're harsh sometimes, but here, go blow off some steam.

It was a large, shady outside area, and people often set up huddles, where they had couches, TVs, tables, and whatever else they desired. A few elementers hung out there and usually changed the weather to fit their will.

Also, it wasn't uncommon to see grills set up with people cooking out, though there were some who preferred to prepare their food over fire and rock.

All income brackets hung out at the bottoms as did many different species. It was a mutual place, no violence allowed, and respect for other people's stuff being the number one rule. "There's no way the bottoms don't know what's going on," I said.

"They'll talk," I said. My eyes flashed fire, and my claws came out again, long and thick, curling around my hands. All I could see was Rome and his sister torturing and tormenting Boya, laughing at his pain. "They'll talk," I repeated. "Either that or I'll rip their fucking tongues out."

Chapter 6

We arrived at the bottoms to see that it was summer here. The place was set up with huddles everywhere, and all around you could hear TVs and people laughing and holding loud conversations.

I could sense other succubi here, as well as incubi, sirens, dranghums, bears, and a host of others. A lot of people were here, so somebody had to know something.

The smell of roasted vegetables filled the air, and I figured a few were in the midst of cooking lunch. There was no law here, and we had no authority, but Boya's life was on the line, so I wasn't about to be nice about anything.

Lin looked over the whole of the bottoms. "Spread out. Don't take no for an answer."

With that, he walked off, and the rest of us went ahead and mixed with the crowd. I walked up to a woman with rat DNA sitting on a green couch, watching TV.

She had brown hair, sallow skin, and I could sense that not much got by her. She appeared to be in her late forties, and the pipe she had in her hand was one I noticed every time I came here.

"Annie," I said, standing just outside her huddle. "May I come in?" You never entered someone's huddle without permission, and even though I wanted answers, I figured I'd learn more if I did it this way first.

She waved me inside, intelligent eyes watching me the whole time. "What do you want now?" she asked once I'd taken a seat beside her on the couch.

"Rome and his sister Kriste, where are they?"

She took a long drag off her pipe, her eyes never leaving mine. "Are you going to kill them?" she asked, and I could sense that her answer depended solely on what I said next.

"Yes." I decided not to lie. I held up my hands, my claws springing forward. Her eyes flickered. As succubi, we rarely showed this side of ourselves, and most knew when we did to get out of dodge without delay. "I'm going to rip them apart with my bare hands, now, where are they?"

Annie took another drag off her pipe. "Heard talk they've been hanging out over near Hailstock. Got a building or two there." She took another toke and shrugged. "That's all I know."

"Thanks," I said. I stood, my pulse racing, because at least now we had something to go on.

I went back to the car where the others were already waiting. Steva ran a hand over his head. "I heard they may be down by the Weeping Wet. Seems Rome holds up there three nights a week."

Iscca had a fireball in his hand and something told me it was the only thing keeping him calm. "Someone mentioned Hailstock to me, not sure how true it is."

I nodded. "Annie said something about Hailstock too, so that could be a clue."

"Could be a trap," Lin said, his voice gruff and hard. "Be on guard, but we'll check it out anyway."

A small bit of music started up and Ninia looked over to where a man and woman were laughing and slow dancing. "I heard he's scaling the streets, just waiting for us to make a wrong move."

Lin looked up, and though he appeared in control, I saw nothing but fury underneath. His jaw was locked tight, eyes small storms, hands flexing back and forward to keep his claws at bay.

Lin didn't show his emotions much, but right now I was sure just the smallest thing would set him off and I pitied anyone who got in his way. "Heard something about Winn Town."

"Okay," I said, nodding. "Let's check out Weeping Wet first since we're closer to that, then we'll go to Hailstock, and if still nothing, we'll head to Winn Town."

The Weeping Wet was a river that held enormous power. The First Families forbid anyone to use it unless your life was at stake. It had awesome healing abilities, but it also amplified your powers, making them three times stronger than normal, though that only lasted for a couple of hours.

It was high noon when we got to the Weeping Wet. Not many were out, but I knew once summer hit, the place would be packed with people setting up barbecues and such.

There were many picnic tables and grills here, as well as large trees casting a nice shade. There was a jogging trail, and also a few play areas for the kids. As we walked we could hear birds squawking in the distance and something told me that Rome and Kriste would not be here.

The last time we'd been here they'd been defeated by us. They both carried an enormous amount of pride on their shoulders, and we'd not only stopped them from taking the power of the soulbar here, we'd also been able to get Mitch and Misha back from them.

"No," I said, shaking my head as we walked. "They won't be here but that doesn't mean they didn't direct one of their minions to send us here."

Ninia kept a steady pace beside me. "Send us here for what?" she asked.

We got to the water's edge, and I looked out at the glowing colorful lake, thinking of how much power was held in that one place.

"They sent us here for this," Steva said, and I followed to where he pointed. High up on a tree branch was the black shirt Boya had been wearing when they'd attacked us.

There were words written on it in red, but I still couldn't see them without bringing the shirt closer. Rising in the air, heart in my throat, I became level with the tree branches.

The shirt was laid out in a way that made the words easy to read and from up here my senses were able to pick up the unmistakable scent of blood. Boya's blood, I'd know it anywhere.

A hurricane of emotions slammed into me at once, and I had to fight to keep from tearing apart everything around me. Those sick fuckers. They'd used his blood to write a message on his shirt, and now they were going to die.

I wasn't messing around here. My hands trembled with anger as I reached out to snatch the shirt up, bringing it closer. "*Give us this one thing, and Boya will be set free.*"

My eyes narrowed as I looked at the words, because what one thing? Surely, they knew the soulbar was with the First Families now, and irretrievable.

Going back to the ground, I handed the shirt over to Lin to see what he and the others thought. Lin looked it over, and I knew, like me, he could smell Boya's blood. His eyes flashed for a moment, and his claws came out, before going back in. "They're baiting," he said.

Ninia nodded. "And bet when we get to Hailstock they'll have another message for us."

Steva sniffed the air, then leaped back toward the tree. "There were three of them here. Wolves, all from the same pack, I can still smell it on them."

Iscca was no longer covered in fire, now he just looked pissed. "But are they working with Rome because they want to, or are they caught in his allure?"

Ninia held up a finger. "It only takes one look in their eyes. If it's allure, we leave 'em alone. Not their fault."

"But," I said, thinking back to the last time Rome and Kriste had wolves, owls, and phoenixes willing to kill for them. "If the wolves and others are doing this because they want money and power, if they hurt Boya and did so because of some off-kilter fuck you to the First Families, then, well, then we'll show them no mercy."

Rome and Kriste's biggest beef was with the First Families. Not only had they killed their cousin, but they didn't like how the First Families ruled over everything. They didn't like how their word was law above anything else, how with a few whispered words they could ruin you, or give you great wealth, didn't like that they held power that most of us could only dream of, didn't like that they controlled everything.

Look, I got it, I really did. Lots of us felt that way about the First Families, but without order there was chaos. I looked out at the Weeping Wet, my mind going over the many ways it could be abused if magical creatures were allowed to use it freely.

Then I thought back to Morse Town and shuddered. If not for the First Families, it would be a bloodbath there. Some of my kind hated humans and if not for the First Families, would've been ripping through Morse, tearing everyone apart.

Even now, some went over there and acted out a bit, and Boya and myself, usually along with Rosen and Mason, would have to clean up the mess and set up a few glamors. Then the First Families would viciously and publicly murder the accuser, letting others know what would happen if they tried it.

I swallowed hard, my bones shaking with rage. I didn't know anybody who actually liked the First Families, but most all respected them and trying to go up against them.... no. My grandmother had more power in her pinky finger than I did in my whole body, which was proven every time I saw her.

"This is about the First Families," I finally said. "Everything is about the First Families with them."

Lin stood with Boya's shirt clutched tightly in his hand.

"Something's waiting at Hailstock," I said to him. "Let's check it out."

Chapter 7

Hailstock was a street in Spray Town. It held six large buildings. Three on the right side of the road, three on the left. There were five of us, so I figured we'd each take a building and check out the last one together.

We parked the car at the top of the street, and as the others got out and walked ahead, Lin put a hand on my arm, holding me back. "We're going to find him," he said, then pulled me close, engulfing me in his big strong arms.

I exhaled, and lay my head on his chest, loving the feel of him, loving everything about him, and feeling nothing but protected in his arms. "I know," I said, squeezing him tightly, and wishing I could stay like that with him forever, that all the bad stuff would go away, then Boya would come back and we could all just be together.

An electric shock went through us and I backed up in surprise. "Been a while since that happened," I said, looking at Lin to see his reaction.

"Body just a little stronger. Drem."

I nodded, but knew I was nowhere near one hundred percent. Drem had helped, but I still felt like I'd been at least a week without sex. Though, I thanked Drem for healing me this much. Still, if my body had built up enough that sparks were flying when Lin and I touched, well that was something.

"Come on," Lin said, pulling me to him again, and I could smell the musty and spicy scent that was him. "Let's go see what they left this time."

Once we walked up, the other four were coming back shaking their heads. "We checked every building," Ninia said. "Nothing."

"Did you check them well?" I asked, wondering if they'd really had enough time to do a thorough walkthrough. Lin and I hadn't been at the car that long, had we?

Ninia nodded. "Pretty thorough, I didn't sense anything."

Steva looked back at the buildings. "I didn't sniff anything, didn't see anything."

Iscca rocked back on the heels of his feet, a disappointed look on his face. "Nothing."

My brows furrowed. Iscca and I had both been given the name Hailstock. That couldn't have been by coincidence, so... I stopped, my body going rigid, before going into attack mode. "Be ready!" I shouted, but the others were already in defensive positions, probably having sensed our oncoming attackers too.

Steva sniffed the air. "There's at least twenty."

I nodded because I'd sensed about that many too.

"Formation!" I said. "Back to back." We needed to stay together because if not, they'd pick us off one by one.

We'd already went up against Rome twice and beat him, so I knew his pride wouldn't let it rest until he'd proven to us, and his followers, that he was the best, the most powerful.

I didn't care about shit like that, but everything he did hinged on him being undefeatable, unstoppable, and we'd already proven he wasn't.

My guess was he didn't plan on there being a third time. He was out for blood now, and once again I cursed the First Families. Because of them and their stupid punishment I wasn't up to full power.

I cracked my head from side to side. Didn't matter. I'd still fight with everything I had. I heard the flap of wings and looked up to see three men with owl DNA and two women.

Then, from around the buildings, came wolves, fifteen of them, moving full steam ahead. "There is no allure!" I said looking into their eyes. "They're doing this because they want to!"

We didn't have time to brace ourselves before they were on us clawing and scratching.

One made to rake her claws across my face, and I leaned back, then used my own talons to claw into her gut, ripping her to shreds. Then I opened my mouth and took every bit of life force she had.

A man with owl DNA swiped down toward me, and I held up my hands and used my telekinesis to part his body in two. Blood shot out, as part of him fell off to the right, the other to the left.

Iscca went up in the sky where the owls were. The remaining four surrounded him, striking him with their talons, going for his neck and chest.

He breathed fire out of his mouth at one, and the Owl's head burst into flames. He threw a ball of fire at another one while whipping a lasso of fire around a different one's waist and setting them all aflame.

Ninia grabbed a wolf and whispered his worst nightmares in his ear. The man's eyes went wide as the violent, bloody, scene became real for him and he tore out his own eyes. Another wolf came for her and she ducked his claw swipe. He then changed tactics and hit her in the face twice rapidly.

Her head lolled back and then she used her telekinesis to rip his hands off. The man let out a howl, falling back as blood spurted out. She then grabbed him by the neck, sinking her talons into his throat, as she opened her mouth and took his life force.

See, that's the thing about succubi and incubi, we could stay recharged during a fight. Depending on how powerful they were, taking another being's life force offered an excellent boost.

My skin prickled, and my heart jumped, but once I was in the thick of the fight, I ran on auto pilot, doing what I had to in order to stay breathing.

Three wolves came on Steva and he let out a roar and released his claws. One slashed him in the back, while another went for his legs. The other one decided to claw at his face.

Steva was a powerful man and would never give up in a fight. He dropped low, catching the one who'd been aiming at his face by the private area and then ripping it out. The guy screamed and fell away. He ducked a blow from the one who'd hurt his leg, then grabbed the man by the head and used his teeth to tear the man's throat out.

The one who'd clawed his back tried to sink his nails into Steva's side and rip it out, but Steva grabbed the man by the arm and then proceeded to bite his whole face off.

Lin used his telekinesis to peel the skin from one man, and his screams lit up the night, horrible and tortured. He grabbed another one close, and whispered something in his ear that made the man's eyes go wide before he fell to the ground, howls echoing from his throat.

Two more came on him, aiming their claws for his face, working together in an effort to tear him down. He sunk his talons into their necks, and blood dribbled over his hands as he pulled them close and took their life forces.

Another wolf came at me and I reached into his chest and ripped his heart out, but before he hit the ground I took a blow to my face that knocked me back.

My jaw was on fire, but I grabbed the woman who'd hit me by the hair and used my strength to rip it from her scalp, then I took her life force.

After that, there were still two left, until Iscca opened his mouth and they went up in flames. The scent of blood and burned flesh surrounded us and I was just getting started. "What was that?" I asked, looking at the others because Rome already knew how well we could defend ourselves so what was the point?

"Distraction," Lin said, wiping blood from his face. "He's planning something. Not sure what that means for Boya."

Chapter 8

B looded and bruised, but bursting with renewed energy, we decided to pay the twins a visit to see if they could remember anything from the months they'd been with Rome.

Lin had called ahead and they'd both agreed to meet us at their father Kevin's house. Kevin and Lin had been in a relationship for a few years, but things hadn't ended well. Still, Lin had come to love the kids, so he was very protective of them and their wellbeing.

That they were better now and no longer under the control of Rome was a weight off Lin's shoulders, and I knew he hated to drag them into this, but we needed answers, Boya's life depended on it.

Kevin lived in a small yellow clapboard house. The yard was always neat, and he had cushions in the outdoor furniture that sat on the porch. He and the twins were standing outside waiting for us and we all got out of the car and walked up together.

Kevin was a very tall man, bald, with eyebrows so thick my hands often itched to put them into pigtails. He didn't like me, never had, but now wasn't the time for that. Not that I'd ever cared anyway. His feelings were his own, they didn't bother or affect me.

He sat in a chair on the porch, watching us, not saying a word. Misha stood by the steps. Over the last few months, she'd grown her hair out a bit. Like her brother's, it was jet black, but where his was cut short, hers now reached her shoulders. They both had olive skin and brown eyes.

Mitch had been on the porch with his father but came down to stand beside his sister when we walked up. I let out a breath when I saw them, because the last time I had, Rome had turned them into barely speaking animals, feral beasts, only able to do his will.

We'd fought him that day, with everything we had, down by the Weeping Wet, then taken the twins to Drem where he healed and restored them back to themselves.

"We've been thinking," Misha said, her eyes shining as she looked at Lin. The twins loved him, he'd always been good to them, and they knew how hard he'd fought both times to bring them home safely. "There is a place Rome would take us to sometimes. It's far out, on the outskirts of Spray Town, nothing but woods and trees there."

Mitch ran a hand over his head. "He had to know you'd come to us and we'd give you this location."

"That means he's ready for you," Misha said.

"He's probably got hundreds, maybe even thousands by his side," Mitch said.

"He's been going out of state, gathering others who are tired of living under the First Families' rule," Misha said.

"Who've lost family and loved ones to them or felt they've been treated unfairly," Mitch said.

"These people, he doesn't have to glamor," Misha said.

"They're as depraved as him, as angry as him, want the First Families gone as much as he does," Mitch said.

"And he takes a special pride in whipping them into a frenzy," Misha said.

"Want us to come with you?" Mitch asked, his face eager. "I'd like to pay him back for everything he did to us, and then some."

"No!" Kevin said from the porch, coming to a stand. "Just give them the address and then they'll go."

Both twins looked at their father, their faces softening. He'd been put through a lot when they'd fallen under the spell of Rome. Neither twin lived here with him or depended on him for their income, but he was still their father, and they still respected what he had to say.

Both nodded and then they told us everything we needed to know.

Chapter 9

Once we had the location, Ninia made a call to the chief telling him to send us backup. If the twins were right, and Rome had thousands with him, we were going to need it.

We pulled off the highway after driving for twenty minutes down a very dark and isolated road. No other cars passed us, and out here the air was still and quiet.

We got out of the car, and from the twins' directions, I knew we were in for a fifteen-minute walk. We needed to wait for backup, but I was sure they'd be here soon, and besides, who knew what would be happening to Boya while we wasted time out here doing nothing?

I cracked my knuckles. Not sure about the others, but I was starting forward right now. It was eerie how quiet it was, and as I walked, I couldn't stop the feeling of trepidation going down my spine.

The others came right along with me, and I figured no one was going to wait on the side of the road until backup eventually came.

"Out here, away from everything, planning something big," Lin observed.

I nodded. "And remember, he probably knows we're coming so we need to be on our guard."

It took us another fifteen minutes before we came to a large clearing, but as we got closer, the sound of raised voices could be heard. I could also sense blood, Boya's blood, and I looked at the others, knowing they probably did as well.

Lin's hands curled at his sides, his talons out in full force now, though from the way his voice stayed leveled you'd never know just how pissed he was. "Not jumping to conclusions. Anything could be happening."

My heart stuttered in my chest, and the closer we got to the sound of the voices and the blood, the more erratic my thoughts became. If he was dead... if Rome and Kriste had.... Fire shot out of my mouth, as wings sprouted on my back, and my talons scraped the ground.

"Control," Lin said sternly beside me, and I took a deep breath and tried to push thoughts of Boya being tortured and mangled out of my mind.

The closer we got, the louder the voices became, and soon we saw why. The twins were right, there had to be a few hundred, maybe even a thousand people here easily.

They were all lined up behind Rome and Kriste, who sat in two large high-back chairs; king and queen of this whole thing. They watched our approach, like snakes waiting to pounce on their prey.

The noise around us was mostly people talking. They had a few grills going, and my stomach lurched thinking about what they were cooking. The grass was gone here, and for what looked like a few miles, there was nothing but cement covering the ground.

Large trees surrounded us, like they were closing us in, and up above I saw men and women with owl, phoenix, and dragon DNA sitting on the branches. No one seemed to be doing much, just talking, eating and arguing with each other.

"Well," Rome said, once all five of us had stepped onto the cement. "We've been waiting quite a while for you three to show up." He looked from me, to Ninia to Boya, ignoring Steva and Iscca altogether, because, in Rome's eyes, anyone not of Cubus blood wasn't worth his time.

Rome was a tall man, with short brown hair, and an aristocratic nose that fit his arrogant, I'm better than all those around me, attitude perfectly.

"Oh, look, Rome," his sister Kriste said, coming to her feet, and clasping her hands together in delight. "They actually think they have a chance. That's so cute." Like him, Rome's sister was tall. She had the same nose as him and wore a long braid that reached past her butt. She was just as cunning as her brother, maybe even more so.

The noise around us stopped as soon as they started talking and I looked around at the crowd, checking their eyes, sensing them out.

"Oh, no one here is glamoured," Rome said, throwing his hands out in front of him. "No need to do that. Everyone here hates the First Families as much as I do. We all came together for the same purpose."

"Which is?" I asked, sensing the crowd growing more anxious by the second.

I looked around. That I didn't even see a trace of Boya, was making me jumpy. I could ask Rome for proof of life, but I knew that wouldn't happen until he was damn ready.

Rome snapped his fingers, and a medium height, medium built, incubi with pale skin and red hair walked up to stand beside him. "This is Ernie," Rome said, putting a hand on the man's shoulder. "Because his brother refused to do the bidding of the First Families, refused to let a land deal drop that he needed for his company to survive, they sent in their goons. Three of them pulled him out of his house, where a member of the First Families was waiting."

Rome leaned his head to the side. "You can guess the rest, of course. His throat was torn out, his body broken in half. He was left in the street for his wife and kids to find when they got home."

My skin prickled at his story, but I didn't believe it for one minute. That the First Families had killed his brother, that part I didn't doubt, but the rest, nope, I didn't think so.

Rome snapped his fingers again, and a woman with dark skin and black hair that reached her ears walked up. She was a phoenix and her wings were purple and blue. "They murdered her daughter."

He pointed into the crowd. "His mother, her brother, his grandmother, and the list goes on."

"What we want is simple," Kriste said before any of us could react. "Elections where the people choose who they want to govern them, where the people lawfully pick who they want making the rules and laws governing us all."

My hands flexed at my sides, as I let out a bitter laugh. "It's a nice concept," I said. "And I agree, something like that would be satisfying, reasonable, but why don't you say what you really want?"

"And what's that?" Rome asked, looking like I'd actually offended him.

This time it was Ninia who spoke. "You want the freedom to take on the powers of the Weeping Wet and other such places, so you can rampage and destroy at will."

Rome clicked his tongue. "I can do that without a foolish lake of water."

"Not without consequences," I said. "You want the freedom to go into Morse Town and other such places, to drain and kill humans as you see fit. Feeding from them, taking from them, whenever you get ready with no one telling you no. The First Families would never allow you such freedoms, so this is your move to just take it."

"Why should we be subjected to their laws!" Rome roared, breaking his composure for just a second. "We are Cubus! We take what we want! We fuck who we want! Damn them if they don't like it!"

"That's sick!" Ninia sneered.

"Disgusting," Lin said, his eyes hard as he looked at Rome. "You need a leash."

"No," Kriste, said, her eyes flashing red. "It's your boy Boya who needs a leash. You and Kia share your bed with him as if he's your equal." She curled her lips in disgust. "The fuck is wrong with you?"

"Where is Boya?" I asked because, I couldn't keep having this ridiculous conversation.

Rome and Kriste shared a fond smile that made my skin crawl. "Want your pet back?" Rome asked, a smirk on his face. "Willing to do tricks to make it happen?"

Beside me, Lin bristled, but I put a hand on his arm to calm him. We were finally getting somewhere, and hopefully, soon we'd learn what they really wanted.

"You can have him back," Rome said, pacing, hands locked behind him. "All you have to do is deliver the First Families to me."

Chapter 10

"**D**o what?" I asked, my eyes bucking a bit at his suggestion. "What are you talking about?"

"It's simple," Kriste said, wrapping a hand around her long braid and throwing it behind her head. "The First Families are all powerful. We know that."

Her eyes roamed around at the thousands of succubi, incubi, sirens, banshees, phoenixes, snakes, wolves, dranghums, owls, and so on. "As powerful as they are, they cannot beat us all. We can't get close to the First Families, but you..." She pointed a finger my way. "You can."

Not really, not unless I was invited, but I got her point. "Go to them and tell them we call Akashic! Every thought! Every feeling! Every emotion laid bare, and Akashic will decide the victor!"

"Huh?" I asked, not sure I understood. Akashic were a set of records that held every feeling, thought, emotion, and act, by all who'd ever existed. No one had called Akashic since ancient times, because no one was stupid enough to go up against the First Families.

By calling Akashic, it meant letting the challenger's deeds be weighed against those of the First Families, and whoever Akashic found lacking would lose in a fight to the death.

To my right, I heard Steva groan, and Iscca let out a snort.

"You? All of you," I asked, waving my hand at the crowd, "want to challenge the First Families in a fight to the death?"

A guy with wolf DNA stepped up, his eyes yellow and unforgiving. "Why should we continue to bow to the humans? Who are they to us? The First Families protect them like they're babes in the crib. Every law is centered around their comfort, of keeping them safe and ignorant of the beast that lurks beside them."

He ran a tongue over his sharp teeth, his claws gleaming at his sides. "I pick 'em off every chance I get." The crowd cheered at this and I looked around horrified at what my senses were telling me. No one here was faking, these people actually agreed with him.

The First Families protected the humans from us because they could not protect themselves. Yet these people here were envious of that, angry, vengeful because they couldn't resort to their viler instincts.

"Back home," a dude with owl DNA said, and I figured he was from out of state. "Back home we round 'em up. Take 'em out in the woods and let 'em go. Then we have sport for the rest of the night. The owl who produces the most bones wins."

I reeled back in revulsion, especially since I could sense how much this excited the crowd. Did these depraved motherfuckers really think the Akashic records would pick them over the First Families?

"So," I said, shuddering in disgust at how many wanted to kill and maim. "You'll give Boya back if I go to the First Families and tell them you challenge them to Akashic?"

Rome smirked as he nodded. "Yup, what do you say?"

"I say fuck you!" I walked forward, body popping with rage, talons out, teeth sharp. "I say never!" If I did some stupid shit like that, walked up to the First Families and parroted Rome's terms, for the sake of Boya's life, they'd see Boya as a weakness, my weakness, and kill him on sight, and I was sure Rome knew that.

Though I could sense there was a small part of him, a slither, that really wanted this, really thought he and the others had a chance against the First Families.

The other part though, the other part was hurt pride. We'd bested him twice in front of his followers, and he couldn't continue to be all-powerful, without bringing us down a peg or two.

We'd beat his ass twice, and a man with pride like his simply could not let that rest. Every single inch of him needed to prove that he was better than us, stronger. He needed to prove it to himself and to his followers. He'd suffered two blows at our hands, and I realized in that moment that he'd never stop.

He'd never quit coming for us until he'd picked us off one by one, so something had to be done. I would not live in fear of him and neither would the other Xelone agents. He had to be stopped.

"No?" Rome asked, looking at me, a sick smile on his face. He shrugged and turned toward the crowd. "All well, we tried." He snapped his fingers, and then I heard the flap of wings. A second later an owl dropped something bloody and pulverized onto the cement. It hit with a bang, not moving as blood flowed from it.

It took me a moment to realize it was a body, as it looked like someone had taken a meat cleaver and just cut and hacked until there was nothing but shredded skin and bones.

It took me a whole other second to realize, to understand that it.... that the body was.... that it was what used to be Boya laying in front of me.

My eyes went red, my blood turned to fire and boiled, my talons scraped the ground, my teeth hung out of my mouth, my height grew, my skin hardened, my heart hammered, and everything turned silver and gold.

Behind me, I could hear Lin let out a roar, and Ninia gasp, as they both grew five feet taller. Steva groaned, Iscca hissed, and Rome and Kriste... they laughed.

"I told you I'd give him back," Rome said, wiping the tears away from his eyes as he continued to laugh. "I didn't say what condition he'd be in."

Kriste threw her head back, a big smile on her face. "And he was so much fun to play with."

At this, the crowd laughed as well, but by now fire whipped around me, and I knew, I was no longer in control of myself. If I could have, I would have told Lin and the others to run, but I wasn't in my right mind to do that.

From below, Boya let out a small pain-filled breath of air, and that's when I lost it. I threw my head back and roared as fire shot out of my mouth. Then I was walking forward, nothing but death on my mind.

They thought I was a fucking joke and they'd come at me like I was. I walked into the thick of them, I was full succubus now, so their little hits and jabs couldn't even put a dent in my skin.

A siren raised her voice to sing me into submission and I grabbed her by the throat and crushed it, slinging her out of the way. A wolf slashed me across the face, but the only thing hurt was his fingers as they came up against my hard, impenetrable skin.

I grabbed him with one hand then broke his body in half on my knee, pulling his spine out and crushing his bones in my fingers.

A phoenix flew my way, and I opened my mouth, scorching her as she turned to dust and dissipated. A snake tried to strike out at me with his tongue and I ripped it out, then twisted his body into a triangle.

The owl who'd dropped Boya swung out at me, and I grabbed his hand, ripping it off, before sticking my talons into his stomach and disemboweling him.

No incubus or succubus came my way, as I was sure they'd hightailed it out of there the moment I began to turn. A dragon opened his mouth to hit me with fire, and I let it wash over me, then used my telekinesis to slam him down in front of me, shredding him like paper.

I walked through them all, ripping off heads, breaking spines, tearing off limbs, and crushing bones. Then I heard Boya groan again, and I looked up to where Kriste and Rome stood, horrified expressions on their faces.

"Did you really think you could beat me?" I asked, my voice thick and hard. "That you could mess with what's mine and not pay the price?" I threw my head back and let out a bitter, painful, insane laugh. "You thought wrong."

Now they looked scared, now they looked frightened, now they looked like two idiots who'd bitten off more than they could chew and could no longer handle it. "You will give him life," I said, then proceeded to suck the essence out of Rome, Kriste, and every follower they had left standing.

Then I went to Boya, poured it all into his mouth, and watched as he changed, reformed, and became himself again.

Before me, Rome and Kriste were empty husks, turning to dust, as were all of those who'd co-signed their bullshit. Good fucking riddance.

Boya began to take shape again, and at the same time, I felt my body break down.

After being in human form for so long, turning full succubus was dangerous and life-threatening unless you planned on killing and feeding for days. It drained you completely. My eyes drooped, my energy waned, and for the third time in as many days, I felt the blackness take over completely.

Chapter 11

"You can have sex again," I heard my grandmother say as I blinked my eyes open. I was laying on a dark blue couch, the scent of pine and lilacs in the air, and I instantly knew I was in Riverwalk where the First Families lived.

"What?" I asked, holding my aching head and coming to a sitting position.

"Well," my grandmother said, her black hair to her shoulders, her face so like my own. "You've been here for a week, so your time is up anyway."

"A week!" I said, my eyes bucking, not sure I'd heard her right.

"Yes," she answered calmly from the blue recliner in front of me, her hands clasped together. "Lin and Ninia brought you here."

She pointed to her head. "Remember, I was with you the whole time. They did as they were told. Then I called Drem and he's been here working on you every day."

I scoffed. Drem, everyone's favorite wizard, I'd forgotten that he often spent a lot of time in Riverwalk doing work for the First Families.

"You handled yourself well," my grandmother said, the white pantsuit she had on without a speck of dirt or lint on it. "Rome and Kriste were a threat and you took them out as any member of the Wyaque Clan would."

I blinked as I looked at her, was that actually a compliment I heard?

"You also survived your punishment, though I'm sure that had more to do with the powers of the soulbar than anything you did."

Ah, and there it was, her usual banter toward me. Although... I leaned my head to the side. Had she known the powers of the soulbar would protect me when she'd handed out the whole no sex thing. Had it all been for show, to prove to others just how powerful those of the Wyaque Clan were?

I looked at her, with just a little bit of hope in my eyes, but she was already coming to a stand. "Leave now," she said, and before I could blink, she'd already disappeared from sight.

I went straight home, ignoring the shock and gasps from others as I made my way up the steps to my room. *Come here*, a voice said in my head, and I almost melted on the spot as Lin's smooth baritone washed over me.

Feeling just a little bit giddy in my newfound freedom to have sex, I pivoted, and then made my way to his room. That was the thing about living here. We often slept in each other's rooms, but each agent had their own quarters, their own space.

I opened the door to Lin's room, and let out a long breath as I saw both him and Boya on the bed. Boya looked good, fully healed, not a scratch on him, and boy, I couldn't wait to devour every part of him.

I took off my clothes as I walked toward the bed. They were already naked, the smell of sex heavy in the air. I crawled onto the bed, and both of them were on me and each other in an instant.

I smiled as their hands and lips roamed all over me thinking that this, this right here was what it was all about.

Author Note

I f you enjoyed this book please check out the short story set in this world, Cursed Magic.[1] Free when you join my mailing list here.[2]

---

1. https://www.amazon.com/Cursed-Magic-N-R-Hairston-ebook/dp/
   B075YDZZ45/ref=pd_sim_351_3?_encod-
   ing=UTF8&pd_rd_i=B075YDZZ45&pd_rd_r=d93388d2-b7a5-11e8-ac55-83
   4a4eb79bb6&pd_rd_w=L3A7c&pd_rd_wg=AfG1h&pf_rd_i=desktop-dp-
   sims&pf_rd_m=ATVPD-
   KIKX0DER&pf_rd_p=18bb0b78-4200-49b9-ac91-f141d61a1780&pf_rd_r=Z
   50ENXV0XXY4V3HJMV8M&pf_rd_s=desktop-dp-
   sims&pf_rd_t=40701&psc=1&refRID=Z50ENXV0XXY4V3HJMV8M
2. https://landing.mailerlite.com/webforms/landing/h2l3b2

Other Titles by N. R. Hairston

O ther Titles by N. R. Hairston
Magic and Mischief Series
A Magical Reckoning,[1] Book One
A Symptom of Magic,[2] Book Two
A Victim of Magic,[3] Book Three
Sun Cursed
Cursed Magic,[4] Book One
Savage Magic[5], Book Two
Lethal Magic[6], Book Three

---

1. https://www.amazon.com/Magical-Reckoning-Supernatural-Betrayal-Mis-chief-ebook/dp/B071P7HQVH/ref=as_li_ss_tl?s=digital-text&ie=UTF8&qid=1495929540&sr=1-1&keywords=a+magical+reckon-ing&linkCode=sl1&tag=fbp02-20&linkId=53cd93b9dc96241660ae8b41ec2bd efe

2. https://www.amazon.com/gp/product/B07489BQVL/ref=se-ries_rw_dp_sw

3. https://www.amazon.com/Victm-Magic-Stories-Supernatural-Mischief-ebook/dp/B07H5FHBFE/ref=sr_1_6?ie=UTF8&qid=1536873999&sr=8-6&keywords=n+r+hairston

4. https://www.amazor..com/dp/E075YDZZ45/ref=sr_1_3?s=digital-text&ie=UTF8&qid=1506478708&sr=1-3

5. https://www.amazon.com/Savage-Magic-N-R-Hairston-ebook/dp/B094DXP7J1/ref=sr_1_6?crid=2BGRD37EYPF31&dchild=1&key-

World Breaker

Rogue Magic,[7] Book One

Bloody Magic,[8] Book Two

Battle Magic,[9] Book Three

World Breaker Beginnings (Novellas set before the events in Rogue Magic, though you don't have to read one to read the other.) Read this series for free when you join my mailing list, here.[10]

Rebel Magic,[11] Book One

Stolen Magic,[12] Book Two

Crooked Magic,[13] Book Three

---

words=n+r+hairston&qid=1620470219&s=digital-text&spre-fix=n+r+%2Cdigital-text%2C148&sr=1-6

6.   https://www.amazon.com/dp/B094DQ663R/ref=sr_1_10?crid=2BGRD37EYPF31&dchild=1&keywords=n+r+hair-ston&qid=1620470219&s=digital-text&sprefix=n+r+%2Cdigital-text%2C148&sr=1-10

7.   https://www.amazon.com/dp/B075YGLN4P/ref=sr_1_1?s=digital-text&ie=UTF8&qid=1506478708&sr=1-1

8.   https://www.amazon.com/gp/product/B094DR-RQH7?ref_=dbs_m_mng_rwt_calw_tkin_1&storeType=ebooks

9.   https://www.amazon.com/dp/B094DS7WLQ/ref=sr_1_8?crid=2BGRD37EYPF31&dchild=1&keywords=n+r+hair-ston&qid=1620470219&s=digital-text&sprefix=n+r+%2Cdigital-text%2C148&sr=1-8

10.   https://landing.mailerlite.com/webforms/landing/h2l3b2

11.   https://www.amazon.com/gp/product/B075YD3B6V?notRedirectToS-DP=1&ref_=dbs_mng_calw_0&storeType=ebooks

12.   https://www.amazon.com/gp/product/B075YTLVZK?notRedirectToS-DP=1&ref_=dbs_mng_calw_1&storeType=ebooks

Dirty Magic,[14] Book Four
Feral Magic[15], Book Five
Lawless Magic[16], Book Six

Rise of the Dragons

Fire and Ash,[17] Book One
Smoke and Flame,[18] Book Two
Dust and Cinder,[19] Book Three

13.   https://www.amazon.com/gp/product/B075YF35XX?notRedirectToS-DP=1&ref_=dbs_mng_calw_2&storeType=ebooks

14.   https://www.amazon.com/dp/B094DSC8ZX/ref=sr_1_5?crid=2BGRD37EYPF31&dchild=1&keywords=n+r+hair-ston&qid=1620470219&s=digital-text&sprefix=n+r+%2Cdigital-text%2C148&sr=1-5

15.   https://www.amazon.com/dp/B094DQHDHY/ref=sr_1_3?crid=2BGRD37EYPF31&dchild=1&keywords=n+r+hair-ston&qid=1620470219&s=digital-text&sprefix=n+r+%2Cdigital-text%2C148&sr=1-3

16.   https://www.amazon.com/Lawless-Magic-World-Breaker-Beginnings-ebook/dp/B094DPBVHN/ref=sr_1_11?crid=2BGRD37EYPF31&dchild=1&keywords=n+r+hair-ston&qid=1620470219&s=digital-text&sprefix=n+r+%2Cdigital-text%2C148&sr=1-11

17.   https://www.amazon.com/Fire-Rise-Dragons-Trilogy-Book-ebook/dp/B076VFSGTZ/ref=sr_1_4?s=digital-text&ie=UTF8&qid=1531259254&sr=1-4&keywords=n+r+hairston

18.   https://www.amazon.com/gp/product/B076V3N5H8/ref=series_rw_dp_sw

19.   https://www.amazon.com/gp/product/B076V14N8H/ref=series_rw_dp_sw

Atina and Ridge

We Got Powers Too,[20] Book One
We Wreak Havoc Too[21], Book Two
We Got Witches Too[22], Book Three

Rebel Writers Anthologies

Street Spells[23]

20. https://www.amazon.com/gp/product/B07F8D55LL/
ref=dbs_a_def_rwt_hsch_vapi_taft_p1_i10

21. https://www.amazon.com/dp/B094DQSMS5/
ref=sr_1_9?crid=2BGRD37EYPF31&dchild=1&keywords=n+r+hair-
ston&qid=1620470219&s=digital-text&sprefix=n+r+%2Cdigital-
text%2C148&sr=1-9

22. https://www.amazon.com/dp/B094DP9PNQ/
ref=sr_1_13?crid=2BGRD37EYPF31&dchild=1&keywords=n+r+hair-
ston&qid=1620470219&s=digital-text&sprefix=n+r+%2Cdigital-
text%2C148&sr=1-13

23. https://www.amazon.com/gp/product/B07F6GXSWV/
ref=dbs_a_def_rwt_hsch_vapi_taft_p1_i11

Acknowledgements

A special thanks to my beta readers, and editors for making this book what it is. Thank You!

If you enjoyed this book, tell me all about it by leaving a review.

Subscribe to N. R. Hairston's newsletter here,[1] to get exclusive short stories, and be the first to hear about deals and promotions. Join my private Facebook reading group here.[2]

1.   https://landing.mailerlite.com/webforms/landing/h2l3b2

2.   https://www.facebook.com/groups/262478357600840/?fref=mentions

About the Author

N.R. Hairston resides in Southern Virginia with her family. She enjoys writing, reading, cooking, and spending time with her loved ones.

Please be on the lookout for upcoming books by N. R. Hairston.

I hope you enjoyed reading this book.

If you'd like to discuss it, join my private Facebook Reading Group here,[1] or find me on linktree here[2].